Thurkill's Rebellion

PAUL BERNARDI

north. Enough to deliver a crushing blow that sent a message to anyone else who might think they could stand against the Normans. Either way, the tidings settled matters in his mind; they had to leave as quickly as they could. He turned back to where his wife still comforted Aelfric's widow.

"Come to me, Hild, my love." Thurkill watched as she made her way over. Though it was still early in her term – Father Wulfric's wife, Raeda, back in Gudmuncestre reckoned it would be a good six months before the baby would be born – he could not help but worry for her. Childbirth was fraught with enough danger as it was, and he did not want his actions making matters worse if he could help it. Despite his worries, he smiled as she approached; the white woollen dress she wore clung tightly to her form, making no secret of the fact that there was, as yet no sign of the baby she bore in her belly.

"Your will, husband?"

Taking her hands in his, he looked into her eyes. "We must leave our home, wife. In a few days, the Normans will come here with an army, looking to wreak vengeance on those responsible for the death of Taillebois and his men. We cannot risk the lives of the people of Huntendune by staying here."

"Leave Gudmundcestre? I was starting to like it there." Eahlmund sniffed pointedly.

Thurkill smiled sympathetically. He knew his friend was referring to Hereswitha, the miller's daughter. She had taken such a liking to Eahlmund that he had managed to overcome his natural distrust of all things female.

"You must make your own choice, friend; I will not order you to follow me even though that is my right as your lord. If you choose to remain here, then I release you from your oath. The same applies to all my hearth-warriors."

There was a hint of pain behind Eahlmund's eyes when he spoke. "There'll be no need for that, Lord. I gave my word to stand by your side, and I would not break that, whether you release me or not." Then, almost as an afterthought, he added, "Though the chances of finding a second woman on God's earth who finds being with me tolerable must be slim."

Hild laughed and threw her arms around his waist, planting a brief kiss on his cheek as she did so. "Don't be foolish, Eahlmund. Any woman would be pleased to have you. I've heard plenty say as much. Though," she wrinkled her nose in mock disgust, "it would not hurt you to bathe more than once a year. That would improve your chances, greatly."

"Hmmph." Eahlmund broke away from the embrace. "It suited my father to bathe but once each year, on the day of his birth. That is good enough for his son too."

"Where would we go, Lord? Where can we be safe from these bastards?"

Thurkill paused before replying. "I don't know, Leofric. Somewhere far away from here, though. I fear we might even have to venture beyond England's borders."

"Across the salt sea, Lord?" Eahlmund's voice was incredulous. "That's where the goat-lovers come from. It would be like a virgin walking into a Viking camp. We'd be well and truly f-"

"There are other places we can go without risking such an outcome, Eahlmund," Thurkill laughed. "I was thinking more of the kingdoms of the Waelesc. Far to the west of here. My father fought against them with Harold, back when he was Earl of Wessex. I remember Scalpi telling me about those battles when I was a boy. A wild bunch, the Waelesc, but good fighters, brave and proud. Though they came off worst in the end, they gave a good account of themselves in every battle."

"The Waelesc, you say?" Alwig's brow was furrowed.

"You think it foolish, Steward?"

"No, Lord. Your words prompted a memory, that is all. Lord Aelfric has a cousin, a man some years his junior by the name of Eadric. I remember he came here for a year or two as a young lad, to learn battle-craft in Aelfric's war-band. A pleasant lad, as I recall, but with a cold eye and a ruthlessness I had rarely seen in any man twice his age. He was from those parts, or at least the lands that border the kingdoms of the Waelesc. Henfforddscire, I think it was."

"You think this Eadric would take us in? Protect us?" Thurkill's voice betrayed the hope that now coursed through his veins.

wielding the huge iron hammers of his trade so that his arms, chest and shoulders rippled with muscle every time he moved. Combined with his leadership skills and booming voice, he had been the natural choice for lead man in the villagers' shieldwall. Urri set a fine example for the other lads and was the rock on which they had all depended. Stepping back now to take the measure of the man, Thurkill knew he would be sorry to leave the blacksmith behind, but the villagers needed him more than he did.

"Well met indeed, Urri. In truth, I had hoped to stay in Huntendune 'til the morrow, but it is sad news that brings me hither so soon. Lord Aelfric was killed, murdered by Norman bastards, this very morning."

Urri's beaming smile was replaced with a frown as his eyes narrowed. "What foul news is this? What could have led to such an evil act?"

"They came from Lundenburh with orders to seize his lands. King William has decreed that Harold took the throne illegally, and so any man who followed him must be marked a traitor and his lands therefore forfeited to the crown."

"But Harold was elected king by the nobles of England. He was the rightful king. This is nonsense."

"I cannot argue with you, Urri. It is but a device to seize what is ours so that William can reward his followers. Many of his warriors joined his army in the hope of receiving land and riches, and William must deliver on his promise or face discord. And what better way to do so than to dispossess his defeated enemy?"

"That does not make it right, Lord."

"Quite. A view also held by Lord Aelfric, and he now lies dead, spitted on a Norman lance for daring to resist them." A tear came unbidden into the corner of Thurkill's eye which he quickly cuffed away, but not before it was spotted by Urri and those others who had gathered to hear the news.

Father Wulfric grunted. "So, the Normans now hold Huntendune? They have taken Aelfric's hall. What of his wife? Is she also dead?"

"Aebbe lives and Huntendune stands free. Whatever the

17

consequences, I could not stand by and do nothing to avenge my lord. So, we put them to the sword. All of them, bar one who managed to escape, I'm sorry to say. And though I may have to answer to Saint Peter for my sins when the time comes, I tell you it felt good. And I would do it again were the same thing to happen tomorrow."

Urri clapped him on the shoulder, a look of pride mixed with understanding on his face. "A lord could not hope for a better man at his side. Aelfric's spirit can rest easy knowing that those responsible for his murder are no more. But what of the one who escaped?"

"He will be well on his way back to his masters in Lundenburh by now." He paused, lowering his head in shame. "And it is for this reason that I must leave Gudmundcestre. The Normans will return in force; they have no choice. They cannot allow the death of twenty of their men to go unanswered."

The villagers erupted in dismay. Shouts of "No" and "For shame" filled the air. Haegmund the miller stepped forward to grab Thurkill by the shoulder, fear and anger in his eyes. "You cannot desert us, Lord. With you here to lead us, we could defend ourselves, just like we did before."

Sighing, Thurkill shook his head. "No, Haegmund. We were lucky before. We were beaten and would have been killed to a man if it were not for Aelfric arriving with his men. Now we have no one to save us and some of our best men have already given their lives to defend the village. This time, the Normans would come in far greater strength and we would soon be overwhelmed not matter how bravely we fought. They would simply burn the village to the ground and slaughter everyone they found here – man, woman and child – if only to set an example for all others to hear."

"We'd have a chance, though? We can rebuild these walls again. That'd keep them out."

Thurkill shook his head. "There is no time, for they will be here within the week. I have already risked the lives of every person in Gudmundcestre once and I'll not do so again. My mind's made up and I shall not be moved on this. Too many have died already because of me. There must be an end to it and the only way is for me to go.

"You will be safe, though. Alwig the Steward of Huntendune has promised to look after you. He will use his skills to convince the Normans that it was a band of renegade Saxon warriors who were responsible for the deaths of their men. He will tell them that those men fled north and east into the fenlands where none may follow. Rumour is there are men in those parts who seek to fight the Normans so it will not be a story that is too far from the truth."

The priest sniffed. "But you'll allow us one last feast to mark your departure? I have a fresh batch of ale that should not be allowed to go stale."

Though he would have rather been on the road without delay, Thurkill bowed to Hild's entreaties and agreed to leave the next morning. She was right; he could not disappoint the people of Gudmundcestre after all they had been through together. But, despite the excellent cuts of meat on offer and the vast quantities of Wulfric's ale with which to wash them down, it was a sombre affair, with little in the way of good cheer on display. Hild did her best to lighten the mood, arranging for songs and dancing in the open space between the hearth and the lord's table, but few were of a mind to truly enjoy the festivities.

Though most understood his reasons for leaving, few if any were happy. At first, Thurkill put it down to fear of what might become of them without him and his warband to protect them. But as the evening wore on, he realised there was more to it. Though they had been in Gudmundcestre for but a few short months, there was genuine affection for them. They had been accepted into the community, and even begun to put down roots, as if they had been there since birth.

Glancing to either side, he saw that his friends bore similar expressions to his own. They, too, had been happy here, content to make a life for themselves among these people. Eahlmund more than most. Even now, he was deep in conversation with Hereswitha, his arm around her shoulder. Even from this distance, Thurkill could see tears shining on the miller's daughter's cheeks, reflecting in the light of the hearth-fire like the dew sparkles in the morning sunlight.

Thurkill was on the verge of going to offer some small words of consolation when the two of them rose to leave the hall. Thurkill looked over to where Haegmund sat, fearing a reaction. The miller was famously protective of his daughter as many a potential suitor had found out to their cost. But on this occasion, he simply smiled and nodded. He had warmed to the young Saxon and welcomed his help in the mill these last few weeks. Just as Hereswitha was sad to be losing a potential husband, Haegmund must have felt, just as keenly, the loss of a son, someone to whom he might have one day passed the running of the mill.

At last, the meal came to an end, the songs finished, and the scops completed their tales of old. The final guests left to go to their homes as the churls cleared away the last remaining platters and empty jugs of ale. Wearily, Thurkill offered Hild his arm to help her to their sleeping chamber one last time. Mercifully, the fires from the battle with FitzGilbert had not reached as far as their hall but there remained an acrid smell of smoke nonetheless, which clung to the rugs and wall hangings with an intensity almost as strong as the fire itself.

"Thank you, husband. I know you didn't want to stay this long, but it was right to bid a proper farewell to these people. They have been kind to us when they had no need to, and it is good that their last memory of us should be happy."

Thurkill kissed her on the forehead. "As ever, you are right, my love. It was my duty and I thank you for holding me to it. Sleep now, though, for we must be up with the dawn. We should not give the enemy too much of a gift of our time."

FOUR

Although the hour was still early – the sun not long having appeared over the treeline to the east – almost the whole village turned out to see them go. The mist of the previous day had cleared, leaving a bright, sunny morning which promised much early spring warmth as the day went on. For now, though, their feet crunched as they walked over the heavily frosted ground.

Despite the crisp chill, Thurkill was already sweating, partly because he had been labouring hard since before dawn, preparing everything for their departure, and partly because he had chosen to wear his thick, woollen cloak rather than have something else to carry. Looking around for perhaps the fifth time, he noted Eahlmund was still not there.

"Where is the lazy bastard?" He could not hide the irritation in his voice. "I told him we had to be on the road by dawn and we're already late."

He was about to send the brothers to look for him when he heard a familiar voice to his left.

"Alright, alright, I'm coming. Can't a man say goodbye in peace?"

Eahlmund came into view from behind the church where there was a path that led to the mill. In his haste, he was still pulling the ties on his trews together. Following closely behind, a sheepish looking Hereswitha carried the rest of his belongings. Her dishevelled hair showed it had not yet seen a comb that morning.

Thurkill laughed, unable to stay angry with his friend for long. "I'll wager you have been saying goodbye since you left the hall last night. If you are done, perhaps we can be on our way now?"

"Certainly, Lord. I crave your pardon for my tardiness." His voice was muffled somewhat as he shrugged himself into the mailshirt that Hereswitha held out for him. Thurkill had ordered that they ride dressed for battle just in case they were attacked on the road; it made for less to carry also. With a final flourish, Eahlmund swept the girl up in his arms, twirling her around before pressing his lips firmly against hers. "Who knows, my love? Maybe one day our paths will cross again."

"Yes, but by then I will have a proper husband and six children." Though she smiled, there was no doubt it masked a great sadness which did little to assuage Thurkill's sense of guilt.

Not willing to wait a moment longer, lest his feelings get the better of him, Thurkill set off on foot, holding his horse's reins loosely in his left hand. They had chosen not to ride at first, so that they might bid farewell more easily to the assembled throng that lining the path all the way to the broken gate. They had not gone more than a few paces, however, before their progress was halted by Elspeth who came running forward, clutching a small bunch of flowers that she must have picked in the woods that very morning. Tears streamed unchecked down the little girl's face as she curtsied before Hild to present her gift. Her maid's sorrow brought fresh tears to Hild's eyes as she bent to stroke her head. Friends since the day they arrived in Gudmundcestre, Thurkill doubted Hild would ever forget her.

Thurkill felt a lump growing in his own throat as he fought to keep his own emotions in check. Was he doing the right thing? Would the village survive without him? No matter which way he looked at it, he came to the same conclusion; if he stayed, they would all die.

"Take me with you, Lady."

Smiling through her tears, Hild hugged Elspeth tight. "I would like nothing more, darling child, but who would take care of your father then? He has greater need of you than me, so I release you from my service and thank you for it. You must be strong now and do your duty by your father. Do you understand?"

Elspeth nodded briefly, before turning to run back to her house, unable to bear witness to Hild's departure any longer.

"Wait."

Thurkill had not taken more than another half dozen steps before the next interruption. Turning to see who had shouted, he spied Urri coming out of his smithy. He was dressed for the road and leading a sturdy-looking pony across whose back was slung his cloak and a couple of leather bags containing the tools of his trade.

"Where are you heading, my friend?" Thurkill knew the answer before he even asked.

"I thought I might tag along with you, Lord. If you'll have me?"

"Gladly, my friend. You know how much I value your skills and your strength. But is your place not here with the other folk? The village has greater need of its smith than me."

"I have no family here, no wife to care for and my girls are full grown. My smithy is in good hands with the lads I have trained these last five years. I could hope for none better to take it on from me, and I am sure they would rather I were out of their way now, too. I have a desire for adventure before I grow too old, to see something of the world beyond these walls. And I'll wager you are not done killing Normans, Lord; work for which I appear to have a talent. It would be a dreadful shame if that were not put to good use."

Thurkill laughed. "You realise my path has no clear destination and is one from which we may not return? I can offer you no surety of protection or wealth as you might expect of your lord. Most likely, all we will find is a cold, wet plot of earth at the end of this road, in which our broken bodies will be laid to rest, if we're lucky. Either that or we'll be left to rot as carrion on which the crows will feast."

"As unappealing as you make it sound, Lord, I believe my fate lies with you for as long as the road shall persist."

"In which case, I bid you welcome to my warband. I have nothing to offer you for now, not even a roof over our heads nor a hearth by which to warm our weary bones."

Urri grinned, "I have had enough fires to last several lifetimes. I am sure I can do without for a while."

***

Once Gudmundcestre was finally behind them, they made good progress. They followed the old Roman road that headed north west. Thurkill remembered tracing its path with his finger on the ancient map that Alwig had proudly showed him before they left Huntendune. The road ran in an almost straight-line past numerous towns and fortresses picked out in black ink on the parchment, until it reached the old city of Chester. Some time before that, he knew they would reach a junction where they would need to turn south to take them into Eadric's lands which bordered the lands of the Waelesc.

Thurkill had thanked Alwig, committing as much of the map to memory as he could. It would be a risk to follow the road, but one he was prepared to take so that they might reach Eadric's domain as quickly as possible. And even if they did encounter Normans along the way, it was unlikely that they would be looking for them in that direction.

And so it proved. They passed few other travellers on the road, and those they did see gave them a wide berth. Even with a woman in their midst, the sight of six men dressed for war in helms and mailshirts, carrying spear and shield, was enough to deter all but the foolhardiest thieves and robbers.

The one concession to safety that Thurkill did insist on was to avoid any towns they encountered. There was a chance that people might remember their passing, and it made no sense to make a present of the information to any would be pursuers. The spectre of FitzGilbert was never far from his mind.

Unsurprisingly, Eahlmund griped about the decision, bemoaning the fact that the towns would most likely have any number of taverns where they might find a bed for the night, a hot meal and copious amounts of ale with which to wash it down. His mood was not helped on the first night when, shortly before they settled down in a small hollow a hundred or so paces back from the road, a thin, but steady drizzle began to fall. Pulling his cloak about him and up over his head, Eahlmund lost no time in making his feelings known.

"To think we could have been warming our feet by a cosy fire right now, with pretty maids waiting on us hand and foot. There's no justice in the world. None at all, I tell you."

So interminable was his bellyaching that it took a branch, flung by a sleepy and disgruntled Leofgar, to shut him up.

***

The shadows were lengthening on the fifth day since leaving Gudmundcestre when they finally took their leave of the road.

Ahead of them, the ruins of an old Roman town were visible. The crumbling stone walls standing like silent sentinels, watching back down the way they had come. To their right, the road stretched off into the distance, continuing its inexorable journey north to the old city of Chester just as Alwig had said, ploughing its lone, straight furrow ever onward. To their left, a narrow, earthen track, little more than two parallel ruts where innumerable wheels had worn away the grass over generations of use, headed south towards a line of dark, forested hills that dominated the horizon.

Thurkill held his hand above his eyes, shielding his gaze from the glare of the low, setting sun as it began to dip down towards the skyline to the west. "Somewhere over there, we should find Eadric's hall at a place called Conendovre. At least, that is where he was living when Alwig last visited all those years ago."

"What do we know of this Eadric, Lord?"

"No more than Alwig told me, Urri. He's supposedly one of the wealthiest men in these parts, holding lands along the border from here, southwards towards Gleawecastre. But, he has, for many years, had an uneasy relationship with the earl in these parts, a man called Richard FitzScrope."

Eahlmund furrowed his brow. "Fitz?" That's a Norman name then, like your FitzGilbert?"

"Well observed, my friend. Alwig said he was installed here by King Edward some fifteen years ago, given lands in these parts to act as a buffer against the Waelesc. FitzScrope has castles at Scrobbesburh and Henffordd, a few days march from here. They are the cause of much resentment amongst the Saxons, not least with Eadric."

"So, we may find ourselves in the midst of another fight, then?" Urri did not sound impressed.

Leofric grinned. "Well, the sooner we get there, the sooner we'll know."

"Aye. If we press on, we can be there in time for supper."

Thurkill frowned. "It will be dark soon, Eahlmund, and I would rather not test the horses further today. They could easily snap a foreleg in the dark with this rutted path. Let's find a stream and settle down for the night. I'd much prefer to meet the man I hope will be our new patron with a clear head after a good night's sleep. It's important we make a good impression, lest he send us on our way."

Eahlmund grunted, though not without humour. "Another night under the stars feasting on nought but cheese and apples? What more could a man wish for?"

The light began to fail much sooner than they had expected, gobbled up by the high hills around them, and it was almost dark when they finally reached their intended target: a heavily wooded dip in the land that Thurkill thought would have a stream snaking its way along its lowest point. He had just turned his head back to the others to urge them to hasten when Hild emitted a terrifying scream.

Her cheeks had drained of colour and, though the sound had died on her lips, her mouth remained agape, her round eyes staring in horror towards the trees. Yanking his head round, Thurkill followed the direction of her gaze, fumbling at the same time to release his sword from within the folds of his cloak, though he could hear no sounds of attack.

And then he saw the cause of her distress.

At first, he could not be certain – the scene imperfect and vague in the twilight – but as he drew closer, he knew there could be no mistake. There, ranging from left to right across several of the tree trunks on either side of the path, were the remains of what had once been a man. By the looks of what clothing remained, he guessed it to be a Norman knight, though it was hard to be certain. On the outer most trees had been nailed the arms and legs, each limb separated from the body by what appeared to be crude hacks of a blade, most likely a woodsman's axe. In the centre, adorning two huge old oak trees, were the trunk and the head. It was the latter that gave the best clue as to the identity of the unfortunate wretch as Thurkill noted the distinctive short mop of hair he had become so used to in recent weeks. There was no way of telling how long ago the man had been killed but judging by the dark stains that streaked down the bark all the way to the grass, he surmised it must have been several days.

Having recovered her composure, Hild reined in her horse alongside Thurkill's, all the while holding a piece of scented cloth to her nose to offset the stench of rotting flesh. "Who would do such a thing? And why?"

"I don't know, wife, but my senses tell me this has something to do with Aelfric's cousin. Things may be worse here than we thought."

"But why mutilate the man and leave him like this?"

"Perhaps it's a warning to others? Perchance, we stand on the edge of Eadric's lands, and he has done this to mark the border, to show other Normans what awaits them should they trespass further?"

"If so, I think I could grow to like this Eadric." Eahlmund had dismounted in order to take a closer look at the body parts. Moving in close, he swatted away the flies that buzzed around the trees, angry at having their feasting disturbed. "It's not clean work by any means, Lord; your axe would have made a much neater job of it."

Thurkill had to look away in revulsion as Eahlmund then stuck a finger into the stump of one of the legs before sniffing it. "I'd say he's been here the best part of a week, definitely starting to smell bad now. His eyes have gone too, and there are marks where the birds have begun to peck at the flesh. Another week or so, and there'll be nothing but cloth and bone left."

Leofric shrugged. "So, what do we do?"

"I don't think we have much choice. We go on and find this Eadric."

"Even if that means becoming part of whatever is happening here? I thought we were looking for a safe place, somewhere to be away from fighting Normans for a while?"

"Until something better comes along, this is the only place we can run to. We have nowhere else to go, and we may not even be welcome here. Either way, let us at least move on before you turn our stomachs any further, Eahlmund. For tonight, we'll camp amongst the trees, close to fresh water. Tomorrow, we'll find Conendovre."

FIVE

"Ooft." The leather-booted foot caught Thurkill squarely in his gut, jolting him awake and causing him to double over in pain as the air was forced from his lungs.

"Sit up, you dog. And keep your paws away from your seax."

In case further emphasis were needed, Thurkill felt the cold steel of a sword's blade pressing against his neck. His thoughts turned immediately to Hild and the others. *Pray God they are unharmed.* The fact that the voice had been Saxon felt no more than a small comfort at that moment.

He tried to make sense of his surroundings, but it was as yet too dark to see much other than a handful of indistinct shapes revealed by what little light from the crescent moon could penetrate the canopy of leaves high above his head. Though his eyes were of little use to him, his other senses slowly began to make up for their shortcomings. The familiar odour of unwashed, male bodies assailed his nostrils while, somewhere behind him, someone was moaning as if in pain and – if he were not mistaken – he could hear Hild's laboured breathing over to his left. *At least she lives.* Thurkill swore to himself that if she had been harmed in anyway, the culprit would not live to see the dawn.

As the pain receded, he managed to push himself into a sitting position as ordered. Immediately, strong hands gripped him on either side, dragging him backwards until his body slammed against the gnarled trunk of a nearby tree.

Gritting his teeth against the pain, Thurkill forced himself to make no sound, not wishing to give his captors the satisfaction of knowing they had hurt him. He still had no idea who they were. Though his assailant spoke the same tongue, he did so with an accent that was so unfamiliar as to be almost unintelligible. But at least he knew them not to be Normans; that much was a blessing.

The next blow was as unexpected as the first; he'd not even realised anyone was that close to him. His head snapped to one side, bouncing off the knotted surface of the tree trunk. Despite the darkness, a blinding flash of light burst behind his eyes, before fading almost as quickly as it had come. It had been a measured blow; enough to hurt but not sufficient to render him unconscious. As he shook his head to clear the fog, he knew these were men not to be trifled with. His life hung in the balance; one wrong move – a word or gesture out of place – could prove fatal.

Aware of movement beside him once more, he tensed in anticipation of the next assault. This time, however, it was a different, unexpected pain. Rough hands grabbed his wrists on either side before stretching his arms back round either side of the tree against which he sat. Stout ropes were then tied around his wrists and fastened at the back of the trunk, completely immobilising him. His back and shoulders began to ache almost immediately, in protest at the unnatural angle into which his body had been forced.

As soon as it was done, one of his captors – he presumed him to be their leader – knelt close to Thurkill, his foul breath forcing him to suppress the reflex to gag.

"Who are you and what are you doing here in the middle of the night, dressed for war?"

Thurkill wondered how best to reply. Whilst not wishing to provoke these men unnecessarily, he also did not want to appear overly weak or cowed. These were not mere brigands; this was becoming clearer with every passing moment. Something told him these men were under the orders of another, one who might hold sway over this area.

A stinging slap to the face reminded him he had yet to respond.

"My name is Thurkill, former Lord of Gudmundcestre and loyal thegn of Lord Aelfric of Huntendune. I seek Lord Eadric of Conendovre for whom I have letters of introduction. I'll thank you to release me and my party so that we may continue our journey."

It was too dark to see whether the speaker showed any signs of recognition at the names of Aelfric or Eadric, but there was certainly no change in his voice. "An interesting story, I'll grant you. Not one that I had expected to hear, that's for sure. Though you sound a bit young to be a lord, these are strange times in which we live. It might not be beyond the bounds of reason."

"You'll release us then?"

"Let's not be hasty, young Thurkill. I merely suggested that your words might have some truth to them, nothing more. It's not for me to say whether you go free. That's up to my lord, on whose lands you now trespass. Don't fret, though; I have sent men to summon him hither, so you'll not have long to wait. Though I should warn you, he does not take kindly to folk wandering about uninvited. Did you not see the warning?"

"We did, but we took that to be a message to the Normans rather than honest Saxon folk such as ourselves."

"Either way, you may still live to regret taking this path. Though not for long, admittedly." He chuckled at his own joke. "But we'll know soon enough. I suggest you sit quietly until then."

"At least tell me that none in my party has been harmed. I will have words with your lord should it not be so."

He snorted. "You're not really in a position to be making threats now, lad, are you? But rest assured they all still breathe. And all but one is the same as when we found you. The other – the man you had on watch – is a little the worse for wear. He heard us coming so we had to make sure he did not cry out. He'll have a sore head for a day or two, nothing more. Big fellow he was too. It took a couple of my lads to deal with him."

Urri. Thurkill smiled to himself. The big man had not been caught napping, but he'd paid a heavy price for his vigilance by the sounds of it. At least the others were unharmed, though he wished he could see Hild or at least sit with her. Although these men seemed decent enough, there was always a fear that a defenceless woman would be mistreated.

***

The next thing Thurkill knew was another kick to the ribs. This time, however, there was no weight or malice behind it, its intent simply being to rouse him from his slumber. He was amazed he had managed to doze off despite the discomfort caused by the bonds that held him firmly in position. Opening his eyes, he guessed that it must have been fast approaching midday, for the sun seemed to be high in the sky, from what he could see of it through the thick foliage knitted above him.

"Time to wake up, boy."

Thurkill recognised the voice; it was the same man who had spoken to him during the night. Like the kick, its tone was more placatory, almost apologetic. He wondered if that meant his story had been accepted. The man – Thurkill realised he knew not his name – then squatted down on his haunches to push the neck of a leather water-skin between his lips. The ropes prevented him from tilting his head properly, causing most of the cool liquid to splash down his chest, but he was grateful for the small amount he did manage to swallow, easing his parched tongue from where it had stuck to the roof of his mouth.

He shivered, involuntarily as a great shadow fell across him, blocking out the warmth of the dappled sunlight. Looking up, he found himself staring into the piercing blue eyes of a huge, almost bear-like man. So thick was his beard that the eyes were almost all that could be seen of his face. They burned with an intensity that made him recoil. Thurkill reckoned him to be of similar height to himself but almost twice as broad across the chest and shoulders.

The hands that hung by his sides looked as big as the shovels that the stable boys used to muck out the horses on his father's estate back in Haslow. He wore no armour other than a leather jerkin that was stretched tight over his massive frame. Over his shoulders he wore a bear-skin cloak which hung down to his knees, its fur matted and stained through long and continual wear.

"So, Aethelgar, this is the whelp who claims to know my cousin, Aelfric?"

"Aye, Lord. Though I have not been able to verify the truth of the matter. I thought it best to wait for you. Do you know the boy?"

"I swear I do not, but then I have not seen Aelfric for a long time. It must be ten years or more since he came with Earl Harold to put down the Waelesc rising. By the looks of him, this lad would have not long left his mother's teat back then."

Thurkill's cheeks burned with shame and anger as laughter rang around the assembled warriors. He fought to keep his emotions in check; to react badly now would not help their cause. There were at least a dozen men, each holding shield and spear, most of whom seemed to bear the scars of past battles. He wondered, idly, whether he had stood with any of them at Senlac.

"Let's have him on his feet, Aethelgar. I want a closer look at him."

Thurkill felt the pressure on his back evaporate as the ropes were cut. Such was the blissfulness of the feeling he could not prevent a gasp escaping his lips. Two of Aethelgar's men then helped him to his feet where he stood rolling his shoulders and stretching his arms above and behind his head, trying to coax some life back into his tortured muscles.

"Well, he's a big enough lad, I'll give him that. Goes some small way to make up for his age, I suppose. Look at that face, though, hardly any sign of a beard at all." Without warning, the man's huge paw grabbed Thurkill's face where it proceeded to rub at his cheek, testing the stubble that grew there. The inspection stopped abruptly, though, when the groping fingers touched the spot where his ear had once been.

"By the Devil's arse-crack, he's no stranger to a scrap, though, if this is anything to go by."

With that, he pushed Thurkill's hair back, exposing the angry red wound. Though it had long since healed, it remained – at least to Thurkill's mind – a blemish that embarrassed him. He was beginning to lose patience with the way he was being treated, and the lack of respect it showed.

"And what of it? It's a badge I wear with pride for it shows I stood with King Harold in the shieldwall at Senlac, defending him to the last. Though I consider the price I paid cheap compared to that imposed on many good men who stood with me that day. Can any of you say the same? Did any of you place your shield between Harold and the Norman horde on that day? For if you did not, I'll thank you to show me the respect due one who did. And while we're about it, I'll have you even the score. You have my name, but you have me at a disadvantage."

His tormentor threw back his head and laughed uproariously, his shoulders shaking and his chest heaving as he fought for breath. "The boy has rocks for balls, that's for sure. I'm beginning to like the fellow, Aethelgar. Thurkill, did you say his name was? Well, Thurkill, allow me to even the score as you so rightly say.

"My name is Eadric, sometimes known as The Wild or – in the tongue of the Normans – Salvage, which I am told refers to my liking for living among the trees. I am the man you seek, the man for whom you have letters of introduction from my cousin, Aelfric. So, if you're done stamping your foot like the petulant child you are, I would see those letters and hear news of my cousin."

Before long, they were settled on the ground around a fire that Aethelgar had built. The rest of Thurkill's party had been untied and provided with bread and ale by means of apology for their rough handling. None seemed to be the worse for wear, least of all Hild, much to Thurkill's relief. To be fair to Eadric's men, they had treated her gently and with respect, so much so that she had no complaints. Urri was the one exception, nursing a bruised head on which a sizeable lump had already appeared. But even he accepted the cup of ale pressed into his hand with good grace and a rueful grin.

All the while, Thurkill thought about how best to break the news to Eadric. He had no idea how close he had been to Aelfric, but he could see his host was a volatile character, no doubt quick to anger if provoked. He would need to tread carefully lest he send him into a rage.

"Hand over these letters then, lad. Let's hear what the old goat has to say. He was always full of piss and wind as I recall; I'm keen to see if that has changed in any way."

"Before I do, Lord, I should tell you these letters have been penned by Aelfric's Steward, a man by the name of Alwig whom you may remember?"

"Ha. I remember. A bald fellow, always fussing about something or other. Aelfric's still getting his maidservant to do his donkeywork then? Somethings don't change, eh? He never was much good at his letters; not that I can boast much skill to be fair."

"No, you misunderstand me. Alwig writes because Aelfric cannot. He is dead."

"What?" Eadric roared. "You'd better explain yourself quickly, boy. How's this come to pass and what part did you play in this foul misdeed?"

"None, Lord. Though I was there when it happened."

"And did nothing to stop it, apparently."

This was not going how Thurkill had intended at all. Before matters could get any worse, he cast caution to the wind and explained what had happened in Huntendune the week before. Eadric listened quietly but intently, his face slowly reddening as if consumed by impotent rage. As Thurkill ended his tale, Eadric rose and slammed his fist into the nearest tree, the younger man marvelling that he appeared to suffer no harm to his hand.

"Bastards!" Eadric roared up at the treetops above him before stomping off into the woods.

When it was clear that he was not coming back, Thurkill turned to Aethelgar. "Should we go after him? I need to know if my people are welcome in his hall."

Eadric's man grinned apologetically. "It would not pay to intrude on his thoughts for a while, Thurkill. I can tell you that from experience. It'll be a day or two before his mood calms enough to be in the company of his fellow man. Best we leave him to his own devices until then."

But Thurkill was not to be put off. "What are we to do until then? My wife is with child, and we need warmth and shelter. Can you not take us to Eadric's hall in the meantime?"

"I would, and gladly, but he no longer has a hall to call his own. Not since the Normans burned it down for his refusal to submit to their earl in Henffordd, a whoreson by the name of William FitzOsbern. He sent his henchman, Richard FitzScrope, to burn it down and kill all that he found there. Of all the Normans, this FitzScrope is the worst of them by far. A foul demon conjured up from the pits of hell would quail in his presence."

"I've met a couple that sound similar."

"I doubt it. Whatever you may have experienced, double it and it would still fall short. Either way, Eadric has sworn to kill him; rest assured, he will not stop until the murdering scum is cut into pieces and pinned to a tree, just like you saw yesterday. That was one of FitzScrope's men, by the way, sent as a warning to his lord."

"But why does Eadric hate him so? I have seen what the Normans can do; it's why we've come west; to be away from them. Why risk destruction? Is that man worth it, however much of a bastard he might be? A hall can be rebuilt somewhere safer, after all."

Aethelgar laughed without humour. "You think this is about a hall? Eadric has no need of such things. He has men and coin enough to build any number of halls. No, this is about far more.

"On the night FitzScrope set it aflame, Eadric was not home… but his wife was. She perished in the fire, unable to escape as the Normans had barred the doors shut. There was no way out for her or those with her. It was a bad death. Their screams could be heard for a long time. And all the while, the Norman swine just stood and watched, laughing as they burned alive. Is that enough of a reason for you, boy?"

Thurkill was silent, recalling the events at Haslow where he had set torches to his own father's hall. Though he had allowed Richard FitzGilbert and his men to escape, it was only so that he might slaughter them as they ran from the flames. Was he any better than this FitzScrope? He reconciled himself with the thought that it had been done to avenge his kin, not as an act of petty cruelty as had apparently happened at Conendovre.

"Anyway, enough talk," Aethelgar concluded. "Gather your people and follow me. I'll guide you to Eadric's new home among the trees. We'll wait for him there."

SIX

The shadows were lengthening when they finally arrived at Eadric's forest camp. They'd been walking for most of the day, and Thurkill had begun to worry for Hild. The pace was brisk and the ground uneven at times with hidden roots and exposed rocks to navigate. Though he was sure she would never complain, Thurkill knew she must be tiring by the end.

He was about to ask Aethelgar to allow a short period of rest when they crested a small rise in the ground to find the camp stretched out below them amongst the trees. Though compact in area, it was a good-sized settlement, with buildings ranging from plank-built houses with thatched rooves to more makeshift shelters comprising several hides stitched together to form sheets which had been stretched between two tree trunks and secured by stout lengths of twine. Judging by the number of structures, Thurkill reckoned the camp must be home to around forty to fifty families.

Roaming freely between the buildings, dozens of pigs, geese and goats snuffled, honked and brayed, hunting for scraps that had been thrown from the kitchens at the end of each meal, or digging deeper in their search for worms and other grubs. Running through the middle of the camp, a small stream – no wider than could be easily jumped by a child – wound its way along the bottom of the little valley bringing fresh, cold water in plentiful supply. Tall silver birch, larch, and ash trees grew all around them, providing a luxuriant covering of leaves that sheltered those below from the worst of the sun's heat and would even keep all but the heaviest rain at bay. The scent rising from the surrounding flora, combined with the sound of bird song from the myriad feathered creatures that festooned the higher branches gave the place an almost magical feel. If he could have but forgotten the circumstances under which the camp had been created, Thurkill would have found it almost idyllic, reminiscent of the tales of fairies who supposedly lived in the deepest, darkest forests in the tales told to him as a child by his aunt.

They were shown to a small wooden building on the edge of the encampment, furthest from the stream. As they passed through the settlement, many of its inhabitants called out greetings to Aethelgar. Others simply paused in whatever tasks they were doing to stare at the newcomers, their expressions betraying interest rather than malice.

Inside their allotted home, Thurkill noted how the wooden beams that formed the walls smelt as if recently cut, a fact reinforced by several drops of sticky, pungent resin that oozed from innumerable knots in the wood's grain, where smaller branches had been hacked off.

The furniture was sparse – no more than a few straw-filled mattresses set along the walls and a small table in the centre, either side of which were set two benches big enough to sit three a-piece. But it was cosy despite that. The gaps between the wooden planks had been carefully plugged with wet clay and moss to stop the cold air seeping through.

Hild smiled as she looked around. "Well, it's not quite what we were used to in Gudmundcestre, but it's nice enough all the same. I'll have it feeling like home in no time."

Thurkill hugged her, grateful that she was making the best of their reduced circumstances, scolding himself for having doubted her. "It's not what I had in mind if I am honest. I feel like a fish that has jumped from the cooking pot only to land in the fire as I fear that things will be anything but peaceful hereabouts... but it's home for now until something better comes along.

"But for now, wife, you must rest. It's been a long journey and the business of improving our lot can wait until the morrow. I'll send the lads out to organise food and ale and, in the meantime, you can sleep. There's the baby to think about."

"Oh, stop fussing, Killi. I'm not made of pottery; I won't break at the slightest knock." Nevertheless, Hild did ease herself down onto the nearest mattress and was asleep before Thurkill had finished giving his men their duties.

***

It was five days before they saw Eadric again. In that time,

Thurkill's group settled in well enough. Though they had not yet been wholly accepted by those around them, they were at least made to feel welcome. Hild had used her natural charm to good effect, soon finding friends among the other womenfolk who had readily shown her the best places to draw water, wash clothes and where to bathe.

The men had not been idle either. Several times they'd joined the other men on hunting parties, using their spears to good effect in bringing down both boar and deer which roamed in great numbers in the surrounding hills. Nor did they shy away from the messy business of skinning and butchering the carcasses on their return, using their seaxes to good effect to open the guts of the animals so that the entrails could be removed. Nothing went to waste, though, as the discarded innards were put to one side to feed Eadric's two wolfhounds.

It was while Thurkill and the others were busy eviscerating a pair of deer, blood spattered up to their elbows as their hands plunged deep within them, that they heard a commotion. Seeing Aethelgar passing, Thurkill hailed him for news.

"It's Eadric. He's back, and it looks like he has been hunting too." Rather than answer any more of Thurkill's questions, Aethelgar simply smiled enigmatically and continued on his way.

Rinsing the gore from his arms in the stream, Thurkill gathered the others around him. "Come on, lads. I would have words with our host so that our position here might be clarified. It's not certain yet whether we are guests or prisoners."

As they drew closer, they could hear a great clamour, the noise of which grew until it was almost deafening. It looked as if the whole camp had gathered to welcome their lord back, and yet that alone could not explain the furore. Pushing through the throng, Thurkill eventually found himself face to face with Eadric. And there, by his side, was the cause of the commotion.

Standing with his head bowed, his wrists bound with strips of twisted leather that had been pulled so tight they bit into the flesh, causing blood to drip down onto his hands, was a Norman soldier. His face bore the marks of a heavy beating; the flesh around his eyes was puffy and discoloured, and his nose looked to have been broken. His mouth was also swollen and bloody, though whether this was from the fractured nose or broken teeth was not clear. The eyes, though, were very much alive, darting from face to face, constantly scanning the crowd as if looking for a means of escape.

But there was none. Thurkill could see the man was on the edge of panic. The colour had drained from his cheeks, lending his bruises an even more vivid hue. *Eadric must have a fearful reputation in these parts,* Thurkill mused. *This man knows his fate is sealed; he does not expect to see out the day.*

All around him, people were already baying for blood, urging Eadric to kill the miserable wretch. But Thurkill found himself conflicted. God knew he had good reason to hate the Normans and all that they stood for, but he could not – in all good conscience – stand by and watch a defenceless man be butchered to satisfy the bloodlust of a rabid mob. To kill a man for sport would mean they were no better than those who now ruled over them.

A thought at the back of his mind nagged at him. Had he not killed Richard FitzGilbert in cold blood? He told himself that was different. That bastard had murdered his aunt and sister for no reason; he'd deserved to die several times over for his actions. But this man had done nothing so foul to his knowledge. His fate was the result of nothing more than an accident of birth. He knew in his heart that he had to speak. His conscience – his honour even – demanded it of him.

"Lord, forgive me but what do you have in mind for this man?"

Eadric spun round to see who spoke, the voice as yet unfamiliar to him. "Ah, Thurkill. Why, I mean to gut the bastard." He grinned with a look of malevolence that was chilling.

"For what crime, Lord?" Thurkill knew he had to maintain a respectful demeanour if he were to avoid angering the volatile man.

"For the crime of being a Norman and trespassing on my land. Is that not enough? In what way does this concern you anyway, boy? You're here as my guest. That does not afford you the right to interfere in my business."

A number of those close to Thurkill growled in support of Eadric's words, angered by this newcomer who sought to challenge their lord. Nevertheless, Thurkill pressed his case noting with relief as he did so that Eadric had – by his own words – conferred guest status on him. Whilst he could not push his luck too far, he felt more confident in his position, knowing Eadric would not easily renege on his offer of hospitality rights.

"My apologies, Lord. I merely sought to establish the reason why this man should be put to death. Has he stolen of your property? A deer perhaps or a favoured horse? Has he raped one of your women? As lord in this land, it is your duty to stand in judgement over all others and to dispense justice on any that are found to be wrongdoers. But it is also your duty to exercise these powers justly and with wisdom. Men should know that they will be treated fairly by your hand. Else how would they ever trust you?"

As he finished speaking, Thurkill folded his arms, pleased with his words and certain they would have the desired effect. His hopes lasted no more than a heartbeat.

"How dare you lecture me, you pup?" Eadric shoved his face right into Thurkill's so that the younger man's face was coated in a thin film of spittle. Thurkill knew better than to rile him further by wiping it off; he had to stand and take it.

"You ask what crime he has committed? Well, I will tell you. His crime was to come here to my country and to my land. Him, and many thousands like him, have killed my king and many hundreds of his best men and nearly killed you, too, by all accounts. They have raped and pillaged their way across England, taking what they want and killing any who dare try to stop them. And if that weren't enough, men like this one killed my wife, not to mention my cousin, Aelfric of Huntendune, as you yourself told me not one week ago. May be not this man, but men of his ilk. And if men like us do nothing, the killing, pillaging and raping will go on unchecked."

Although the Norman had little or no understanding of the words spoken, he must have known that his life hung in the balance, poised precariously on the edge of a knife with only the outcome of this argument to determine on which side he fell. His eyes remained fixed on the young Saxon whom he knew had spoken in his defence, imploring him to save him.

That hope was misplaced, though, as Thurkill did not have the power to save him. He could not defy Eadric's word; he had already risked much to this point and to go further might see him and his people forced from of the camp or worse. But the idea of cold-blooded murder still rankled. He recalled the dismembered knight they had found nailed to the trees. He had little doubt that a similar fate awaited this poor bastard too. As much as he detested the Normans, he had no wish to be party to the savage killing of a defenceless man.

"Your will, Lord." As he spoke, Thurkill bowed stiffly in recognition of Eadric's authority before turning away from the gathering, the jeers of those around him ringing in his ears. One or two of the more belligerent even took to jostling him, although they ceased when he stared in their direction. Despite their safety in numbers, few dared challenge the hulking warrior to his face.

"Wait."

Thurkill stopped in his tracks, his gut churning at the thought of what might be to come. Too late now, the voice in his head berated him for becoming embroiled in business that was not his to be concerned with.

"I'd not finished speaking with you, boy. On reflection, I see your words carry merit. You're right to remind me of my duty to the law and before God, who stands in judgement over all of us. For this reason, I've decided I will not kill this man. Not without a fair trial at least. And I decree that his trial will be decided by combat, as ancient tradition allows."

Thurkill's heart sank, for he knew before Eadric even uttered the words what he would say.

"And it is my command that you, Thurkill, will be my champion. I promise you that if the Norman manages to kill you, then I shall declare him innocent and see him safely returned to FitzScrope in his castle in Henffordd. I trust this sits well with your sense of justice?"

SEVEN

The trial was set for dawn on the morrow. Thurkill knew he needed rest to be fresh for the ordeal, but no matter how hard he tried, sleep just would not come.

As he lay awake, listening to the wind howling around the eaves, jumbled thoughts trampled through his brain like a herd of stampeding wild boar. Images of all manner of different outcomes fought for precedence in his mind, each presenting a different picture of what the next few hours might bring. It was his own fault, though. Eadric's proclamation had caught him in a web of his own making and now his life hung in the balance just as much as the Norman captive. He would have to kill the wretch; assuming, of course, that the bastard did not kill him first.

Grudgingly, he had to admire the simplicity of Eadric's solution. It had a symmetry that would have been pleasing if he did not stand to lose everything as a result. The irony was not lost on Hild either. Though she had not said as much, Thurkill could see disappointment in her eyes. One day he would learn to stop allowing his mouth to talk himself into trouble.

After tossing and turning for what felt like hours, Thurkill finally abandoned all hope of sleep. Sighing heavily, he pushed the fur covers aside and rose to his feet, doing his best not to wake the gently snoring Hild by his side.

"At last. I thought you'd never give up," Eahlmund's whispered voice floated over from the other side of the hut, heavily laced with sarcasm.

"Your pardon, my friend. There're too many things on my mind to sleep. I'm going for a walk to clear my head."

Eahlmund grunted. "Wait there; I'll come with you."

"There's no sense in both of us being awake. You'll need your wits about you should I lose the fight tomorrow. God alone knows what will happen should that befall me."

"I wouldn't be surprised if it's today now, actually." Eahlmund huffed, changing the subject. "Anyway, your need is greater than mine; I can sleep all I want when I'm dead. Though, with luck, that won't be for a while yet."

Outside, they were buffeted by the gusting wind, forcing them to pull their cloaks more tightly around their bodies to stay warm. Together, the two friends walked through the camp, following the line of the stream. After fifty or so paces, they passed the night watchman who barred their path until he recognised them.

That obstacle passed, they walked on in silence, the sound of their feet muffled by the soft grass, made damp by the night's moisture. A companionable silence lay between them until, eventually, they came across a cluster of small, moss-covered boulders nestled in the undergrowth by the water's edge and sheltered from the breeze by a steep earthen bank. Thurkill sat on the nearest rock, shivering as the cold surface of the stone penetrated his clothing.

"Your pardon, Eahlmund. Once again, I'm failing in my duty to protect you and the others from harm. When we set off from Gudmundcestre, I had hoped to keep us all safe for a little while longer than this."

"Well, you know what they say, Lord? Those with no coin do not get to choose what meal they eat."

Thurkill could not help but smile. As ever, Eahlmund's spirit seemed unbreakable. Whether it was an act, Thurkill did not care. He was grateful for the support of his oldest and closest ally.

"Though, if you're asking my opinion – and speaking as a friend, of course – it might not hurt if you were to learn to keep your big mouth shut every now and then."

Thurkill bent to pick up a loose stone which he then launched into the dark, rushing waters. Its weight made a satisfying plop, spraying his leather-clad feet with fine droplets. If he'd wanted to take offence at Eahlmund's jibe, he could not. His friend had offered him heartfelt advice dressed up as a joke, making it that much easier to swallow. Besides, it was nothing more than he'd already thought.

Eahlmund was right. His misplaced sense of honour had landed him in the mess in which he now found himself. If only he'd held his tongue, none of this would have come to pass. The unfortunate Norman would be dead, his body parts distributed around several tree trunks. Did one life more or fewer truly matter?

The problem was, however, that Thurkill still believed it did.

Eahlmund continued, "Anyway, what's more important right now is making sure you beat this fellow. I was watching him closely, Lord, and he's no match for you, I'm sure of it. You're a good head taller and have the longer reach in your arm. He'll have to duck inside your defences to land a blow, and I can't see him doing that."

"And why is that?"

"Well, I'd say he's seen at least ten more summers than you, if not twenty. You should have the edge in terms of speed and agility. If I were you, though, I'd look to end it as quickly as you can. He should tire more quickly, but the longer it goes on, the more chance there is that you'll make a mistake, slip or he'll get lucky. I'd pile in from the word 'go' and smash his skull with a single blow of my axe."

Thurkill smiled. "I admire your enthusiasm and your faith in my battle-skills. I find little fault with your plan, other than one thing."

"Which is?"

"The wretch will be fighting for his life. He's been offered an unexpected chance of survival, and he'll give all that he has to seize it. Fear lends strength to a man, enabling him to achieve feats he might otherwise think beyond him. I doubt it'll be as easy as you hope."

"I still give him little chance against the famous scourge of the Vikings at Stamford."

Thurkill fixed Eahlmund with a hard stare, trying to fathom whether his friend was jesting at his expense, but his face was inscrutable – making it even more likely that he was.

"Anyway, even if he were to win – which I still say is impossible, by the way – do you really think Eadric will let him live?"

Thurkill shrugged. "I fear I'll not care if that comes to pass. The Norman has no way of knowing that, though; all he knows is that killing me takes him a step closer to his freedom. Look, friend, the sky lightens to the east. I must make ready."

***

The first souls had already begun to gather by the time they returned, doubtless eager to secure the most advantageous places from which to view the coming spectacle. Back inside their hut, Thurkill quickly donned his padded leather jerkin, before shrugging into his heavy mailshirt, taking comfort from the familiar feel of the armour, like it was a favoured pair of boots. To reduce the burden on his shoulders, he cinched his belt tightly around his waist, his fingers nimbly working the smooth leather into a sturdy knot that would not come loose. Straightening up, he bounced on his toes a few times, partly to loosen his muscles, partly to shift the iron-ring encrusted garment into a more comfortable position.

Satisfied, Thurkill picked up his shield, slotting his left forearm through the weathered straps attached to the rear of the board, made greasy from hours of sweat-stained use. The golden paint that depicted the wyvern of Wessex design was battered and flaking, reminding him he'd not had time to see to its upkeep in recent weeks – a fact that ought to bring shame on any warrior worth his salt. Finally, he grabbed the hilt of his sword. The act of closing his fingers around the grip brought back memories, not all of which he wished to recall. Like his shield, the blade needed work, notched here and there as a consequence of prior conflicts; but it would suffice for today. He knew its edge to be keen enough. A few hours with one of Eadric's whetstones the previous evening had seen to that.

He did not relish the business of killing, but it was a business to which he was well suited all the same. And if he had no choice, then he would perform its rituals with care and diligence. He would not be found wanting for lack of preparation.

His tasks complete, Thurkill turned to face his companions. "If this goes badly, my friends, you must look to yourselves. Our position here is frail at best, and with me gone, I fear for the rest of you. Eahlmund…" he turned to face his oldest, most trusted companion, "I charge you with Hild's safety and that of our child. This is no small burden, and I have little by way of advice for you. But do it you must. Raise the child as your own, if that is what Hild wants, and – if it's a boy – name him for me so that he might have remembrance of his father."

Holding back her tears, Hild walked over to Thurkill carrying his iron helm. Such was his height that he had to go down on one knee to enable her to reach. Before placing it, however, she kissed his forehead and whispering in his one remaining ear so that none of the others might hear her words.

"You'd better not die, husband. As sweet as Eahlmund is and as good a father as I'm sure he would be, I would rather lie with my own man each night. Go with God, my love."

With that, she pushed the helm down on his head, making sure the leather padding cap on the inside fitted snuggly before pulling the chin strap tight to stop it from shifting.

With a final grim-faced nod, Thurkill turned to go, each man in turn gripping him by the forearm to wish him luck as he made his way towards the door. He noted that they all – Urri, Eahlmund, the brothers, Leofric and Leofgar, and even young Eopric – had their swords belted at their sides. They would be ready for whatever outcome prevailed.

Outside the hut, Thurkill headed back towards the clearing where the trial was due to be held. As he walked, he took the opportunity to swing his sword in wide circles, loosening the muscles which were stiff from lack of use. Though it had been some days since he'd last had cause to use the weapon – that fateful day back in Huntendune when Taillebois' man had slaughtered Aelfric in cold blood – he did not doubt that this body would remember soon enough.

As he drew closer, the sound of chanting and shouting assailed his ears. It sounded as if Eadric was whipping his people into a frenzy in anticipation of the coming fight. With a sinking feeling in the pit of his stomach, Thurkill realised that this whole event would be little more than sport for these people. The trial itself was incidental to them; they cared not about justice, or who won or lost. They wanted to see a contest worthy of its name, with a man killed at the end of it.

Mirroring his mood, the leaden grey clouds above began to

unload their cargo. Heavy drops of rain thudded rhythmically against his helm as a woodpecker hammers its beak against the bark of a tree. Now he would have to contend with the added danger of losing his footing on the wet ground.

Pushing through the crush of bodies, Thurkill was pleased to hear the crowd's chanting replaced by shocked gasps. The sight of a Saxon huscarl dressed for war was new to them. Added to which, Thurkill stood taller and broader than most and, accoutred in his gleaming armour, his appearance could not fail to strike dread into a weaker man's soul. Thurkill resolved to revel in the awe he had created; it would be no bad thing if these folk feared him, he decided.

He came to a halt in the centre of the make-shift arena which was, in fact, little more than a patch of well-trodden earth that had been cleared of whatever stores had been kept there until now. Saying nothing, he stood in front of Eadric, shield held at the ready and sword drawn, its tip pointing at the ground midway between the two men. There was no sign of the Norman.

Eadric grunted a greeting. Though the outlaw's face betrayed no emotion, Thurkill had seen a glimmer of surprise in his eyes. Perhaps now he would start to receive a little of the respect that he felt was due to him. In the short time he had been there, Eadric had treated Thurkill with little more than contempt. Though it might be the last impression he was able to make, Thurkill felt no small sense of satisfaction that his host might now see he was not just the boy he supposed him to be.

Out of the corner of his eye, Thurkill saw his companions taking up station behind and to the left of Eadric. He briefly inclined his head in their direction to acknowledge their presence, a gesture too small to have been seen by many but which Eahlmund, nevertheless, answered with a small nod of his own. They were well positioned, Thurkill noted, to intervene should the need arise. Urri had even taken up position right behind Eadric's shoulder, out of his sight but close enough to grab him in a heartbeat. It amused Thurkill to think these people were so poorly disciplined as to allow their lord to be so exposed to danger.

Like a clap of thunder, the sombre mood was torn asunder by a great shout that began to Thurkill's rear before rumbling around the entire circle. Moments later, the crowd parted to admit the captive soldier into their midst, stumbling in response to a none too gentle shove. Thurkill turned to face him, appraising the man that stood by his side. Eadric's men had done him proud, finding a helm, sword and shield similar to his own which, combined with his own hauberk, made the two men evenly matched.

Looking into his opponent's eyes, Thurkill saw no fear; rather, he appeared resolute and determined, as if resigned to his fate. *The man knows he has nothing to lose,* Thurkill mused. *He will fight as if the very devil comes for him and will be all the more dangerous for it.*

Meanwhile, the jeers and howls of the crowd had grown to a deafening crescendo as the prospect of bloodshed intensified. Eadric, his dark hair plastered to his face by the incessant rain, finally held up his hands to call for peace.

"Friends, in keeping with our ancient customs, a man accused of a crime may elect to undergo trial by combat in order to prove his innocence. It is for this reason that we are gathered here to bear witness before God. Ralph the Norman proclaims he is innocent of the charges laid against him, that he did – along with others of his ilk – lay waste to, despoil, and otherwise pillage these lands and people, thereby ignoring the rights and wishes of their lord."

A chorus of hisses and abuse greeted these words. It was a piece of theatre, designed solely to stir up the crowd's fervour, and they had not failed in that regard. Once again, Eadric had to appeal for calm before he could continue.

"Whether we think him guilty or not, this is his right. I have selected Thurkill, newly arrived in our community, to be my champion. Few could be more worthy, for this man fought with Harold at Senlac, standing in the huscarl ranks and defending our king to the last. What's more, Harold personally rewarded him for his courage and skill against the Viking champion on the bridge at Stamford. It is fitting that a man such as he will represent me in this trial."

At least he has read Alwig's letter; I should be grateful for that, I suppose. Thurkill's thought as the crowd roared its appreciation.

Eadric then addressed the two combatants directly. "You are each armed with sword, shield and seax. These are all that are available to you. Should you lose them, or should they break, you will have to rely on your wits alone. None here will help you. This is the only rule; everything else is up to you."

Raising his voice, he then roared. "The contest will end only once one of you is dead... though I recommend you make quick work of it as I am hungry. Breakfast awaits and I'm eager to be out of this pissing rain."

Eadric waited while his words were haltingly translated for Ralph by a man with some skill in the Norman tongue, after which Ralph nodded to signify his understanding. With that, Eadric brought his arm down in a sharp cutting motion to signal the trial to begin.

Before Eadric's arm had finished moving, Ralph was on the move, hurtling towards Thurkill with his sword raised high above his head, screaming a fearsome battle cry in his own tongue. Even though Thurkill had expected just such a move – it was exactly what he would have done in his place – he was still caught off guard, stumbling back a few steps as he desperately blocked the blade on his raised shield. The blow's impact reverberated up his arm, causing his jaw to clamp painfully. If he had been in any doubt before, he knew now he was in a fight.

All around him, the crowd screeched its delight, anticipating a thrilling contest.

Strangely, Ralph chose not to follow up his attack, instead preferring to back off a few paces where he began circling his opponent as if looking for an opening. It occurred to Thurkill that Ralph might be caught in two minds. Whether to conserve energy to try to match the Saxon for stamina or to try to finish the fight as quickly as possible. Surely, he must choose the latter. The Norman had not been well treated since his capture and must be fatigued from lack of sleep and food. He had to gamble on a quick victory for, of the two of them, he would surely tire more quickly.

It was as if Ralph had been reading his mind, for suddenly he was charging at him once again. This time, however, instead of aiming a sword swipe at Thurkill's head, he dropped his shoulder at the last minute and barged straight into the Saxon with his full weight behind his shield. Thurkill had positioned his own board to deal with a strike coming from above, and so Ralph's raised iron boss caught him square in the left shoulder. Once again, he staggered back, dropping his arm as the impact deadened the feeling in his muscles. *By God's hairy scrotum,* Thurkill cursed, blinking the rain out of his eyes. *He has the measure of me.*

The crowd had also smelt blood. To Thurkill's shock and dismay, several of them were even cheering for the Norman, urging him to finish the job. Taking heart from their cries, Ralph now pressed home his attack, perhaps sensing he had his opponent where he wanted him. Roaring incoherently, the Norman launched a flurry of blows at Thurkill's head.

The pain in Thurkill's numbed shoulder as he tried to lift the dead weight of his shield was excruciating. The muscles were steadfast in their refusal to do his bidding. He prayed that the feeling would return soon, for without his shield he'd be dead before too much longer.

As he parried blow after blow, Thurkill caught a glimpse of Hild standing between Eahlmund and Leofric. If he hadn't already known it, the expression on her face told him just how badly the fight was going. The colour had drained from her cheeks, and her mouth was suspended open in a rictus of pure terror. The sight was enough to shock him to the core. *Come on, man. Pull yourself together before he guts you like a pig.*

But there was no respite, no time in which to gather his thoughts. The one glimmer of hope in his mind was that, having to move his shield arm in a series of rapid, jerky movements had unexpectedly started to ease the pain in his shoulder. Though it still ached horribly, he did at least have some much-needed flexibility back. Tensing his wrist and forearm behind his shield, he realised that he'd not struck a single blow yet. It was high time he shifted the momentum of this battle; he had to put

Ralph on the defensive before all was lost.

A sudden searing bolt of pain made him gasp out loud. Hobbling back, he risked a glance down at his thigh, where already, the light brown cloth of his trews was beginning to stain a deep red hue. *Shit. You've let him get in under your guard. For God's sake, man, focus!*

Gingerly, he took another step back, testing the strength in his leg and fearing it might buckle under his weight. Happily, it held and held well. Though the wound stung with an intensity that made his eyes water, it could not have been too deep. He knew he'd had a lucky escape, though.

Even as that thought occurred to him, a plan began to form in his mind. He took another step, limping heavily to exaggerate the extent of the wound. For a further piece of mummery, he forced a grimace each time he placed his foot and accompanied each step with an audible grunt. The crowd whooped with enthusiasm, anticipating the spectacle of a man about to be eviscerated on the point of a sword.

Meanwhile, Ralph had stepped back once again, to survey the result of his handiwork. Seeing Thurkill's supposed discomfort, he allowed a wicked grin to form, his lips pulling back in a fierce snarl and exposing his yellowing, uneven teeth.

Even with his head bowed and with his matted strands of hair masking much of his face, Thurkill could see that the Norman was blowing hard. Ralph's early exertions were starting to catch up with him; he was paying the price for his initial flurry of attacks. But even so, the look of triumph in his eyes was unmistakable. He believed his foe beaten; or, at least, cowed. Ralph would doubtless believe it a simple matter to finish the job now, no matter how fatigued he might be.

With a howl that echoed around the clearing, Ralph stormed forward once more, murderous intent in his eyes. Thurkill watched him come, determined to play out his subterfuge to the last moment to ensure the deception was complete. Turning side on to keep his wounded leg behind him, he raised his shield ready to receive the attack. He concentrated on making it look a slow and cumbersome manoeuvre that was completed only just in time.

Once again, the blows came thick and fast. Splinters of wood dug from Thurkill's battered shield flew out on all sides. All the while, he retreated as awkwardly as he could, making it seem as though the end were both inevitable and imminent.

Just as he was about to launch his attack, Thurkill found himself sprawled on his back, the wind forced from his lungs, staring up at the laughing, toothless face of one of Eadric's men. The bastard had stuck out a foot to trip the Saxon as he retreated. As he lay there, momentarily dazed, Thurkill committed the man's features to memory, swearing to himself that – should he survive – he would open a new smile across the man's throat. But for now, he had not a moment to lose.

Taking the chance offered to him, Ralph closed the distance between them and readied himself to stab down on his prostrate opponent's exposed belly. Before he could land the blow, however, Thurkill released his grip on his shield and rolled away in the opposite direction. It was a calculated risk, but it worked. Committed to the move, Ralph buried his sword deep into the soft earth, made glutinous mud by the pouring rain. As the Norman struggled with both hands to free the blade, Thurkill lurched to his feet and came rushing in from the side. *Why does he not forget the damned sword and grab his knife?* It mattered not, though, for Ralph's fate was sealed.

A look of abject fear seized control of his face as he realised – far too late – that it was all over. But still he did not let go of the hilt, but rather redoubled his efforts to free the blade. With a triumphant yelp, Ralph finally managed to yank his sword out of the ground, but it was heavy, made unwieldy by thick lumps of sodden earth which clung obstinately to the steel.

Before he could even turn, Thurkill was upon him. He slashed his blade across the back of the Norman's thigh, opening a deep gash that immediately hamstrung him. Using his momentum, Thurkill then swung back in a sweeping motion that caught Ralph just beneath the chin. His sword bit deep into the flesh of the doomed man's throat, stifling his scream before it could even form. In the same moment, his eyes rolled back, and the colour drained from his face. He was dead before he had crumpled to the ground.

Thurkill did not join in the celebrations. While mayhem reigned around him, he fell to his knees, mentally and physically exhausted. In all his time as a warrior, he'd never felt so close to death as he had then. Not even in the final moments at Senlac. He could only speculate what might have happened had Ralph been properly rested. Relief flooded through his limbs, washing away the stress of the duel, though leaving him exhausted and aching all over.

"You are one lucky bastard; I'll say that for you."

Thurkill looked up at Eahlmund's grinning face. Despite the smile, he could see the strain behind his friend's eyes. He was all too aware how close Thurkill had come to losing his life.

Hild, however, made no attempt to disguise her true feelings, as she punched him on the arm as tears streamed down her cheeks.

"Don't you dare ever frighten me like that again, do you hear?"

Thurkill groaned, almost too weary to form the words. "Believe me, wife, it was not my intention. He was a brave and formidable opponent. He did not deserve death at my hand."

"Nonsense." Eadric laughed, reaching down to cuff him round the head. "Justice has been done and God has seen fit to judge the Norman guilty. Do you dare say otherwise? Would you challenge God's Holy law now?"

Thurkill chose to keep his peace. There was little sense arguing the point any further. He did not and would not feel guilt for Ralph's death – he didn't care for the man one way or another – but he still clung to the principle of truth and justice and, no matter how he looked at it, he had killed a man innocent of any crime other than the language he spoke. Wearily, he bowed his head in tacit acceptance of Eadric's authority. He was a stranger in this land and must look out for the safety of his followers. Eadric was the only thing that separated him from a life of outlawry. It would not do to push him too far.

"Still, that was some scrap, eh? I confess, I thought the bastard had you for a time there. You fooled us all, pretending that cut to your leg was worse than it was. It was a ruse I'd have been proud to have thought of myself. Still, it would've been awkward had you been killed, for I would not have been able to let him live."

Despite everything, Thurkill could not stop himself. "But you'd given him your word, Lord."

Eadric sighed. "You've a lot to learn, lad. Life is not so simple as you think. Honour is something to be hoped for rather than expected. Knowing that Ralph had seen our camp here, do you really believe he'd treat us with honour and not give away our location to his masters? Of course not. He would be back here within a day with that bastard, FitzScrope at the head of an army.

"It is my duty to protect these people, and if that means one more hairy-arsed goat-shagger must die, then that is a price I'm prepared to pay. No doubt, I'll be having a frank discussion with Saint Peter when I present myself at the gates of Heaven, but that can wait until the time comes."

"So why bother with the trial? Why not just kill Ralph and be done with it?"

"What? And spoil everyone's fun? We love a good fight here and that – let me tell you – was one of the best. Besides, I needed to teach you a lesson, boy. Can't have you shouting the odds in front of all my people and then not be taken down a peg or two, eh? I should've expected it, though, for Alwig said in his letter that you can be a feisty whoreson at times."

With that, Eadric strode off, roaring with laughter and calling for bread and ale.

EIGHT

Thurkill could not suppress a grunt of pain as Hild tended to his injury. Sitting on their cot with the leg of his trews cut away to avoid any dirt or pieces of cloth getting into the wound, he was able to see the full extent of the damage. He'd been lucky. The gash was as long as his palm was wide, but it had penetrated no deeper than the breadth of his little finger. Ralph had struck him at the full extent of his reach; any closer and it could have been fatal. He'd seen many men bleed to death from just such a cut – some of them in less time than it took to milk a cow, great arcs of blood spurting forth in time with each beat of the heart.

"Hold still. Honestly, you're worse than a child who's fallen and grazed their knee. 'Tis little more than a scratch."

Though she spoke with a calm authority, his wife could not hide the worry in her eyes. Thurkill knew how afraid she'd been but, nevertheless, she remained steadfast now as if unwilling to lay bare her emotions. Instead, she concentrated on washing his leg with a cloth dipped in water from a carved wooden bowl before binding it with fresh, clean strips of linen which she wound around his thigh several times. Finally, she pulled the ends tight and tied them off in a knot at the back. Eadric's healer had given her a poultice made of herbs mixed with honey which she had professed would stop all evil humours from infecting the wound. He was to leave it in place for two whole days and if, when he removed it, the leg did not smell of rotten eggs, then all would be well.

"Christ's cock, does it have to be quite so tight, woman?" The pain he felt added a note of irritation to his voice that was not meant.

Hild took it in good part, though. "I'm not sure Father Wulfric would be pleased to hear such profanity pass your lips, husband. You know as well as I that the skin on either side must be drawn together like this to help it heal. The closer it is, the sooner it can begin to knit together once more."

Thurkill grunted but did not complain further, knowing her to be right. Besides, after the initial discomfort, the pain was easing to a more manageable level now, little more than a dull throbbing sensation to which he would soon become inured. In a week or two, it would be little more than another scar to add to his ever-growing collection.

"What now, Lord?" Eahlmund was standing at Hild's shoulder, a hard to fathom expression on his face.

"Your meaning, friend?"

"Do we stay and make our home here amongst these people or not?"

"I'm not sure we have much choice. Back east, the Normans hunt us for the murder of Taillebois in Huntendune. Then, there is the small matter of Robert FitzGilbert to consider. Though I don't know if he were injured in the fighting at Gudmundcestre, he certainly cheated death. You can be assured that he will not rest till he has his revenge or dies trying. There's no future for us back there. I see no other option than to make the best of it here with Eadric. They may live outside of the law but where else can we go? Here we have some safety, at least. Eadric's camp is well concealed in these woods and he has men aplenty to defend it. I can think of no better place at present, but I would willingly listen to other ideas."

***

That night, Thurkill sat with the others around the fire pit over which was turning on a spit, the suspended carcass of a deer which had been killed earlier that day. Any remaining worries he might've had in respect of his status among Eadric's people had faded away over the course of the evening as time and again, folk came up to him to offer their congratulations on his victory. Whatever he may have thought of their allegiances at the time, it was clear they had not really wanted him to lose.

One of the last to come over was a weasel-faced man who looked vaguely familiar. As he spoke, Thurkill wracked his brains to try to place him. He wondered if he had been one of Aethelgar's men whom they had met on the first night. The mystery was finally solved when – as he finished speaking – he opened his mouth and grinned foolishly. The sight of the man's gums, missing all but a few teeth, brought the memory back in a rush. The man who had tripped him during the fight.

Thurkill got to his feet slowly, but deliberately, careful not to give any clue as to his intent. Then, grabbing the man's outstretched hand with iron strength, he hissed, "You've some nerve to stand there before me, my friend, after you so nearly got me killed today."

With the young Saxon towering over him, the grin froze on the man's face. Stuttering, he sought to assuage Thurkill's anger, while vainly trying to pull his tortured hand away. All those within earshot stopped to watch the altercation as the weasel whimpered through pain and fear. "W...well... well, it was just a bit of fun. I meant no harm by it. And it all turned out well in the end, did it not?"

Thurkill nodded sagely as if weighing the words closely. Releasing his hand, he allowed a smile to form on his lips. "That is true, it did. Likewise, you will know, therefore, that this is also just a bit of fun and that I mean no harm by it."

With that, Thurkill took half a step back, bunching his fist as he did so, before driving it with all the strength he could summon directly into the scrawny wretch's mouth. Such was the power behind the punch that he was knocked off his feet, ending up on his arse, his mouth bloodied and his eyes streaming with tears of pain and shock. One of the few teeth he still possessed was then spat out along with a great gobbet of blood and phlegm.

Roaring with laughter, Eadric slapped Thurkill on the back. "I warned Aelwulf he had that coming. I think he hoped you might've forgotten or perhaps had not known who the culprit was. But you always reap what you sow, as my father used to say."

"The man's a fool for I had forgotten until he came to me seeking to buy my favour with his ingratiating words. If he'd but stayed out of my way for a few days, it might have gone better for him."

"Ha. I doubt he'll learn from his error, though. He's not known for having the sharpest scythe in the field. Anyway, enough of him; tell me what it is you want from us here, Thurkill, son of Scalpi. You can see what we are and what little we have. Though I have a lord's status, I cannot offer you patronage, advancement or even gifts, save what we take from those Normans we kill.

"I'll not lie, though. I have need of good fighting men and, despite what we saw here today," he chuckled at his own joke, "your battle-skills vouch for themselves. But is that what you want, lad? You have a young wife, one that is with child if I'm not mistaken. Are you sure that the life we have here will be good for you? For her?"

"But it was not always like this, was it, Lord? Alwig told me you were once one of the most wealthy and powerful men in the lands that border the Waelesc."

Eadric sighed. "Aye, 'twas so. I don't deny it. There were few in these parts that could rival me. That was until old King Edward brought his Norman friends with him when he returned from exile half a lifetime ago; one of whom he made Earl of Henffordd with plenty of land to go with it. There have been Norman lords in these parts ever since, and now they're multiplying like rabbits and pushing the rest of us – those who were born here and whose fathers can trace their lineage back to King Offa's times and beyond – to one side. I was a fool to think that William of Normandy would lift a hand to protect us, though he promised as much when we submitted to his authority."

Thurkill stared in open-mouthed astonishment. "You swore fealty to William? Were you at his coronation? I don't recall seeing you."

"Aye, lad, though I went to no crowning. We were summoned to Saint Erkenwald's Abbey in Berchningae not far to the east and north of Lundenburh. William was staying there while his great fortress was built by the great river. There had been some trouble at the coronation, so I was told."

"Aye, that there was, but it was not Saxon doing. It was his soldiers who acted like thugs, setting fire to the houses around the abbey for no reason."

"Hmmph." Eadric's expression showed his lack of surprise. "I was there along with many others, including the Earls Morcar and Eadwine. There, we submitted to William, placing our lives and our property in his hands and, there, he restored that property to us from his favour and swore to treat us well and fairly.

"All was well until we found out, a few days later, just what 'restored to us from his favour' really meant. His lick-spittle minions were quick to inform us that if we wanted to keep our lands, we would be required to redeem them from him at a sum of his choosing. We were then sent back to our estates to raise the coin within a month or face forfeiture."

Thurkill nodded sympathetically. "A similar thing happened to Aelfric in Huntendune. He paid with his life when he tried to resist."

"It's the same the whole land over, my friend. The Normans have their victory and now their true colours are revealed. The grand promises from the coronation are gone. Instead, William distributes our lands amongst his followers as if he were serving them the best cuts of meat from his table. And before I could even raise the money, things went from bad to worse when William FitzOsbern was appointed Earl at Henffordd. Him and the king's half-brother, Odo of Bayeux, are William's most trusted and most powerful lords. And I suspect he's been placed here because the king fears us wild folk on the borders."

"I suspect he's right to fear you if my experience of the last few days is anything to go by."

"It's kind of you to say so," Eadric replied with no hint of irony. "As soon as the deadline passed, FitzOsbern wasted no time unleashing his devil-hound, Richard FitzScrope, on me. In truth, I believe they hoped I wouldn't pay. FitzOsbern wanted my lands to reward his own men and he was going to have them by any means, fair or foul. But though I gave no money, the price I actually paid was more than any amount of silver or gold. FitzScrope took something much more valuable; now he has my lands, and my wife lies beneath three feet of English soil."

The bear-like man whispered these last words before falling silent, apparently lost in his own thoughts. Moments later, Hild walked over to where Thurkill sat, taking to the stool by his side and kissing him gently on the cheek. Eadric watched her as she glided like a swan across the ground in her flowing white dress, a look on his face that was a mix of pain and sorrow. Even in the darkness of the night, Thurkill could see Eadric's cheeks were wet with tears, reflected in the light of the fire whose flames danced in front of them.

Then with a great effort of will to regain his composure, Eadric croaked, "Take good care of her, Thurkill. I pray you do not lose her as I lost mine. There's no pain deeper, nor anger greater than that which is caused by the death of a wife. And mark me, I will make them pay, all that had a hand in it, or I shall die trying."

Thurkill felt a lump growing in the back of his throat as he contemplated what it must be like to walk in Eadric's boots. Though he'd known grief enough through the loss of his own family, he could not imagine how he would bear losing Hild. He could not love another as much as he loved her. It was like they were two halves of the same puzzle and, together, they formed a whole that was far stronger than they would ever be apart. Taking Hild's hand in his, he squeezed hard, feeling her return the grip.

"And I will help you, Lord. My sword is yours, should you want it." The words surprised Thurkill; he had not meant to commit so soon and so readily and a part of him cursed himself for his impetuosity. *One day, your mouth will get you killed; you see if it doesn't.*

But the fact was, Eadric's words had moved him, penetrating the deepest recesses of his soul. Any last misgivings he had about his part in Ralph's death had been laid to rest. So far, he'd not met a single Norman worthy of his respect or trust. He did not care if every last one of them were killed. If his fate were to die ridding England of their scourge, then so be it.

NINE

Richard FitzScrope removed the bone-handled knife from the sheath which hung from his belt by two twisted leather thongs. Without pausing, he leaned forward towards the steaming leg of mutton on the wooden platter in front of him, where it had been set only moments before by two kitchen servants. With his left hand, he grabbed hold of the bone protruding from the hunk of meat, wincing as he did so at the heat that seared his palm, before then using the knife to hack off a thick slice of the succulent flesh. The blade made short work of the mutton; its edge having been whetted that very morning.

FitzScrope dug the point into the tender slice of meat and lifted it back towards his trencher, turning it as he did, so that he might inspect the underside. Grunting with satisfaction, he noted the flesh was just the right shade of pink. The Saxons had a habit of burning everything to a cinder and he'd grown so tired of eating dried out, blackened meat that he'd been forced to send for his own cook from his estates back in Normandy. *At least Hugh knows how to prepare a decent leg of mutton, unlike these backward fools.*

Using long slender fingers, FitzScrope picked up the piece of meat and leaned forward to take a bite, making sure that the meat's juices dripped down onto the bread rather than his chin or – worse still – his clothes. He prided himself on his immaculate appearance and to have stains on his tunic would be unacceptable.

The meat literally fell apart in his mouth. It was cooked to perfection; just long enough for the fat to have melted, but still leaving its exquisite taste infused through the flesh. He closed his eyes to savour the texture and flavour as he chewed slowly, before finally swallowing. Finally, he took a long draught of red wine, also from his estates back home, enjoying the warm, fruity aroma that assailed his nostrils.

"Are you quite alright, FitzScrope? You look like you're having some sort of spiritual experience." Sitting to the knight's left, William FitzOsbern had paused in his own meal to stare at his subordinate with a look of undisguised bemusement on his face. FitzScrope was aware that the older man could never resist poking fun at him because of his fastidiousness, not least because the earl knew was often quick to take offence. But, on this occasion, FitzOsbern was to be disappointed in his sport, as nothing could detract from the joy FitzScrope felt at that moment.

"You'll excuse me, Lord, but I would contend there's nothing wrong with enjoying a well-cooked piece of mutton occasionally. And is this not the finest you have tasted? I'll say one thing for these Saxons: though they may be useless in the kitchen, they know how to raise sheep fit for a lord's table. It's one of the few things I like about this god-damned pit of hell."

"They do indeed. And my compliments to your man, Hugh, too. At first, I thought you were mad bringing him over just to cook for you, but your wisdom is plain to see now."

"I'd recommend you do the same if your Saxon cooks are anything like mine. Life's too short to be spent eating burnt meat, eh?"

"Hmmm," FitzOsbern had gone back to his own food, his mind seemingly having moved on. "Speaking of short lives, FitzScrope, when are you going to rid me of this fellow, Eadric the... what do they call him?"

Wiping his fingers delicately on a cloth held out for the purpose by a waiting serving girl, FitzScrope picked up his goblet, draining the remains of the rich dark wine in a single gulp. Almost before he could place it back on the pitted surface of the old oaken table, it was whisked away to be refilled. The Lord of Scrobbesburh castle had a reputation for violent retribution against any that committed even the most trifling mistake, and none wished to incur his wrath by being anything less than fully attentive.

"He appears to be known by any number of names, Lord. Eadric the Wild being a popular one among his own people, but we more commonly call him Eadric Silvaticus on account of the fact that he likes to live amongst the woods and forests hereabouts. He's really no better than a rutting wild boar if I'm honest."

"Well, whatever his name, when are you going to put an end to him? I hear plenty of tales among your folk here that he has no respect for our authority. If I'm not mistaken, only yesterday news reached us of another of your men being found cut into pieces and nailed to a row of tree trunks. Fellow by the name of Ralph if I heard correctly."

FitzScrope could feel his ire rising, certain that the earl was goading him once more. God knows he'd tried to deal with the outlaw. Had he not burned down the man's hall at Conendovre? He could hardly be held to blame if the pig-shagger had not been at home. The fact that his woman had perished in the blaze had been some small consolation at least. He'd hoped that act would drive Eadric into the open to seek retribution, but the old fox had been too wily for that, knowing that he would stand little chance against mounted knights on open ground. Instead, he'd continued to skulk amongst the trees. FitzScrope had sent patrols to search for him but they had either come back empty-handed or had been captured and brutally murdered, like this Ralph.

Rather than rise to the bait, FitzScrope fought hard to keep a lid on his anger. It would serve no purpose to give the earl the satisfaction of having needled him to the point of losing his temper. "The net is ever closing, Lord. He can't hide forever."

"That may be but, in the meantime, we are a laughingstock, man. How can we hope to impose our authority on the people if we cannot bring one man to heel?"

"He's not just one man, he has several…"

"Interrupt me again, and you'll find yourself in Ralph's place." FitzOsbern had not shouted; he had not needed to. The glower with which he fixed the younger man was enough to make his point. "I do not care if he has four men at his call or four hundred. The fact is that all the castles in the world are useless if we cannot bend the people to our will. Do I make myself clear?"

FitzScrope sat brooding, every fibre in his body itching to bite back at the grey-haired earl. Instead, silence reigned in the room, the only sound the steady drip-drip as the rainwater found its way through the wooden roof above their heads into the pail that had been placed on the floorboards to catch it. Even the servants had stopped in their tracks, unused to seeing their master bested in this own home. Here and there, one or two of them glanced uneasily at each other, their expressions bearing the realisation that one of them would doubtless pay the price for their lord's impotence later than night.

Eventually, FitzOsbern broke the spell. "I don't care how you do it, Richard, but be sure you put an end to this man's charade before the summer is out. I do not expect to hear his name again unless it is to tell me that his head has been placed on a spike on the walls of this castle."

***

FitzScrope stared into the flames, his mood as dark as the night that had closed in around the wooden keep that sat atop the vast earthen motte, forming the centre-point of his castle in Scrobbesburh. FitzOsbern had long since left, heading south to his own castle in Henffordd, leaving him alone with his thoughts. None of his captains had dared keep him company. He knew his reputation and was not surprised that no one wanted to be near him in this mood. Even the servants had disappeared except for one young woman who hovered in the shadows holding a pitcher of wine. Staring at her through his bushy eyebrows, he could have sworn she was shaking, though it was hard to tell amid the gloom of the shadows cast by the few candles dotted around the sparsely furnished chamber. Still, she probably had good reason. Chances were, he'd have her in his bed before the night were out, whether she was willing or not. In fact, he preferred it when they put up a fight; it stoked the fire in his loins to burn yet brighter. What use was there in being the lord of a godforsaken shithole like Scrobbesburh unless you could avail yourself of the few delights it did have to offer?

He was on the verge of stirring himself in her direction when the sound of boots running up the wooden stairs from the lower feasting hall distracted him. God-dammit, the wench would have to wait. Who was it now, by Christ's balls? Who needed him to wipe their arse? It'd better be important or he'd have whoever it was whipped until the bones of his back showed.

"Lord, Lord, I bring news." A breathless knight burst into the room, his face a mixture of fear at having disturbed FitzScrope and eagerness to win his praise.

"I'm sure you have, man, but is it worth my time? You'd best hope for your sake that it is. Well?"

The colour drained from the man's cheeks, but he pressed on nonetheless, hopeful that his words would win favour. "It's Eadric, Lord. We have word of where he will be in three days."

FitzScrope sat bolt upright, all thoughts of the girl forgotten for the time being. "By what means do you come by such information? Is it to be believed?"

"It hails from a source that can be trusted, Lord. By the time the information was acquired, the man was close to death. He would have done anything to make the pain stop."

FitzScrope chuckled, relishing the thought of the torture that had been inflicted upon the unfortunate wretch. "Where is he now, this man? I would question him myself before I commit my soldiers to chasing shadows in the dark."

The knight looked down at his feet. "I'm afraid that will not be possible, Lord. The dog's heart gave out not one hour ago. It appears we were a little overzealous in our work."

"Oh… well, these things happen. It is of no matter. Assemble a conroi of forty knights and let us be about God's work."

FitzScrope bounded out of his chair, knocking over his goblet as he did so. He cared not, though, for plans needed to be made, soldiers assembled. He hared down the stairs to the lower floor, hard on the heels of the messenger. *Finally, I get to remove this Eadric from the playing board and shut that smug bastard, FitzOsbern, up into the bargain.*

TEN

The news that Eadric had sworn fealty to William came as a shock to Thurkill, at least initially. But then several English lords had submitted when Edgar capitulated at Beorhthanstaed and many more still had done so at the coronation in the abbey at Westminster. It made sense that William would have summoned all other lords and notables to pledge their oaths as soon as possible thereafter. Once given, the oath could not be broken, or risk being declared outlaw or traitor. Nevertheless, many Saxons were now being pushed into revolt by the actions of their new overlords. First Aelfric, and now Eadric. And who knew how many others found themselves with the same stark choice?

From what he could gather, a state of near open war existed between Eadric and the Norman Earl of Henffordd. The dismembered bodies were evidence enough of that. But what hope did the former thegn have of winning? Already, the Normans were said to be strengthening their dreaded castles in the area, at Henffordd to the south and at Scrobbesburh to the north. When they were done, Eadric would be caught in the middle with nowhere to run.

Even built of wood, they would be formidable redoubts which the Normans could garrison with tens if not hundreds of knights, making them nigh on impregnable. What made it worse was that FitzOsbern was forcing the local townspeople to build them without pay, under the pretence that it was for their own good as the castles would bring peace and stability. But it would be a peace that was imposed under threat of violence more than anything.

"What troubles you, husband?"

Hild had come back from the river where she had been washing their clothes. Thurkill rose to relieve her of her burden, before proceeding to lay out each item over a piece of twine that had been stretched between the trunks of a pair of alders behind their hut. The warm breeze blowing through the camp would soon dry the garments.

"I worry for us, Hild. I had hoped that we might find peace here, away from the Normans. I thought we would find something like what we had at Gudmundcestre, that you would once again be the wife of a village lord and that we could rebuild our life amongst the hills and forests on Eadric's land. But instead, I have brought us to yet more danger at a time when you need calm and rest for the baby."

Hild came to stand behind him, circling her arms around his waist and pressing her cheek into his muscular back. "And what other path was open to you, Killi? We could not stay where we were, for our sake as much as for the people of the village. We could not wander the land aimlessly either. You know better than anyone that without the protection of a lord to speak for him, a man is defenceless in the eyes of the law."

"But is that not what we are now anyway? Eadric is no longer a lord. He lives outside of the law. By pledging my sword to him, have I not sealed our own fate too?"

Patiently, Hild straightened the clothes that he had failed to hang properly. "I ask again: what choice did you have? Besides, Eadric is strong. He has many men in his warband, and he is secure here deep in the woods. The Normans wouldn't dare come after him unless they could muster many hundreds, which I doubt is possible so far from Lundenburh. And with you, Eahlmund and the others, his strength just grew even more. We're safe here, Killi, and we should make the best of it. There are plenty more who have it worse."

Thurkill knew she was right, but it pleased him to hear her reassuring words. As ever, he felt the burden of responsibility for the lives of her and his little warband weigh heavily on his shoulders. Smiling, he finished hanging out the rest of the damp clothes, careful to learn from his earlier mistake.

"You've done a fine job with these trews, my love. There's hardly any trace of blood now and the rent has been neatly stitched. With prayer and God's help, we'll make a goodwife of you yet, huh?" Just in time he ducked the slap that Hild aimed at his cheek before running laughing into the hut.

***

Thurkill was awoken by someone shaking his shoulder. Instinctively, he reached for his seax which he kept close at hand by the side of his cot.

"Steady, Thurkill. There is no danger; I am here to bring you to Eadric. It's time."

It was too dark to see clearly, but Thurkill recognised Aethelgar's voice, the man who had captured them when they first came to Eadric's lands several days ago. His calm tone allowed Thurkill to relax the tension in his muscles. "Time for what, pray? Apart from sleeping that is."

"You'll see. Bring Hild and join us by the river as soon as you can."

There were at least thirty people, men and women, waiting by the river when Thurkill and Hild arrived. Several of them carried torches – thick lumps of wood around which had been wound strips of cloth dipped in tar which burned slowly but fiercely, illuminating the night to reveal the solemn expressions of those that carried them. Without a word, the column of people began to move as soon as the couple arrived, led by a man short in stature, who was – as far as Thurkill could tell – wrapped in a dark woollen cloak, the hood of which was pulled down low over his head to mask his features. A priest or monk perhaps, Thurkill surmised, his curiosity aroused yet further.

No one spoke as they walked. At first, Thurkill tried to engage those around him but he received little by way of reply. Shrugging at Hild, he gave up, lapsing into a companionable silence. The night was not cold, but he was glad for his cloak all the same for there was a chill edge to the breeze that swirled around them as they processed through the trees by some ancient path. Once or twice, he whispered in his wife's ear to make sure she was warm enough until she grew tired of his fussing and dug him in the ribs with a hissed warning to desist.

Thurkill had no idea as to their destination. The path – a narrow dirt track, worn into the earth by centuries of usage – seemed to be heading downhill but, beyond that, he was both literally and figuratively in the dark. Outside of the small circles of light cast by the torches, he could see nothing. At first, he wondered whether they marched to battle, but with equal numbers of women and men, he quickly discounted that idea. Moreover, the mood of those around them was too relaxed and benign to presage any imminent violence. Eventually, he realised he had no option but to wait and see, and to put his child-like curiosity on hold.

Finally, after what seemed like an age, they emerged from the woodland into a sizeable clearing. Set in the middle of the meadow was a small stone building which had a pitched roof covered with earthenware tiles. By now, the first light of the new day was dawning, meaning there was no longer any need for the torches. As his eyes slowly became accustomed to the morning twilight, Thurkill was able to take in his surroundings.

Beyond the trees, steep hills rose on all sides, making this a little sanctuary of sorts. The building seemed to be a church, for the highest point of the end nearest to him was adorned by a crudely fashioned cross. But then he also saw that the branches of the surrounding trees were festooned with brightly coloured strips of cloth, reminding him of the tales his aunt used to tell him as a boy. Though she'd always been a staunch follower of the Christ-saviour, Aga had maintained a quiet respect for the ways of the old people. Thurkill remembered her saying that followers of the old gods often had their ancient shrines deep in the middle of the darkest woods where they would decorate the trees and leave offerings. This, he realised, must be what she had meant. *But what is that doing next to a church?*

As he drew closer, Thurkill realised that another, much smaller, group of people were gathered in front of the church, waiting for them. Looking more closely, he realised that each of them was dressed in the same dark woollen robes as the priest that had led them to this spot. Up at the front of their party, Eadric held up his hand to signal them to stop while he went forward with the priest to speak with the others. Glancing around while he waited, Thurkill noticed he was standing next to Aethelgar.

"What is this place, friend? And why have we come here?"

Keeping his voice low, Aethelgar explained, "This is the church of the Lady Mildburh of Wenloch, a much-revered saint in these parts. She was the eldest daughter of King Merewahl who ruled here some four hundred years ago. Legend has it that she was to be wed against her will to a Waelesc prince, but she escaped across the river Hafern which then became so miraculously swollen that her pursuers could not cross. Then to protect herself from him, she entered the monastery here, which had been founded by her father and her uncle, King Wulfhere of Mercia."

Though not familiar to Thurkill, it was a story that was not uncommon. It was the same where he grew up, long dead saints who were still worshipped in the area in which they had lived and who were said to still have powers.

Aethelgar continued, "It's said that she was endowed with the gift of healing. There are stories of blind men whom she made see once more. People also say she holds sway over the birds, entreating them not to eat the grain sowed by the local farmers. She was buried here and, even to this day, these trees fill with the most wondrous sound of birdsong every dawn and dusk."

"But why are we here now, today?"

"This is her feast day, Thurkill. The one day on which you can pray to her and it is said that your prayers will be heard. Eadric has come here with offerings and prayers so that she may intercede on our behalf against the Normans. These ancient lands are hers as much as ours and it is an insult to her memory that they are now despoiled by the foul invader. But listen." Aethelgar cocked his head to one side. "Do you hear that?"

It was true; all around them the air began to fill with the sound of birdsong. Around them, people lifted their heads hoping to catch a glimpse of them. It was not hard, for almost every ribbon-bedecked branch was now laden with all manner of colourful birds, each one chirruping as if trying to outdo its neighbour. Thurkill had not seen them arrive; in fact, he could not say whether they had been there all the time. The sound they made was magical, though, filling his senses with peace and tranquillity. *Perhaps this Mildburh does have the power that Aethelgar claims?*

At that moment, the sun finally rose above the line of the trees, casting its light directly onto the cross that stood proud of the gable end of the roof. It had been built facing east so that it would catch the first rays of the morning sun. At the same time, the monks threw back their cowls to turn their faces to the sunlight, and Thurkill saw that they were not monks at all but nuns.

Seeing his confused expression, Aethelgar whispered, "This foundation is a convent, my friend. Mildburh eventually went on to become the Abbess here. These nuns are the latest in a long line of attendants who care for her tomb and her legacy. They will take us into the church now to lead the prayers."

Inside, it was cold and gloomy, despite the growing light outside. Windows had been built into the walls, but they were small and narrow and set high towards the roof, letting in almost no light at all. But within moments, the darkness receded into the corners, banished there for good as the nuns lit candle after candle in every nook and corner of the church. As his eyes grew accustomed, Thurkill could not suppress a gasp of astonishment.

Open-mouthed he stood rooted to the spot but turning in a full circle to take in the spectacle before him. Every wall had been white-washed and then painted with the most incredible colours and artistry. Wherever he looked, he saw wondrous scenes, some of which he recognised from his studies of the bible and some of which he assumed conveyed aspects of Saint Mildburh's life. Yes, there on the wall to his left was a picture of the saint, her arms spread wide with several birds perched on her arms while many more hovered around her head. Another scene on the opposite wall showed her looking out over a field of wheat, protecting the crop from voracious crows who would otherwise strip the stalks bare.

Looking down, Thurkill reached for Hild's hand, squeezing her fingers tightly between his. Glancing sideways, he could see that she, too, was enraptured by the whole experience. He had not considered himself to be particularly spiritual; he believed in God, of course. He'd always listened dutifully to the bible lessons he had attended as a child and he was ever careful to say his prayers... though, at times, he felt as if he were just saying the words without really understanding their meaning. But at that moment, he felt closer to God than he ever had before.

Everything seemed to make sense to him, to come into focus. Right then, he believed he could feel the presence of Saint Mildburh, feel that she was watching over them and would bless their endeavours.

Bowing his head, he prayed with an intensity he had not thought possible. *O blessed Saint of holy memory. Spare me that I may do God's work to expel the Normans from these lands. Grant me the strength of body and mind to guide my sword true to its target. And keep Hild safe and healthy that we may be blessed with the gift of children.*

The rest of the service passed in a daze for Thurkill. The fact that it was conducted in impenetrable Latin did not help but, more than that, he found he was unable to focus on anything but the sights and smells around him. Every one of his senses was under attack with such a surge of emotional energy that he feared his heart would burst through his chest. Although the doors to the church were closed, he fancied he could still hear the birds singing. Subconsciously, he brushed his hand against his cheek, realising with a start that the skin felt wet. He'd not even realised he was crying.

ELEVEN

Once the final prayer had been intoned, Eadric thanked the nuns and bade them farewell, leaving them with a pouch of silver pennies by way of offering for their upkeep. Emerging from the church, he led his followers a short distance to the south and west on a much wider and far more well-worn path back through the woods. Soon, the trees thinned out to reveal a small cluster of wooden buildings grouped around a much larger hall, similar in design and size to Thurkill's hall back in Haslow.

Inside was a bustle of activity. A heavy iron pot full of porridge was simmering away, suspended over the central hearth by a long iron chain fastened to the huge oak crossbeam that stretched across the width of the hall under the rafters. Several tables, positioned along the walls, were piled high with freshly baked loaves, the scent of which made Thurkill's stomach do back-flips. With the morning's solemnity, he had not realised just how hungry he was, having not eaten since the previous evening. The sun had already climbed high into the clear blue sky, telling him that breakfast was long overdue. And, to his delight, he realised that the row of small earthenware pots by the side of the bread were filled with clear, golden honey.

Aethelgar saw his expression and grinned. "The nuns keep many bees here and produce more honey than they can use. They use the surplus to pay for the villagers' labour. I tell you now, Thurkill, you won't have tasted finer in all of England."

Pride shone from Aethelgar's face, serving only to make the rumbling in Thurkill's belly that much more insistent. Thankfully, it was not long before they were seated. Thurkill grabbed a loaf from a passing tray, borne aloft by a churl, though he had to drop it quickly onto his platter as the crust was still piping hot. Breaking it in half, he smiled to see the soft, fluffy white bread within. He breathed in deeply, savouring the smells that took him back to his Aunt Aga's kitchen. Having given one half to Hild, he then had to wait impatiently – his seax upturned in his hand, the butt of its hilt resting on the tabletop – for the honey pot to make its way along the line. Hild smacked his wrist, playfully.

"Patience, husband. You're behaving like a spoilt child."

"I'm ravenous, Hild, and Aethelgar says this is the finest honey in all the land. No doubt the bees are blessed by Saint Mildburh herself. It's so long since I last had some, I've almost forgotten what it tastes like."

"Well, that's as may be. But there's plenty, and no one's going to steal it away from you. So just wait your turn before you embarrass me anymore."

When the moment finally arrived, Thurkill dug his knife deep into the pot, feeling the glutinous honey grip onto the blade and offer no small amount of resistance as he pulled it free. Long tendrils of the sweet sticky substance fought to stay within the pot as he drew his seax clear. The honey had a deep golden hue and was so clear that he could almost see through it as if it were glass. Grunting with satisfaction, he smeared the knife over his bread, covering the soft white flesh as liberally as he could. It was just the same as he remembered Aunt Aga's. Seeing the look on Hild's face, he paused, bread midway to his mouth.

"Leave me be, woman. There's plenty left in the pot for everyone else."

With that, he sank his teeth into the bread, groaning in ecstasy as he did so. The honey was spread thick and a good deal of it oozed from either corner of his mouth where he did his best to halt its inexorable escape with his tongue. Still more dripped down his fingers on to his hand, leaving a gooey mess that no amount of licking seemed to resolve.

Reconciling herself to inevitable defeat, Hild sighed and returned to concentrate on her own plate where she broke off small morsels of her bread on to which she then dabbed a moderate amount of the sweet honey before placing the whole into her mouth. No mess, no drips, no fuss. Thurkill grinned at her inanely, little golden globules glistening at her all over his thin, straggly beard and moustache. The look on her face showed that she doubted whether he had ever been happier than in that moment.

***

After the meal, they gathered on the banks of a nearby stream to enjoy the late spring sunshine that beat down with its midday intensity. It was a scene of great peace and tranquillity, punctuated only by the gentle rush of the water cascading over the stone riverbed and the soporific snoring of several of the men, their bellies filled with huge quantities of porridge, bread and honey. Thurkill felt sleepy, too, his eyes heavy-lidded with yawn after yawn forcing its way from his mouth. He felt at peace for the first time in weeks.

He lay back on the lush turf, one arm behind his head. His other was curled around Hild's shoulders as she lay on her side, nestled up against his body, her head resting on his chest. From his angle, he could not tell whether she was asleep, but her slow, even breathing suggested she might be, so he was careful not to make any sudden movements in case he woke her. Time and again he had to resist the urge to waft away bees, colour butterflies and even the odd dragonfly that circled his head, attracted by the remnants of honey on his face.

The bump in Hild's belly was growing quickly now, though you could not tell from behind as everything was gathered at the front. He'd been assured by many of the older women in Eadric's camp, that this meant she would bear him a son. Inwardly, he hoped this was true; a son to carry his name, to continue the family line to the next generation. Though, if he were honest with himself, he did not really mind whether the child was boy or girl. As long as it was hale and Hild survived unscathed, he would give thanks to God for his good fortune. There would be plenty of time to have a boy should the first one turn out to be a girl.

"So, what did you make of this morning's service, Thurkill? Do you have any saints like Mildburh where you hail from?" Eadric's speech was slurred as if he too were on the point of succumbing to sleep.

"It was like nothing I've ever seen before, Lord. Yes, there are saints in Kent, none more so than Augustine who first brought Christianity to the English from Rome. But I've been to Cantwaraburh to hear prayers held in his honour in my youth and they were nothing like what I saw here today. It was magical; everything in the forest joined in with the nuns. Trees, birds, even the wind seemed to whisper her name."

Eadric chuckled knowingly. "What you have there, my lad, is the magic of the land intertwined with the glory of God, joined together as one, indivisible and all-powerful."

"How do you mean?"

"Mildburh lived at a time when the Word of God had not long been heard in these parts. Her father, King Merewahl, was one of the first hereabouts to take to the waters of baptism. But that didn't mean that everyone in his kingdom changed their ways and gave up on the old gods overnight. It took generations for the priests to carry their message to every corner of the land and, even then, there were those that refused to change. Or, if they did, they did so only outwardly, going to church on Sundays, saying their prayers, being baptised and so forth, while on the inside, they kept faith with the old ways. And nowhere more so than in the forests where it was said that the old gods made their home amongst the birds and the trees.

"Mildburh comes from a time where the old and the new lived alongside one another, not necessarily in harmony but not always in conflict. It's said that Mildburh did much to bring the two together, taking what was good from each and forging a stronger whole out of the two; just as a blacksmith makes a sword from many layers of iron and steel. And this persists to this day as you saw. The old ways speak to us through the trees and the birds in partnership with the nuns and the church who speak for the new."

It all made sense to Thurkill. He lay back once again and closed his eyes, his mind soothed by the gentle sounds of the stream finding its way over and around the stones. To his left, he could hear a faint knocking sound. Opening one eye he turned his head to see a thrush, standing on one of the flat-topped rocks in the middle of the rushing stream. In its beak, it held a small snail, the shell of which it was beating against the rock in the hope of revealing the prize within. It worked with a persistence that was interrupted only by occasional furtive glances to either side, watching for unknown threats. Idly, Thurkill wondered how long the shell would withstand the assault.

Seeing the direction of his gaze, Eadric grunted. "As it is for that snail, so it seems for us too, eh? All around the Normans peck at us, intent on finding a way in to destroy us. We have to hope that our shell is strong enough to protect those within."

Thurkill frowned. "Do you think we can resist? Or will our shell break in the end."

Just then, a crack sounded from the rock. The thrush stood triumphant over its prey; the shell had broken in pieces leaving the snail's soft, brown flesh exposed. Already, it twisted and turned in on itself as if it could somehow avoid the inevitable. Its efforts were in vain though as the thrush pecked down sharply, spearing the doomed snail on its beak before fluttering off to its nest where its hungry young eagerly awaited the coming feast.

Thurkill thought better of mentioning what they had both just witnessed. "Would it not be opportune to come to an agreement with the Normans? Reach an understanding? That way, fewer would have to die."

As the words left his mouth, Thurkill knew it was a mistake. A cloud came over Eadric's face, his jaw clenched and the lines on his brow knitted together. With a great effort of will, he managed to control his temper, perhaps only because he had no wish to wake those around him. "Do you not think I consider that almost every day? I am aware of my responsibilities to my people, and I do not take them lightly. I can't afford to. Already, I carry many deaths on my conscience and every night I lie awake thinking about how I will face God when my time comes. How will I justify my actions to Him? How can He open the door to Heaven for me after all I have done?"

The emotion in Eadric's voice overwhelmed him so that the words caught in his throat. Thurkill knew exactly how he felt; the same thoughts had plagued him back at Gudmundcestre when FitzGilbert brought death and destruction to his people because of his own actions. He nodded empathetically. It was a heavy burden for one man to bear, but it was the burden of any man who led others into battle.

Eadric was silent for a few moments, a little tic causing the corner of his eye to twitch. Eventually, apparently composed once more, he continued, "But everything that both my head and my heart tell me, says they are not to be trusted. I have wanted to believe that perhaps this FitzScrope is the one bad apple in the barrel, but I fear he is not untypical of their kind. A little more savage than most, perhaps, but not wildly different. Whatever my conscience assails me with today would be nothing compared to what would happen if I submitted and they came to kill everyone. That, I cannot and will not allow.

"But, enough of my problems. What of you and yours, Thurkill? Have you thought any more about your future? I know you've given me your oath, but I'll not hold you to it if you wish to leave. You're welcome to stay amongst us for as long as you wish, of course. God knows Il have need of good fighting men."

It was Thurkill's turn to furrow his brow. "I truly do not know, Lord. My mind is filled with thoughts and doubts, each fighting for supremacy. What I know for certain is that there is Norman blood on my hands and that my identity may well be known to them. Then there is FitzGilbert. He is still out there, still intent on avenging his brother's death. I'm certain he'll not rest until one of us is in the ground. I feel safe from him here, but I know he'll not give up. Finally, there's Edgar, the true King of England. Although he bent the knee to William at Beorhthanstaed before Christmas, I wonder if he's given up all hope of being king again one day? Should he summon men to his banner, I know I would have to answer his call.

"But, most important of all right now is Hild. Her time is near, and she needs calm and rest more than anything. Whatever else should happen in the next few weeks, I cannot put her at risk."

"Hmmm, she is a fine woman, that one. You're lucky to have found her, and I understand your wish to keep her safe. There's nothing more precious in this world than the love of a good woman. You will only truly know that if you were to lose it… When is her time?"

"A matter of a few weeks at most, Lord."

"Then rest assured, Thurkill, that the feast we shall have to celebrate the baby's arrival will be spoken about for generations to come."

TWELVE

The sun had long since passed its zenith when they began the long walk back to Eadric's forest camp. The going was slow, but not unduly so. Not only did they have full bellies to contend with, but the heat of the afternoon sun seemed to suck the energy from them, making them more sluggish than normal. Under cover of the woods, it was even worse, as what breeze there was could not penetrate the branches. There, the heat was stifling.

But there was no rush; they could enjoy a leisurely stroll through the trees and across the meadows, safe in the knowledge that they were deep within Eadric's domain. Nevertheless, the wily Saxon was taking no chances. Before they set off, he had dispatched riders to alert the camp of their return. He'd also sent a handful of scouts to guard their flanks. Though he doubted any Normans would be foolhardy enough to risk being this far from their castles, there was no harm in being careful. Caution, he'd said, had allowed him to live a long and happy life so far.

Thurkill walked hand in hand with Hild towards the rear of the group, enjoying the feeling of the dappled sunshine on his face. By his side, his wife chatted gaily with the wife of another man who was also pregnant, swapping stories of babies kicking inside them and the strange feelings, emotions and cravings they had experienced over the weeks and months. From what Thurkill could gather, it was the other woman's first time too, making them ideal companions as they would be able to help each other through the days and weeks to come. Though he was no expert, Thurkill judged her time to be closer than Hild's; her bulge seemed even more pronounced and surely close to the point of bursting? Eadric had offered to find her a mount for the journey, but she had stoically refused, claiming that the exercise would do her good and might even encourage the child to begin its journey into the world.

"What do you think, Thurkill?"

Guiltily, he realised he'd been paying no heed to their conversation; he had no idea what he'd been asked. "I beg pardon, my love; what do I think about what?"

Hild laughed. "I swear he's the same as all men, Agatha. Never listens to a word I say, dreaming about swords and shieldwalls and the like, I'll wager."

Thurkill felt his cheeks redden as those around him chuckled as his expense. "Forgive me, Hild. I was but marvelling at your beauty."

"A likely story, but one that buys my forgiveness, nonetheless. I asked what name would you wish for our child, husband? Whether it be boy or girl?"

Before Thurkill could answer, a blood-curdling scream rang out from the head of the group some fifty or so paces ahead of them. Immediately alert, Thurkill grabbed Hild by the upper arm. "Stay here with Agatha. Do not move."

He ran forward, drawing his sword from his sheep's wool-lined scabbard as he went. Reaching the front, he stopped next to Eadric who had his arm around the shoulders of a sobbing woman, consoling her as best he could as she wailed in distress. It didn't take Thurkill long to find the source of the woman's desolation.

A short way in front of them – where the path split into two – was a grisly sight. A man seemed to be standing upright, leaning against a tree trunk but, on closer inspection, Thurkill could see he was dead. Not only dead but drained of blood if the grey pallor of his skin was anything to go by. At first, Thurkill could not understand why the body had not collapsed to the ground, but then he realised the poor bastard had been tied to the tree in three places by thin twisted lengths of twine: one around his knees, another around his chest and the third around his forehead.

The cause of death needed no divination; his throat had been opened, almost from ear to ear. It was a deep gash too, down as far as the bone of his neck. Mercifully, he must have bled to death quickly. But that cut had not been the end of the wretch's suffering. His trews had been yanked down and, where his manhood should have been, there was nought but a bloody mess now. As a final affront to the man's honour, his severed member had been stuffed into his mouth. It was a clear message, intended to both outrage and dismay.

Thurkill felt a sense of fury take hold of him. He itched to dip his sword in the blood of his enemies, to make them pay for this atrocity. But first, they must spare this man any further indignity.

"Cut him down. Let us bury him with honour."

"He stays where he is!" Eadric's anguished shout stopped the two men who had come forward to do Thurkill's bidding dead in their tracks.

Angrily, Thurkill rounded on him. "In God's name, Eadric, has he not suffered enough already? Surely we should take him back with us so that his woman can wash him and dress him for burial?"

Eadric's voice was softer now, but no less intense for it. "His widow is here with us now, Thurkill. And I say we leave him here. This is a message intended for me, and it tells me that we are betrayed. The men who did this – and I doubt not that FitzScrope is behind it – must be nearby for this is one of the men I sent back this morning to ready the camp for our return. The body is yet warm, I daresay. Perhaps, even now, they watch us from the trees, ready to fall upon us in our disarray. We must move and move quickly. I fear we will soon be attacked but the closer we can get to our own people the more likely we are to survive."

As much as it galled him, Thurkill knew Eadric was right. Somehow the Normans must have learned of their visit to Mildburh's shrine, and they had come for a reckoning that was long overdue in their minds. If that were the case, it promised to be a hard fight. The Saxons numbered but thirty souls of which almost half were women, and two of them with child at that. Fewer than twenty warriors, no matter how hardy and experienced, would be hard-pressed to hold their own against the small army that Thurkill knew FitzScrope must have sent. He would not have committed his men so deep into Eadric's lands without being sure of victory. He wished Eahlmund, Urri and the others were with him. That would have gone some way to balancing the scales.

Meanwhile, Eadric was issuing his orders. The scouts had come in from the flanks, two of them reporting soldiers moving away to their right. They couldn't say how many but the noise of metal clanking against metal had been unmistakable. Eadric kept the scouts back after that; there was little point sending them out again as they knew the enemy was there. They would be more use here, in the fight to come.

All around him, Eadric's warriors were readying their weapons and loosening their muscles. It was as well that Eadric had insisted that each man travel with shield and helm. There'd been grumbling at the extra weight to carry in the summer heat, but the wisdom of the decision was now laid bare. All thoughts of weariness were banished as each man focussed his mind on what lay ahead.

"Our best chance will be to leave the path for the safety of the trees," Eadric opined. "They've long been our friend and won't abandon us now. In amongst the larch, the oak and the alder, we'll be able to move freely and quickly, while the larger enemy force may well be slowed down and may split into smaller groups. We move now and we move fast. Protect the women with your lives. I need not remind you what fate awaits them should we fail."

As they moved off, Eadric grabbed Thurkill by the sleeve and whispered, "Place yourself near the rear, my lad, with your woman, Agatha and the others. If this goes as I fear it will, I would have you save as many of them as you can. When the fighting starts, we'll keep the Normans busy up front so you can slip away into the woods. Lead them home and keep them safe. Get back to the camp and warn them of what comes. Will you do this for me?"

Thurkill faced Eadric, his eyes blazing. "Is there no one else, Lord? I would rather take my place at your side. I have never run from a fight and I would not begin now."

Eadric sighed. "Forget honour, boy, for there will be none to be found here today. Only cold and brutal murder at the hands of these Norman scum. If I am to die here, I would rather do so knowing that some had been saved. Besides, your wife needs a husband and a father for her child. Do not let her down."

Thurkill's face burned with anger and shame. Everything he'd been taught told him that his place was by Eadric's side. He was duty bound to defend his lord, to the death if necessary. There was no honour in leaving the battle without your lord; men had been shunned for less, thrown out of their communities to fend for themselves outside of the law.

But he also knew that the presence of the women changed things. It was a complication that could not easily be squared away. No man could – in all good conscience – put his womenfolk in danger. To die shoulder to shoulder with one's comrades was all well and good, but to leave the women to the mercy of bloodthirsty Normans was unacceptable. However much it rankled, Thurkill knew in his heart that his path was clear.

He lowered his head. "So be it, Lord. Your will be done."

Eadric grinned like a mad man, clapping Thurkill on the shoulder with his huge paw of a hand. "Good man. Now, come on. Let's see what the goat-shaggers have in store for us, eh?"

They did not have long to wait. They'd gone no more than a hundred paces into the woods when they heard a huge roar, followed immediately by the clash of metal on metal. From his position at the rear, Thurkill craned his neck, desperate to see what was happening. He wanted to get a feel for the strength of the enemy, but the densely packed trees and the press of bodies ahead of him left him thwarted. His fingers tightened around his sword grip, until the whites of his knuckled shone through. He felt as much use as a toothless dog with a juicy bone. Every ounce of his body, every sinew, strained to be released from the leash that Eadric had placed around his neck. His soul burned with impotent fury as he knew men would die while he stood and waited.

The women were gathered behind him, perhaps hoping his great bulk could somehow shield them from peril. With him were two more of Eadric's men; he did not know their names, but they looked less than impressive. Short, rat-faced men, both. Understandably, it seemed Eadric had not spared him his best warriors. Their faces had drained of colour as their eyes darted in all directions, scanning the trees for the first sight of the enemy. Thurkill wondered if they might yet surprise him and prove to be stout of heart and strong of arm but he felt it more likely they would shit their breeches and run.

His thoughts were distracted by Hild tugging at his sleeve. Turning to face her, he saw no panic in her eyes, just calm assurance. In her right hand, she held the short antler-bone handle of her seax, its angled blade glinting in the leaf-dappled sunlight. He smiled with pride, knowing that she would not give her life cheaply, nor would she allow herself to be taken. Men would die by her hand before she was done.

"Whither now, husband? Standing here meekly, waiting to accept our fate holds no appeal for me."

"Nor I, Hild, but I would know what we face before we run. Maybe Eadric will have need of us if the numbers are more evenly matched than we had first feared."

"You know that is not likely, my love. This attack has not happened by chance. That poor man tied to the tree is evidence enough of that. They do not fear us; they do not skulk in the woods. They have men aplenty, and they mean to kill Eadric and all those with him."

Thurkill nodded; the wisdom of her words was not lost on him. Before he could reply, however, Aethelgar came barrelling through the undergrowth, his face awash with blood and a wild look in his eyes.

"Why do you dither? Fly, man, fly. Take the women away from here before it's too late."

"Are you hurt, Aethelgar? How goes the battle?"

Aethelgar brushed away his concern. "Fear not for 'tis not my blood, but the fight is lost all the same. There're too many of the bastards; there's no hope we can prevail."

"Eadric still lives?"

"For now. He sent me back to make sure you followed his orders. He was worried your sense of honour would twist your mind and bring you running to the sound of the sword-song. That I find you still here tells me he was right to be concerned. Go now! It may already be too late."

The anger in Aethelgar's voice caused Thurkill to take a step back, abashed. It was true; he had dallied, unwilling to turn his back on his lord. Snapping out of his torpor, he turned to the men with him, surprised to find them still by his side.

"Lead us away from this place. Take us deep into the woods where none may follow. Hurry."

The two spearmen needed no further encouragement. They took to their heels, cloaks billowing behind them. As quickly as he could, Thurkill urged the women to follow before their guides were lost to sight. He prayed that Hild and Agatha would be able to keep up.

"Will you come with us?"

Aethelgar looked back up the path to where the screams of the dying could be heard, his mind seemingly torn in two. Eventually, he shrugged. "I may as well, Thurkill. Eadric will have no use of me by the time I return, I fear. My sword will be better used at your side. You have room for one more, I trust?"

Relieved, Thurkill grinned. "Gladly, my friend. A good sword should never be turned away at a time like this."

Together, they hurried after the women, pushing their way through the tangle of low hanging branches that clawed at them as they passed. More than once, Thurkill winced as a limb snapped back into his face after having been pushed aside by his companion in front of him. Brambles snagged on his trews as he ran, pricking the skin with their sharp barbs despite the thickness of the wool. But if he'd hoped they would escape unnoticed, he was mistaken. Before they had gone very far, Thurkill heard a shout from ahead, followed by the screams of several women. Gripped by fear, he rushed forward, lungs heaving as he forged a path to the front.

"Come on, Aethelgar. The bastards have flanked us." Either the Normans had guessed that survivors might be trying to escape in this direction, or they had sufficient numbers to throw a cordon around the whole area to catch any fugitives. He hoped it was the former.

Bursting through a thickly tangled bush, Thurkill quickly took stock of the scene before him. One of his two spearman was down, unmoving, whilst the other was hard pressed by two soldiers who hacked at him in turns, waiting for him to tire so that they could finish him. Behind them, Thurkill could see more of the bastards crammed into the narrow space between the trees, unable to bring their weapons to bear in the tightly confined area. Fear gripped him as he realised that Hild was also in the middle of the melee. His heart stopped as he watched her dart in low beneath the reach of the Norman on the left and stab her blade hard into his thigh. A bright arc of blood splashed across her face and body as she slashed down with the blade, opening the flesh down to his knee. The man went down, his eyes filled with surprise which soon turned to pain as he frantically pressed his hands into the gaping wound, hoping to stem the blood that now pumped from his leg with unstoppable force.

But Thurkill could not dwell on his fate for the next soldier had already come forward to take his place, aiming his sword directly at his wife. It was all he needed to spur him into action. Yelling incoherently, he stormed forward, sword raised over his head, with Aethelgar by his side.

Sensing what was coming, Hild threw herself to one side, away from the oncoming Norman and clearing a space for her husband at the same time. The Saxon on the right was less fortunate, though, finding himself sandwiched between Aethelgar and the Norman he'd been fighting up to that point. They smashed into the Normans, driving them back so hard that those directly behind them were also sent sprawling to the ground.

Thurkill smashed his sword hilt down hard on the nearest man's shoulder, hearing the satisfying crack as the bone snapped with a sound like a dry twig trodden underfoot. Not pausing to see the effect of his blow, he powered forward, shoving the iron boss of his shield into the next man's face and grunting with satisfaction as he saw blood and teeth splattering on all sides.

But now his path was blocked; he could go no further. Three more men barred his way. They had recovered from their initial shock and were looking to fight back. Thurkill's lungs burned with exertion as he gasped for more air; his tongue was cleaved to the top of his mouth for want of water. But he could not stop;

the fate of the women rested with him and Aethelgar. If they did not deal with these men soon, it would not be long before more of the whoresons arrived to annihilate them.

Realising that the space was too tight to wield his sword to any great effect, he dropped it. In its place, he grabbed his seax. With a blade that measured almost the length of his forearm, it would have no difficulty bringing death to the enemy. He'd grown up with it, used it ever since his father had given it to him on the day of his tenth birthday. So familiar was its weight and so snug its fit in his palm, it felt as if it were an extension of his arm.

Grinning in anticipation, he hurled himself at the nearest man, swerving to one side to avoid the wild, despairing thrust of the Norman's spear before punching the blade deep into his belly. Placing his boot in the middle of the dying man's chest, he pulled back on the seax, the flesh gripping on to the blade, unwilling to let it go. He yanked it free with only moments to spare, the squelching sound almost enough to turn his stomach.

He ducked as the next man swung his sword at him, the blade missing his head by no more than a hand's breadth. Hearing a dull thud, Thurkill looked up to see that the blade had become stuck in the soft bark of the tree behind him. As the Norman sought to twist the blade free, Thurkill jabbed his knife between the man's legs where his mailshirt afforded him no protection. Screaming in agony, the Norman let go of the sword pommel, clutching his ruined groin instead. It was then a simple matter for Thurkill to finish him by pushing the blade into his eye socket.

Suddenly, the fight was over. Aethelgar had dispatched the last remaining soldier, and the path ahead was clear. Thurkill lost no time retrieving his sword and returning it to its sheath. For as long as they remained within the press of the trees, he'd place his trust in his short but deadly seax.

Then, looking round for Hild, he was relieved to see his wife back on her feet, pale but apparently otherwise unharmed. Rushing to her side, he checked her for wounds before she batted his mauling hands away with good-natured impatience. "I'm fine, you oaf. Though no thanks to you, charging past like a bull with the scent of a cow on heat in its nostrils."

Thurkill chuckled, happy that they had survived the encounter with no greater loss than one of the two warriors left to him by Eadric. But he knew they were not clear of danger yet; who knew how many more Normans were out there, standing between them and their sanctuary? And who knew how soon before FitzScrope realised that a few of their quarry had escaped and came hunting for them? The sooner they were away, the better.

Aethelgar was of the same mind. "We have no time for chatter, you two. We must warn the camp else all may be lost 'ere the day is done."

THIRTEEN

They worked their way forward, with Aethelgar taking the lead. At the rear, Thurkill walked alongside Eadric's remaining spearman, a man by the name of Ochta, he discovered. He'd developed a grudging respect for the rat-like fellow, not least because he was brother to the man who had been slain in the earlier skirmish. Ochta had accepted the loss as if it were of no more import than the death of a pig or lamb; the need to save the women had greater import at that time. Thurkill had to admire his calm stoicism, whatever he must be feeling inside.

But he was a dour chap, nevertheless, offering little more than single word responses to Thurkill's questions or observations. Eventually, he gave up trying to engage Ochta in further conversation, choosing instead to focus on his surroundings. He had no idea where they were, nor how far they had yet to travel to reach their objective. Either way, he imagined it would be dark long before they arrived.

Suddenly, Ochta shoved his arm across Thurkill's chest, forcing him to halt. He cursed himself for allowing his mind to wander. He could hear nothing out of the ordinary, though. No more than the rustling of leaves and branches in the breeze and the sounds of birds calling to each other high in the treetops around them. He turned to face his companion, his eyes asking the question that he dare not utter for fear of making a sound. The spearman nodded in the direction of Aethelgar who had also come to a stop a dozen or so paces ahead.

Gesturing that Ochta should stay where he was, Thurkill crept forward past the women, taking great care over where he placed each foot lest he snap a dry twig or disturb a loose stone. At the same time, he turned his head from side to side, straining to hear any unnatural sounds with his one good ear; but there was nothing. Reaching Aethelgar's position, Eadric's man held up his hand to stop him, before pointing ahead. With his other hand, he held up two fingers.

Peering through the undergrowth, Thurkill could at last make out the cause of Aethelgar's angst. Twenty or so paces away, through the serried ranks of the dark, brooding tree trunks, two Norman soldiers stood with their backs to them. Doubtless, they were two more of the many guards that FitzScrope had stationed around the whole area to mop up any survivors.

Leaning in close, Aethelgar cupped his hand around Thurkill's ear to shield the sound of his words. "We have no option but to take them, my friend. They stand directly in our path back to the camp. To go round them takes us too far out of our way."

Thurkill nodded, noticing that his mouth had once again turned dry. How much longer could they ride their luck? The chances were that Eadric, and the rest of his men had already been killed and Thurkill had little doubt that the same fate awaited them. But while they lived there was yet hope. For as long as he had air in his lungs and strength in his arm, he would do whatever he could to protect Hild and the others.

Wordlessly, the two men drew their seaxes, knowing that they would have to get close enough to use them without alerting their quarry. They would have kill them simultaneously, so that neither had the chance to sound the alarm; it would be painstaking work with a high chance of failure. In their favour, though, was the fact that the ground underfoot was mossy where it was hidden from direct sunlight by the curtain of leaves above their heads. With luck, the soft, spongy plant would mask any noise their feet might make.

Quickly, silently, the two men rid themselves of anything that could give them away; off came belts, buckles, brooches and their mailshirts, leaving them in nothing more than their tunics, trews, and leather boots. Then they moved off, leaving Ochta to lead the others back to a safe distance. As they stood waiting, the sky darkened and a summer shower began; the raindrops were warm but heavy as was typical of the time of year, thudding against the canopy of foliage above their heads. It had been muggy for much of the day, an oppressive heat that only relents once the clouds have burst. Thurkill could not have dared hope for such luck. Smiling, he offered a silent prayer to Saint Mildburh for he felt her hand behind its timing. The rain rattled its way to the floor as it cascaded from leaf to leaf; its noise going a long way to deaden the sound of their approach.

Placing one foot carefully in front of the other, the two men crept forward. The rain had soaked through Thurkill's clothes by now, making the fabric rub uncomfortably against his skin as he moved. They stole from tree to tree, using the cover they provided to conceal their movements. That both men were dressed in faded browns and greens, only helped them to blend in with their surroundings still further.

Though their quarry was but twenty paces away, it took an age for them to manoeuvre into position. Every step of the way, Thurkill feared that one or both men might turn round, bringing a disastrous end to their plan. But miraculously, their luck held. The two men appeared to be deep in conversation, if not actually arguing with each other. The man on the left – Thurkill's target – was gesticulating wildly at the other, though he at least had the discipline to keep his voice down.

Another few moments of agonising anxiety finally brought the two Saxons within reach of their prey. Amazingly, the two soldiers had not moved, or even flinched. They stood, sullen now – their argument apparently resolved, or at least paused for the time being – and their shoulders hunched against the downpour.

Thurkill's lank hair was plastered to his head and face as the rain continued to pelt down from above, but he cared not for the inconvenience for it had been a godsend. He doubted whether Aethelgar and he would have been able to get so close without its camouflaging effects.

Slowly, and making every effort to avoid the slightest sound, Thurkill switched his seax to his left hand so that he might wipe the palm of his right between his legs where the cloth of his trews was driest. It would not do for the smooth bone-handle to slip in his wet grip at the vital moment. Straightening up once more, he looked over to where his companion stood, two paces to his right. With a barely perceptible nod, he indicated that he was ready. For his part, Aethelgar held up the thumb and two fingers of his left hand; it was critical that they acted as one to ensure that the surprise was complete.

Aethelgar then lowered one finger and then the other so that only the thumb remained. Then that too was gone and, at that moment, both men threw themselves forward, closing out the remaining distance between them and the Normans. Thurkill had known what he would do before he moved; it was the only sure way to kill the soldier in one move. With his left hand, he reached round to grab the man by the forehead, pulling back hard to expose his throat as much as possible. At the same time, he swung his right arm, slashing his seax blade across the white skin with deliberately excessive violence. So deep was the blow that Thurkill almost gagged as he felt the blade's tempered steel bite deep into flesh, stopping only as it met resistance against the bone. It did the job, though. So brutal had he been that the man had not uttered a single sound before he died.

Glancing across, he saw that Aethelgar had adopted the same approach. Even now, he was gently lowering the gore-spattered corpse of the second soldier to the ground, where the blood continued to pulse from the deep gash, soaking into the soft, mossy ground. Thurkill nodded to him with a look of grim satisfaction. His companion's face was ashen, perhaps mirroring his own, he mused. Thurkill didn't suppose he would ever get used to the act of killing, however well-suited to the trade he was. It was an evil that was borne out of necessity though.

"Come on. We need to be gone from here before anyone comes looking for these two."

Aethelgar's words cut through Thurkill's thoughts. He was right; they could not afford to linger. The rest of the Norman warband could be upon them at any moment.

As they trotted back to Ochta and the others, Thurkill could not help but wonder what had become of Eadric. In his heart, he knew the older man was most likely dead; how could he have survived the fight? Even though he had not known the man for long, Thurkill was surprised to find a sense of melancholy descending over him. In their short time together, Thurkill had grown to respect the man and even to like him. And now he had failed his oath to defend him. True, Eadric had released him from that bond so that he might save Hild and the other women, but that only went so far to assuage his guilt. Guilt at still being alive when others, those who had fought so that he might rescue the women, were most likely dead, their bodies mutilated and nailed to trees for all to see.

Not even a hug from Hild could shake his mood, though he could not deny it helped. She looked tired, though, her features drawn and her face white with shock and fatigue. The strains of the day combined with the weight of the baby she carried had taken their toll. He wished he could allow her to sleep, if only for a while. But they had to move fast. There were scores, if not hundreds, of Normans in the woods still, and he would not allow them to slake their thirst for Saxon blood any further.

FOURTEEN

By the time they reached Eadric's woodland camp, Hild had passed beyond exhaustion. For the last hour or so – ever since the sun had finally set, in fact – Thurkill had been supporting her weight, half-carrying her as she stumbled and limped along the narrow, overgrown path by which Aethelgar led them. His shoulder and arm ached incessantly, but he would not spare himself the pain. In some small way, it helped atone for the guilt he felt for putting his wife through such a trial.

But he could not allow her to rest, not until he knew they were safe from the Norman threat. As much as it irked him, he had to force her to keep moving. He knew he had the strength to carry her on his back, but she was so heavy with child that to do so would have caused her more discomfort and pain. Even on the few occasions he did offer to stop, if only for a short while, she had refused, knowing that to do so would place everyone in danger. For the last mile or so, a small whimper escaped from her lips with every step, each sound reaching into his chest to crush his heart. She was so tired, he doubted whether she knew it was even happening

They were escorted back to the centre of the camp by the guard who'd heard them crashing through the undergrowth. All was quiet, most people having already settled down for the night. It struck Thurkill then that they could not yet know of Eadric's fate. None of the scouts had made it back alive to tell them of the danger they now faced. He wanted to shout and scream at the top of his voice, but no words came. He was past the limits of his endurance. It was as much as he could do to carry Hild back to their home where he lay her down as gently as he could, covering her with blankets before he hobbled back out.

Thurkill marvelled to watch Aethelgar stepping into Eadric's shoes. Though he must also have been fatigued beyond measure, his sense of duty to his master would allow him no respite. Grabbing the night-watchman by the shoulder, he began to relay orders to double the guard and to gather the rest of the community as soon as possible. The guard looked at him nervously but did not stop to question his commands as he rushed off to do his bidding.

Later, as he sat by the hearth pit, Thurkill could not stop himself from yawning continually. To distract himself, he looked around at the faces of those that had assembled, dimly lit by the smouldering embers of what had been the evening's cooking fire. Ignorant of the full extent of their plight, their faces bore only signs of mild curiosity that they should have been roused from their slumber.

Thurkill counted them, stopping when he reached one hundred. Only a third to a half of them would know how to wield sword or spear to any great effect. There was no way they could defend the camp with so few fighting men. He wondered what else they could do but disperse into the woods and trust on God and Lady Mildburh to protect them.

When no more came, Aethelgar held up his hand for calm. As faces turned in his direction, Thurkill heard a few gasps of shock as people took in his dishevelled and bloodstained appearance. It was then that folk also began to realise that Eadric was not amongst them. Aethelgar lost no time in sharing the news, before panic could set in.

"Friends, I bear sad tidings. Eadric is dead."

As Thurkill knew would happen, the throng erupted in shouts and wails, many voices demanding to know how it had come to pass? It was several moments before Aethelgar could continue.

"The Normans ambushed us on our return from Wenloch. We were betrayed, for FitzScrope knew where to find us. To win time for the womenfolk to escape, Eadric led the men against the main body of the enemy whilst commanding Thurkill to bring them to safety. The fighting was fierce and brutal, and I fear none survived." Aethelgar hung his head, the emotion in his voice all too apparent.

The crowd was shocked into silence, broken here and there by the sound of sobbing as friends remembered those who had travelled with Eadric whom they would never see again. Others stood, shaking their heads in disbelief, unwilling to accept that their leader had gone. These people had considered him to be invulnerable, a beast of a man who could never be brought low. Indeed, Thurkill had overheard children telling each other how Eadric had been known to transform into a bear on nights when the moon was full. Doubtless, they were just stories that fathers told their children to scare them into being good, but it all served to add to the aura of the man.

"But you did not actually see him killed?"

Thurkill recognised the hopeful tone of the voice as belonging to Urri. Since his arrival, the blacksmith had forged a strong presence in the camp. There was always need of men with his skills, meaning he was never short of work. He had already taken on two brothers, not much younger than Thurkill, to be his apprentices.

"I did not, Urri, but I cannot in all faith offer you hope. Eadric's head is a much sought-after prize, and I cannot believe the Normans would let him live. But, whatever the truth of it, we cannot stay here. Though we are well hidden, there is every chance that the bastards will discover our whereabouts. If they have taken captives, they will not hesitate to torture them until they reveal our location. There is no time to lose. We must go now. Gather what you need, for we leave at dawn."

***

The mood amongst the villagers was sombre as they gathered, shoulders slumped, and backs bowed under the weight of their belongings. Most things had to be carried as there were only two wooden carts available, one of which Thurkill had commandeered for Hild and Agatha as both ladies were incapable of exertion after the previous day's exploits. Though he was careful not to show it, he was concerned for his wife's health. He knew she would never complain, but he could tell she was suffering. Her normally rosy cheeks were pale and sallow while her eyes lacked their normal sparkle. Nevertheless, she still found the energy to smile at his puerile jokes, though he could tell that even that was an effort for her.

Seeing his worry, Aethelgar clapped him on the shoulder, reassuring him that she was but tired. "A few days' rest, and she'll be like a new-born lamb once again, my friend."

Thurkill grinned, determined to put on a brave face, though his gut remained twisted with worry. All the same, there was little more he could do for her for the time being. At least she would be comfortable, nestled snugly in a bundle of furs on the back of the cart. To take his mind off things, he asked Aethelgar about their destination.

"Caves set into the hills to the north of here. Not far from Eadric's hall at Conendovre, in fact. It's only known to a few of us and was always intended as a last refuge. It's no palace, but the caves are warm and cosy with room for plenty. They'll serve us well until things settle down."

"Is it far?" Though she might be well cosseted amongst the furs, Thurkill still feared for Hild in case the journey were too long.

"No. We should be before the sun sets."

Just then, a commotion broke out to their rear. Instinctively, Thurkill's hand fell to this sword hilt, though, if the Normans had found them already, all was already lost. Even so, he would not die easily. Many would feel the bite of his blade before he was done.

But two men wo approached were not Normans. Relaxing, Thurkill recognised them as having been with them at Wenloch the previous day. Both were wounded, judging by the grubby, blood-soaked strips of cloth that were wrapped around their limbs. They hobbled as they walked, supporting each other as they walked towards them. Moments later, two of the waiting women shrieked, dropped their burdens, and ran forward to embrace the injured warriors.

Incredible. How could anyone make it back from the slaughter? Thurkill pushed his way through the crowd to where the two men were now being tended to by their wives, arriving just as Aethelgar spoke to them.

"Well met, Hrothgar, Cedda. God be praised that not all perished in the fight. Tell me, how do you come to return alive from that foul place when all hope seemed lost?"

It was Cedda, the least injured of the two, who answered. "Truly, God and the Lady Mildburh were watching over us, Aethelgar. Soon after we'd been injured, Eadric went mad, for he charged headlong into the centre of the Normans. I think he'd seen FitzScrope and hoped to end matters there and then. Whether it be true or not, he carried the rest of our lads with him further along the path, leaving us on our own with just the dead for company. With our wounds, we were no use to anyone, so we crawled as best we could into a thicket of brambles, hoping to hide until it was over."

"You did well, Cedda. God be praised the whoresons did not find you."

"Though they searched for a good while, I can tell you. I had to lie there with a rock sticking into my arse and thorns in my face, but I dared not move lest we be discovered."

Aethelgar chuckled, grateful for the humour to lighten the mood. "If only they were the least of your injuries, eh? I'm sorry we can't tarry to allow you rest, but we'll find room for you in one of the carts. But tell me, before we go," Aethelgar lowered his voice, his face assuming a sombre expression, "did you see Eadric at the end? Was his death proud and honourable?"

Hrothgar's head jerked up. "You don't know? Eadric lives!"

"How so? Don't play games with me, Hrothgar."

"It's true, Aethelgar. I swear it by Lady Mildburh and with Cedda as my witnesses." He glanced at his companion who nodded feebly. "When the Normans were hunting for survivors, I could see they already had half a dozen or so captives. Though I couldn't see clearly from within the brambles, there's no doubt in my mind that one of them was Eadric."

"How so?"

"He was a head taller than most and with shoulders like a bull. And, then I heard him growling and cursing the bastards that held him. It was unmistakable; even after one of them cuffed him round the head, he would not stop."

Thurkill grinned, imagining the scene. "He was not injured?"

"That I could not say; my view was not clear enough to be certain."

"By the saints," Aethelgar exclaimed, "why did they not kill him? Even having captured him, you'd think they would finish him there and then. They've wanted him for so many weeks now."

"Perhaps they have plans for him? If it were me, I'd want to make a spectacle of his death. A public execution to send the loudest message to the rest of us."

"I fear you may be right, Thurkill." Aethelgar's face showed how glum he was feeling.

"But while he lives, there is hope, yes? Where will they have taken him?"

A small spark of light returned to Aethelgar's eyes. "They have two of their damnable castles in this region. Scrobbesburh to the north and Henffordd to the south."

"Which is closer?"

"Scrobbesburh. It's but half a day's march from here."

"Then that is surely where they'll take Eadric and the others. They've been in a hard fight and will want to rest and take stock. We won't have long if we wish to save him, though. How many men can you muster within a day?"

"We have around thirty here. If I send out runners now, I reckon on another forty to fifty by nightfall. But they would not be trained warriors."

"Though they'll have handled spear or sword before?"

Aethelgar nodded.

"And stout men, with oak for limbs and fire in their hearts?"

"As much as any true Englishman. I swear it."

Thurkill smiled. "Send your runners now, then. Have the men come to us at the caves. I suggest we plan to attack this castle at Scrobbesburh tomorrow night."

FIFTEEN

Richard FitzScrope leaned against the wooden timbers that formed the small, but sturdy keep of his castle in Scrobbesburh. Arms folded across his chest, he stared at the figure lying on the floor before him. There really was no denying this Eadric Silvaticus was a huge beast of a man. No wonder he had been so hard to bring down. No fewer than four of his men had tried and failed, their broken corpses testament to their folly. In the end, it had taken six soldiers, surrounding him from all sides, to take him. And even then, two of them had suffered heinous wounds for their trouble.

But now, at last, he lay there, trussed up like a slaughtered pig. With his obvious strength, they were taking no chances, lest he were to break free to wreak havoc in the small storeroom that served as his prison. As he watched over him, FitzScrope could not help but feel a warm glow of satisfaction spreading through his bones. Finally, he had the bastard in his clutches. Finally, he would make him pay for all the pain he had caused, for all the soldiers he had killed. But what was most pleasing of all was that he could shut FitzOsbern's smug mouth once and for all. He'd already sent a messenger on horseback down to Henffordd to summon the earl hither and he longed to see the look on his face when presented with this particular gift.

It was the only reason the Saxon yet lived. Normally, he would not have hesitated to slit his throat right there on the field of battle, but his brain had kicked in, telling him there was greater advantage to be had keeping Eadric alive. At least long enough for FitzOsbern to witness his execution. Besides, the public death of such a revered local figure would have a huge impact on the townspeople. The Normans were here to stay and the sooner the Saxon dogs became used to that idea, the better. They would learn the cost of resistance.

With that thought, he strode over to the small window that looked down over the centre of the small market town, to the place where the local tradesmen and farmers came on Sundays to sell their wares. The gallows he'd ordered built that morning had been finished, save for the rope which was – even now – being fitted. Standing on an upturned tree stump, a soldier was slipping the noose into place over the sturdy cross beam.

FitzScrope allowed himself a small chuckle as he imagined how Eadric would look standing on that same stump when the time came. He had a good mind to kick it away himself, so he'd have the best view as the bastard dangled, choking for breath, eyes bulging as he fought for air. The very thought of it gave rise to a feeling of genuine pleasure. It was a shame the old fool, FitzOsbern could not move his fat arse more quickly, for the moment when he ended Eadric's life could not come soon enough.

Just then, a low groan behind him broke his reverie.

"Ah, I'm glad you could join us once again, dog. We have much to discuss."

Though they had killed or captured more than a dozen men, FitzScrope knew that was some way short of Eadric's full strength. He suspected the rest would melt away into the woods and hills without their charismatic leader, but it wouldn't hurt to press home his advantage. If he could learn the location of their camp – a fact that had eluded him for months – perhaps he could put a stop to their insurrection for good. He didn't really expect to learn anything useful from Eadric, though; he had the look of one who would rather die than betray his people. No, he was far more likely to get the information he needed from the others who had been taken along with their lord. They would surely succumb to the pain inflicted upon them by his men. Nevertheless, there was no harm in amusing himself a while longer with this one.

Groaning, Eadric struggled on to his side so he could face his captor. Despite himself, FitzScrope could not suppress a gasp as he set eyes upon the Saxon's face. It was a bloodied mess. Both eyes were closed to nothing more than slits, the flesh around them puffy and discoloured. It was hard to discern the form of his mouth and nose amongst all the blood and phlegm that caked the whole lower half of his face. FitzScrope could see his men had been thorough in their work, perhaps eager to please their master. But there were limits to this sort of thing. After all, the dog needed to be alive if he were to be killed in the marketplace. Even he might struggle to hang a corpse without anyone noticing.

He realised Eadric was trying to speak. Slowly, deliberately, the Saxon managed to lean over to one side, hawked and then spat a congealed mess on to the rushes that covered the floor. FitzScrope made a mental note to have them changed for freshly cut stalks as soon as this was over. The voice, when it came, was little more than a hoarse whisper, so quiet in fact that the Norman had to lean forward to hear the words. When he did, the venom they conveyed was unmistakable.

"You'll get nothing from me, you filthy Norman whoreson."

FitzScrope sighed, though he had expected nothing else. "I could save you a lot of pain – not to mention a good deal of my time – if you would but tell me where I can find your lair. My men are out there searching for it even as we speak, and I do not doubt they will find it sooner or later. But it would be so much easier for everyone if you were but to give me what I want here and now. You need suffer no more."

He could see the Saxon's jaw was moving. Perhaps he was about to say something useful after all? Spitting out the tooth he'd dislodged with his tongue, Eadric croaked, "You're going to kill me anyway, so why should I make things any easier for you? Just get on with it, by God's hairy ball sack."

FitzScrope smiled at the profanity. Though he considered Saxon to be an ugly tongue, full of harsh, guttural sounds that he found difficult to master, he could not deny just how inventive it could be when it came to insults "Very well. Don't say you weren't given every chance to cooperate."

With that, FitzScrope turned away, indicating to the two waiting soldiers that they should begin their work once more.

SIXTEEN

Thurkill sat down heavily, wincing as the sharpness of the stone surface dug painfully into his backside. Still, at least it was cool within the cave, in stark contrast to the scorching heat of the day. His forehead and nose tingled and were sore to touch where they'd been exposed to the sun's glare for the last several hours as they made their way, with maddening slowness, to their new home. His throat was parched, but he had to sit patiently, eyes watching enviously, as the water skin was passed around the group before it came to him. As he waited, he surveyed each man before him, trying to look within their souls to divine their innermost thoughts and feelings.

His little warband were all there, the scars of shared past battles evident on their bodies. Eahlmund, who'd found him close to death, after the battle at Senlac Ridge. The brothers, Leofgar and Leofric who, along with little Eopric, had fought FitzGilbert's thugs at his father's estate at Haslow. And then there was Urri, solid dependable Urri, the blacksmith from Gudmundcestre who had chosen to throw in his lot with Thurkill rather than stay in the village of his ancestors. Just young Copsig and Eardwulf were missing, both of whom had been killed fighting in his service. A sadness gripped him as he remembered the two men. Staunch, loyal fighters both, they had deserved better than to die on the end of a Norman blade.

And now he would have to lead his men into danger once again. He had not seen the castle at Scrobbesburh – or, for that matter, any castle – and its defences were sure to be formidable. Men would die, no matter how well planned or executed was their assault. He was not so worried about his own hearth warriors – they'd had their fill of hard fighting several times over – but could the same be said for the rest of Eadric's men? Several of his best warriors had been lost with him in the ambush near Wenloch and, without their experience and skill, would the others have the mettle to press home their attack? To gut a man face to face when the fighting was at its hardest took real courage. He supposed they would find out soon enough.

He took the still-bulging skin held out to him by Eahlmund to his right. Nodding his gratitude, he tipped back his head to take a deep draught of the cool stream water, savouring the sensation as it eased his cracked lips and rinsed the dust from his mouth. His thirst slaked, he took what was left of the skin over to where Hild lay on a straw-filled mattress towards the back of the cave. Given how small the entrance was, Thurkill was amazed by how spacious the interior was. There must have been over forty people within, not to mention great piles of supplies and a good few livestock too, and yet it did not feel crowded. It had even been possible to screen off a decent-sized area to provide a degree of privacy for the ladies. And it was here that he found his wife, being tended to by two other women, one of whom he recognised to be Agatha. She was mopping Hild's brow with a damp cloth to keep her cool, while the other was mixing a thin potage for her to eat.

As he approached, Thurkill's heart was filled with worry. His wife looked to be burning up. Her face was drenched with sweat despite Agatha's best efforts, and yet she appeared to be shivering at the same time. A fever had taken hold of her and now had her in its firm grip. Having no skill in healing matters, there was little he could do other than fetch and carry for those who cared for her. He had rarely, if ever, felt as helpless as he did now, watching his beloved wife struggling against this unseen enemy that attacked her and the child within. He would rather face a conroi of Norman horsemen on his own twice over than endure another moment of this torment.

Swallowing his fear, he handed the water-skin to Agatha. "How is she? Does she improve?"

The other woman, whom he now recognised as Aethelgar's wife, Sunhilda, smiled up at him, the strain clearly visible behind her friendly mask. "It is early yet, Thurkill. She has been through a lot in the past few days and what she needs more than anything now is rest. We will do what we can, of course – as if she were my own sister – but she is in God's hands." Seeing the look on Thurkill's face, she added. "But she is strong, a fighter no less hardy than her husband, I'd wager. If anyone can beat this fever, it will be her."

Thurkill smiled his thanks at Sunhilda, unable to trust his voice to remain steady. He went to kneel at Hild's side where he took her hand in his, shocked at just how cold and clammy it was. With his other hand, he smoothed away a few lank strands of hair from her forehead before kissing her twice: once on her brow and once on her distended belly. She did not react to his touch, though; she had no awareness of anything that went on around her. She was deep in the grip of the illness.

His eyes wet from unchecked tears, Thurkill rose and turned away, trying to keep his face and emotions hidden from those around him. As despair fought to gain hold of him, he felt the strength drain from his legs and his vision begin to blur. Reaching out with his hand, he took a moment to steady himself against the craggy wall of the cave, oblivious of the many painted scenes etched out on the surface. He shook his head, hoping to clear the fog that had swamped his brain.

He could not imagine life without Hild. She was the one thing he prized above all else. Without her by his side, what would become of him?

A lump formed in his throat, so large that he feared it would choke him. He felt cold, as if the hand of Death reached out for him. He felt weak, his legs threatening to wobble like a newborn foal's. And yet, incongruously, beads of sweat broke out on his forehead. At first, he feared that he had succumbed to the same sickness that clawed at his dear wife, but no sooner had the feeling taken hold of him, it seemed to abate just as quickly. His breathing became less laboured, and his heart slowed to something approaching normality. If it were not for the dull ache that had seized hold of his lower back and thighs, he would have sworn that he had imagined the whole thing.

"What ails you, Lord?"

Looking up, Thurkill saw his old friend, Eahlmund, by his side, a look of real concern on his face. He ought to have known that he would not escape the attentions of his closest companion. Forcing his mouth into an approximation of a smile, he pushed himself away from the wall. "'Tis nothing, friend. A little tiredness, nothing more."

Eahlmund nodded, though his eyes betrayed his scepticism. "How fares Lady Hild?"

"She sleeps, for which the Lord God be praised. She's in good hands and, in time, I'm sure she will recover. But enough of such things." He was eager to change the subject in case his voice should betray his ragged emotions. "How go the plans to rescue Eadric?"

***

Later, in the cool of the evening once the broiling sun had dipped below the surrounding hills, Aethelgar gathered the leading men together to discuss the next day's attack. Thurkill crouched down on his haunches next to him, intent on taking in every detail, if only to distract himself for Hild's trials.

The land around Scrobbesburh was not familiar to him and he would need to learn from others and learn quickly. As they talked, platters of freshly roasted venison were passed round, accompanied by loaves of bread that were past their best, but soon softened when dipped in bowls of goat's milk.

"The town lies on a small area of raised ground that sits within the arms of the river Hafern. It is surrounded by marshland through which no army can safely pass, lest the weight of their armour suck them down to a watery grave. There is but one approach to the town: a narrow, raised path that snakes its way through the bog to the gates from the east."

"What of the defences?"

Recognising the voice, Thurkill glanced across the group to see the spearman who had helped him rescue the women from the ambush at Wenloch. Catching his eye, Ochta nodded in greeting.

"There's a ditch running around the town. Behind that, there is a raised earthwork into which has been planted a wooden palisade. It is not much changed since the days of the Lady Aethelflaed who first built these fortifications."

Ochta grunted. "We'll be hard pressed to break them down then. They stood firm against the Vikings in their day, and they will stand just as firm against us. We have no siege weapons, nor do we have time to build any."

"With courage, determination and brute strength, we can

overcome."

"Indeed, we can, Thurkill," Aethelgar agreed, "but what is also in our favour is that the Normans have begun work on a new castle in the north east corner of the town. Already they have raised a mound of earth on top of which they have built a wooden tower. A keep, I think they call it. But they have knocked down part of the palisade and several the houses to make room for it, and the repairs have not yet been completed. Our scouts tell us that we will find little to bar us from entering the town in that sector."

Ochta sniffed. "So, we just have the tower to deal with, as that is surely where they will be holding Eadric."

Aethelgar leaned across to where the other man sat. Wrapping one arm around his shoulders and ruffling his hair with his other hand, he laughed. "Worry not, Ochta, for I have a plan."

SEVENTEEN

There were close to four score men when they set out soon after midday. The news that Eadric had been taken had passed quickly from village to village across his lands and men flocked to the cave in their droves. Aethelgar had turned away those who were too old, those who had no battle-skill, and those who had no weapon other than some rusting farm tool. Though they were eager, they would be more hindrance than help. It promised to be foul work and Aethelgar did not want to attack with a poorly disciplined rabble.

Thurkill had no idea how many Normans held the town, but he reckoned that Eadric's men would outnumber them by around two to one. Though the enemy would have the advantage of the wooden defences to even things up, he was confident their venture would meet with success. They would have the benefit of surprise after all, as most of the garrison would be asleep when they attacked.

Despite the anxiety he felt ahead of any battle, he at least had a purpose now, a goal on which to focus his mind away from the helplessness that consumed him while he watched his wife suffer.

There had been little change in her condition when he'd checked on her that morning. She remained in a deep but troubled sleep, her skin still pale and clammy to the touch. Sunhilda, who looked exhausted beyond all measure, told him that Hild had woken in the night to call for food and water. Though she had managed only a few mouthfuls of each, Sunhilda declared it to be a positive sign. Aethelgar's wife had then urged Thurkill to be on his way but to keep Hild in his prayers and – with the help of God and the saintly Mildburh – perhaps his wife would have recovered by the time he returned.

Now, surrounded by Eahlmund, Leofric, Leofgar, Eopric and Urri, he felt more at ease. It was good to have these stalwarts with him; men he knew he could trust to stand firm when the time came. They strode along with the easy gait of men used to long marches and comfortable with the weight of their mailshirts. To ease the burden while they walked, each man had slung his shield across his back and carried his spear sloped over his right shoulder.

Thurkill gazed on them with a mixture of pride and humility. He had been through a lot with these lads in the last several months; he would rather have no others stand with him in the shieldwall than these stout fellows. Though he wondered what the day would bring, he knew that whatever the outcome, his men would play their part and would do so with honour and courage.

He prayed that they would all live to feast the victory, for he had never attacked a stronghold such as this before and knew little of the craft or sacrifice it would demand of them. He remembered how difficult his own villagers had made it for the Normans when they assaulted Gudmundcestre. He was under no illusions as to how hard it might be.

They reached their first destination shortly before nightfall, a thickly wooded vale a short distance from the town's defences. There, the scouts who had gone on ahead to make sure their approach was not observed were waiting for them. To make doubly sure, the Saxons had taken a wide arc round to the east of the town, crossing the Hafern a few miles further upstream and then following its meandering course to reach the meeting point.

The men stood shivering in the gloom. Though the night air retained much of the day's heat, the waters of the river had been waist deep and icy cold. Every man was soaked through to the skin from the belly down. One or two had even lost their footing on the slippery rocks of the riverbed, ending up fully submerged and spluttering until those nearby could pull them upright before the sharp current swept them away. Now there was little more they could do to get warm other than stamp their feet and flap their arms about their bodies; there was no possibility of fires being lit this close to the town.

It would be some hours yet before they launched their attack. To pass the time, Aethelgar and Thurkill busied themselves by moving among the warriors, reminding them of every detail of the plan. For those that had not fought before, they also offered words of encouragement to bolster their spirits.

Thurkill remembered his first battle and how he had felt in the hours before the shieldwalls clashed together. It took guts to stand face to face with a man who was intent on killing you; they would need to take courage from wherever it could be found. Thurkill knew that the best strength of all would come from the men to the left and right. Knowing that you could depend on them as much as they depended on you could make all the difference in deciding whether to stand or run.

Their rounds completed, Thurkill and Aethelgar conferred once more with the other leaders under a huge oak, going over the details one final time. It didn't matter that they had been through it several times already; it was essential that nothing was left to chance. In the darkness, everyone needed to know where they were meant to be, else they ran the risk of friend killing friend.

"We'll move in three groups." Aethelgar's voice was calm and assured. If he felt any nerves, Thurkill could not detect them. A steady hand on the tiller would help keep the others focussed.

"Ochta, your group goes in first and deals with any watchmen you find on the walls. Absolute silence is critical. One shout or scream, and all is lost before we even begin. Make sure all your men are clear on that." He paused to wait for the other man to nod his acceptance.

"Good. Once that is done, have your men wait by the base of the tower mound, where the gap in the wall is. You must keep that route open. Should anything go wrong, that is our only way out. You must defend it, with your lives if necessary.

"Once we have the wall, my group will force entry to the tower. Thurkill, you and your men stand ready behind us to deal with whatever you find within. You must rescue Eadric and any others who are with him. Then, together, we will fight our way back to Ochta. I imagine that all hell will break loose soon after we go in, so we'll have our hands full for sure. Stay close, use your shieldwall where you can, and with luck, we'll be safely out with Eadric before the rest of the Normans can work out what's going on. Any questions?"

Both Thurkill and Ochta shook their heads. They knew the plan inside out; they were ready to go.

"Good. Go back to your men and have them rest."

***

Thurkill found that, no matter how much he wanted to, he could not sleep; he was far too tense. The tight feeling in the pit of his stomach never left him at times like these. Oftentimes, he welcomed it, like he were greeting an old friend. He knew the value of taut nerves, that feeling of being on the edge of the knife blade. Amid the screams of the dying and the blood, piss and shit of the dead, a man with his wits about him could mean the difference between life and death.

All around him, men snored, while others grumbled or farted in their sleep. Every now and then a man would get to his feet and stumble a short distance away, avoiding the prone forms of his companions as best he could. Then there would be a short pause before the sound of retching, or of bladders or bowels being voided reached Thurkill's ear. They were not the first and nor would they be the last to suffer fear ahead of a battle. The prospect of a violent and painful death would often turn a man's guts to water.

Oblivious to the concerns of others, however, Thurkill whiled away the hours sitting cross-legged with his back against the big oak tree. In his hand he held his seax, the edge of which he scraped repeatedly against a piece of sandstone, honing the edge until the merest touch on his finger would draw blood. It was dull, methodical work that required a level of concentration that kept his mind off the horrors that lay ahead. There was nothing he could do to stop images of Hild filling his mind, though.

He longed to be by her side but, at the same time, he knew there would be little or nothing he could do if he were there. He knew that his desire to just hold her hand was more to assuage his needs than hers. In all honesty, it was better for everyone to be here helping to rescue Eadric... but that knowledge could not stop his heart from being slowly shredded by his desperate longing.

Eventually, when the darkness was at its most dense,

Aethelgar appeared by his side and placed a hand on his shoulder. "It's time, my friend. Rouse your men."

Gratefully, Thurkill uncurled his limbs and pushed himself upright. He'd been sat in the same position for so long that he had to rub his calves and thighs vigorously until he could feel the sensation returning. Finally, he stretched his arms up above his head while arching his back, loosening the muscles of his upper body. He would have need of all his strength and agility before the night was out.

Soon, the men were ready to go. Assembled into their three groups, they set off at short intervals towards the walls of the town, visible in the distance by dint of the watchmen's fires placed at regular intervals along the palisade. Thurkill knew that their value for the sentries was limited. If the Saxons stayed outside of the pool of light they cast, there was little chance they would be spotted. Their purpose was little more than to provide warmth and comfort for those who had to spend long hours in the dark and cold of a night's watch.

Thurkill led the rearmost group with Eahlmund and Eopric at his side. Urri and the two brothers brought up the rear. Making up their full complement were a score or so of Eadric's best men, those who were the most skilled fighters or the quickest of mind and feet. As the raiding party, it would be they who bore the brunt of any fighting to be done, once Aethelgar had fashioned an entrance to the tower.

Thurkill didn't know many of the men in his group, but he was impressed by what he saw. Several were of a similar stature to him, but every one of them – irrespective of size – had the look of a fighter. He could tell these were men who'd tasted the bloodlust before. They would not shrink away when the time came to stick a blade between a man's ribs. Even though he knew not their names or their history, Thurkill felt he could rely on them. If only Harold had had more of such men at Senlac Hill, things might well have been different.

Suddenly, he realised Aethelgar's group in front had stopped. Fearing that they had been discovered, Thurkill dropped to his knees, signalling for the others to follow his example. He strained to listen for signs of men running or fighting, but there was nothing. His heart was hammering its way through his rib cage, while his head was filled with the sound of his own rushing blood. He was gripping his sword hilt so hard that his knuckles shone white, even in the gloom. Pushing the tip into the soft earth, he wiped his palm against the rough cloth of his trews. He could not believe how sweaty it had become.

Moments later, a man dropped back from Aethelgar's group to report that Ochta's men had reached the wall and had already taken up a defensive position, close to where the new wooden tower had been built atop the man-made mound. It was time to move up, time to be about the grisly business of the night.

Gathering the men around him, Thurkill whispered his final orders. "Stay close. If you get lost in the dark, we won't come to find you, so don't wander off. Remember your duty; we are here to rescue Eadric and any of his men who still live. We have no other purpose, so do not allow yourselves to be distracted by anything else you might see or hear. Our success depends on speed and surprise. If we can be in and out before the whole garrison knows what's happening, our chances of living 'til tomorrow will be greatly increased. Dally and we die. Are we clear?"

He was met with a chorus of nods and the odd whispered "Aye, Lord". Grunting with satisfaction, he turned to follow Aethelgar's man along the narrow path that was marked by stones placed at intervals on either side. In the dark, they had to walk slowly, using their feet to feel for the stones, keeping them on course in the middle of the causeway that ran through the marshy ground on either side. Even now, in the first flush of summer, he could feel the softness of the turf beneath his feet; he could only imagine how much worse it would in winter.

They reached the wall without mishap. As one, they crouched down behind the rough-hewn stakes to take stock of their situation. Aside from the light of the braziers, everything was pitch black. A thick layer of cloud had formed as daylight faded, hiding from view whatever moonlight might have been visible. From where he crouched, Thurkill could see two fires close by. The nearest was no more than twenty paces to his rear, up on the palisade's walkway; the second shone out at the top of the tower that stood at the centre of the circular mound of earth. Though they were close enough to be heard, the glare from the flames would prevent the watchmen from seeing much, if anything, beyond the pool of light cast by the fire.

They remained where they were, watching and listening, for what seemed an age. On the other side of the gap in the wall, Thurkill could vaguely make out several crouched forms, bunched together. They were Aethelgar and his men, waiting – like he was – for Ochta's group to do their work. Craning his neck, Thurkill stared at the area around the nearest fire. Though he could not be certain, he fancied he could see two or three dark shapes huddled around it. Just then, there was a flurry of silent, jerky movements. Half a dozen shadowy forms rushed forward into the light, overwhelming those who had been standing facing the warmth. In quick succession, the sentries fell. But just as Thurkill was thinking how well executed the attack had been, an ear-splitting scream rent the cool night air. At the same time, the brazier toppled over, sending sparks and burning logs in all directions.

"Shit!"

Suddenly, Aethelgar was by his side, dragging Eahlmund to his feet. "Come on. This place will soon be swarming with Normans. We must move now if we're to have any chance of rescuing Eadric."

Wasting no time, Thurkill bounced to his feet, urging his men to follow him. The plan to wait by the wall until Aethelgar had found a way into the tower was a thing of the past, discarded as soon as the alarm had been sounded. They would have to improvise.

Within the walls, all was still eerily quiet, though he knew it would not last. The Normans up on the wall had finally been silenced, and Ochta's men were now streaming back down to guard the gap that Thurkill had not long since vacated. That part of the plan, at least, still held. They had to keep the gap open if they were to have any hope of escape.

"Quick; over here." He turned in the direction of the shout, to where he could make out Aethelgar's lanky frame over by what looked to be a fenced off enclosure. As he drew closer, he saw that it housed a pair of bulls, huge creatures for which the area was said to be well-known. Immediately, he guessed what his companion was thinking. Ordering his men to keep watch, Thurkill opened the gate allowing the two men inside where they untied the halters that tethered the beasts to a central stake.

As they led the docile creatures out of the enclosure, two more of Aethelgar's men ran forward, carrying a heavy wooden yoke and several coils of rope which they used to harness the animals together. Then, with the flat of his sword, Aethelgar slapped them across the rump, urging them towards the tower while Thurkill and several others hauled on the ropes from the front. What with the steepness of the incline and the recalcitrance of the beasts, it was slow going to the say the least.

"Come on, lads. Put your backs into it."

No sooner had he spoken, however, than the man immediately to his left yelped and went down on one knee. Thurkill was about to berate him for his lack of effort when he noticed an arrow protruding from his shoulder. The watchers on the tower had recovered from their shock and had begun to organise their defence.

"Shields," Thurkill roared. Those men that were not hauling on the ropes ran to the front and raised their hide-covered linden boards so that they covered both themselves and the men pulling the oxen. Straight away, arrows began to thud into the shields as more and more archers appeared on the walls, but none found their mark.

Thurkill's muscles strained with the effort of heaving on the rope. His palms burned as he fought to keep a grip on the rough fibres. Although they were over halfway there now, the going was becoming harder with every step. The longer they took, the more likely it was that they'd be attacked from the town as well as the tower. To guard against such a threat, he ordered the rest of his men, under Urri's leadership, to form a shieldwall as a loose protective screen.

At last, they reached the wooden stakes that formed the walls of the tower. In a move that Thurkill considered canny, the archers had now shifted their aim to the oxen, hoping to bring them down before they could be put to work. So now the shield bearers had their work cut out trying to cover the bulls as well. A few shafts struck home but they had little effect other than to enrage the animals who now bellowed piteously, pawing at the ground in their desire to be away from danger.

Aethelgar threw one of the two ropes at Thurkill, yelling at him to secure it to the nearest stakes on his side, while he did the same on his. With the ropes secured, they each grabbed the bulls' halters and pulled on them, exhorting them to move. This time, however, they did not need much persuading. Straightaway they began to lumber away from the tower, taking up the slack until the ropes pulled taut. The poor beasts strained against the yoke but to no avail. Even their great strength was not enough to make the posts budge.

"They're set too deep in the ground." Aethelgar howled in frustration, oblivious to the shafts that thudded around him.

Thurkill could hear the posts creaking, but it was true; they were stubbornly holding firm. They had to move fast if they were to succeed. Every moment lost brought them closer to failure and death. Already, he could see, in the distance, Norman soldiers running towards them from the town. They had to make a breakthrough in the next few moments, or all would be lost.

All around him, men held their shields over their heads but otherwise were uncertain what to do. The whole enterprise hung in the balance. Just as he felt the hand of defeat clutching at his arm, desperation forced an idea to the front of Thurkill's mind.

"You men," he yelled at the spearmen standing idly by the tower. "Get digging. Use your seaxes, helmets, hands, whatever you can." Leading by example, Thurkill dropped to his knees and began tearing at the turf around the base of the posts. Aethelgar had said the tower had only recently been built; perhaps the earth had not yet settled and hardened?

Immediately, his idea bore fruit. Using his shovel-like hands to good effect, he scooped away huge clumps of earth and grass, ignoring the pain as several of his fingernails tore on the rough soil. Catching on quickly, several others flung themselves down on either side of him and began to dig, widening the gully he had started. Others crowded around them, protecting them as best they could with interlocked shields. But still the bulls could make no head way.

"Keep digging. Dig, for your lives depend on it." Jumping up, Thurkill drew his seax. He didn't want to do this, but there was no choice. A sizeable group of Normans was advancing from the town, and they were still stuck outside the tower. If they did not break in soon, they would have to run. Taking up a position in between the yoked oxen, he braced himself. "I'm sorry boys; I know you're doing your best."

With that, he stabbed down hard into the flank of each beast. Deep enough to cause a reaction, but not so deep as to cause fatal wounds. The effect was immediate, though. Both animals bellowed in pain and anger. Together, they surged forward in a gargantuan effort to escape from the knife-wielding maniac. The ropes snapped taut once more, but this time they could not check the bulls' frantic struggle to flee the horror. With a great wrenching sound, the posts around the corner of the tower began to move.

"Ready!" The men knew exactly what to do. Thurkill's group ran to him, forming into a wedge behind him, swords and shields at the ready. Meanwhile, all those with Aethelgar raced to the foot of the mound to join Urri's shieldwall where it awaited the on-rushing Normans. They were not a moment too soon, for the enemy was upon them almost before they had overlapped their shields.

Thurkill had to push them from his mind, though. He had to trust in their skill and strength to hold the Normans at bay while he went about his own business. As he stood there, looking up at the wooden construction that rose above his head, he realised he had no idea how many Normans were inside or where they might find Eadric. It looked as if it were only two stories high with enough room to house twenty or so men comfortably, but who knew what they would find? How many other Saxons were in there with Eadric? How many guards had been set to watch over them? Would they find FitzScrope? All would soon become clear, however; of that he was certain.

EIGHTEEN

With one final effort from the now-petrified bulls, the corner stakes finally gave way. For a moment, the fighting seemed to stop as all eyes turned to the tower. But then, the spell was broken by the man next to Thurkill who yelped in triumph and ran towards the narrow breach that had appeared in the tower's wall. Too late, Thurkill reached out to grab him, his broken nails snagging painfully against the hothead's mailshirt as he surged past.

"Wait!"

Thurkill had seen – or rather heard – what the other man had not. With the load-bearing corner posts yanked out of their moorings, the structure had been fatally weakened at that point. The creaking was growing louder and more insistent with every heartbeat as the timbers of the second story groaned in protest at the extra strain they were being asked to bear. It was an uneven struggle, though, and one they were destined to lose.

Just as the foolhardy warrior reached the gap, the whole section above his head collapsed, crushing him under the weight of several huge logs. At the same time, three Norman archers who had been defending that corner of the tower were thrown clear, landing in a jumble of limbs close to Thurkill's position. Judging by the sickening cracking noises, several limbs had been broken, but he was not willing to take any risks all the same.

"Leofric, Leofgar, finish them. Everyone else, with me."

Leaving his companions to deliver the killing blows, Thurkill led the charge into the now ruined corner of the tower. Once inside, he found himself in a large open space which, judging by the casks, bales of cloth and other materials, was used as a storeroom. There was no time to take in any more detail, however, as a small clutch of soldiers came barrelling into the room via the door in the far corner. Thurkill knew he had to hit them before they had a chance to organise themselves. So, without waiting to see who else was with him, he threw himself forward, ploughing into the lead man with his shield. His impetus knocked the Norman off balance, forcing him back into his companions. Howling incoherently, Thurkill followed up his attack, thrusting his sword into the face of the man to his right. Hot blood splashed back over his face, but he cared not for the bloodlust was upon him. Teeth bared, he launched himself at the remaining Normans, cutting and hacking his way through them until none was left standing.

With the room cleared, Thurkill approached the door, keeping his shield up as a precaution. It was as well that he did for, as soon as he passed the threshold, he was attacked by a canny soldier who had been waiting on the other side armed with a woodcutting axe. The blow was so hard that the axe head split his shield, the blade protruding through the wooden board close to where Thurkill's hand gripped the leather strap.

Seizing his chance, Thurkill twisted his shield hard to the left, dragging his assailant's arm out wide as he failed to let go of the axe haft in time; it would be the last mistake he would ever make. A look of terror spread across the Norman's face as he realised too late, that his whole body was now exposed. Laughing maniacally, Thurkill thrust his sword point deep into the man's unarmoured gut, pushing hard against the flesh and forcing him off his feet. So deep had the blade penetrated that he had to stamp down on the dying man's chest until the soft flesh relinquished its grip on the metal.

"Lord." Thurkill spun round to where Eahlmund was standing, a few paces behind him. To his left was another door, while in front of him, a wooden staircase led up to the next story.

"Which way?"

Thurkill hesitated, conscious of the fact that the rest of his men were already bunching behind him, eager to find their master. *Where would they be holding him?* There was no time to hold a debate, though, as the sounds of a fierce and brutal conflict at the base of the mound were reaching their ears. They had to act swiftly before Aethelgar, and his men were overwhelmed.

"We split up. Eahlmund, take half the men and head through that door. I'll take the rest up these stairs. Go."

Eahlmund grabbed the biggest warrior and shoved him

towards the door. "Through you go, my friend. We're right behind you."

Grinning stupidly at his friend's antics, Thurkill ran for the stairs, taking them two at a time. As he neared the top, he felt the uneven wooden slats starting to buckle under his weight. Without the support of the retaining wall, the whole structure was in danger of collapse. He reached out with his right arm to steady himself only to clutch at nothing; there was no rail or rope to save him, just open space down to the passageway below.

Somehow, he managed to right himself as his toes teetered on the edge. But before he could fully regain his balance, a soldier clad in full-length mailshirt and conical helmet appeared above him. Taking advantage of Thurkill's predicament, he threw himself headfirst at the Saxon, his iron-helmed head catching Thurkill square in the chest. There was nothing Thurkill could do to stop himself falling, but by some miracle, he managed to twist in the air as he fell, ensuring that he landed at least partly on top of the other man, his shoulder punching into the Norman's face. Even so, he still felt as if the air had been pushed from his lungs by the force of the impact. What's more, a jolt of pain spread across his chest like a bolt of lightning from where the point of the helmet had struck him hard on the breastbone.

Half dazed from shock, Thurkill struggled to focus. His head throbbed from where he had bashed his skull on the hardened earth floor. All around him there was chaos and shouting as men fought above his head. As his brain slowly began to function again, he felt the Norman beneath him frantically fumbling with his belt. *He's trying to free his knife.*

Panic gripped Thurkill as he fought to regain control of his limbs. His arms flapped uselessly by his sides, like a young bird, newly fallen from the nest, whose wings had yet to learn the art of flight. As he tried to push away from his assailant, his vision blurred, and a wave of nausea threatened to engulf him. Swallowing down the bile that rose in his gorge, he realised he must have banged his head harder than he had first thought. Just then, a glint of metal caught his eye, and a wickedly sharp-looking knife came into view.

An image of Hild flooded his brain. *Was this the end? Would he ever see his wife again?*

He could feel the strength slowly seeping back into his limbs, but it was too late to be of any use. With a look of malevolent glee spreading across his face, the Norman slowly drew back his arm to deliver the killing blow. Thurkill refused to close his eyes or even turn aside; he would not give the bastard the satisfaction of thinking him afraid to meet his doom. Instead, he grinned at him, wide-eyed and diabolical, daring him to begin his dance with the devil. But then, rather than plunging the knife into his body, the Norman hesitated, a look of fear spreading across his face. Thurkill could not begin to fathom what it meant. Why was he not dead? Why had the Norman not killed him?

Just then, Eahlmund surged past him up the stairs, aiming a kick at the Norman's head as he did so. It was a blow that would have felled a horse, so a mere man stood no chance. The Norman's head snapped back, his neck breaking with the sound of a dry twig snapping under foot. The knife fell from his lifeless hand, clattering to the floor where it stuck upright, its point dug into the soft earth.

Thurkill smiled weakly up at his saviour, still too groggy to muster sounds let alone coherent words. Never one to waste words, Eahlmund grabbed him by the scruff of his mailshirt and hauled him to his feet, before continuing to bound up the steps towards the sounds of battle. Thurkill grabbed his sword and made to follow but found that his legs were not yet ready to support his weight. His left knee buckled, and he felt himself lurch to the side, colliding with the wall. He lent there for a moment, breathing deeply in through his nose and out through his mouth, whilst shaking his head to clear the wooziness. Slowly, the dizziness dissipated enough to encourage him to try once more.

The scene that greeted him when he turned the corner at the top of the stairs was like something out of the old testament. There was blood everywhere, splattered over the walls, gathered in pools on the floor, coating the faces and bodies of those who still fought. The dead and dying lay on all sides;

Norman and Saxon alike, limbs entwined, brought together in death's tight embrace. To his right, he could see fires burning in the town through a huge breach in the wall. Ahead of him, a desperate struggle played out in the far corner of the room. He guessed it must have been the main living quarters in the tower, used by the lord for feasting or holding court, for there were wooden benches and trestle tables on all sides, many of which had been upended in the melee. Large, patterned fabrics had been hung from the walls, presumably to keep out the chill winds that forced their way through the spaces between the logs. But these, too, were now tainted with blood.

The Normans, a round half dozen of them, had taken up position in front of another door. The fervour with which they were fighting told Thurkill that they had been commanded to defend what lay within that room with their lives. *That will surely be where we find our prize. But how to get to it?*

The Normans with their better training appeared to be making light work of keeping the Saxons at bay and time was running out. Much longer and they would have no hope of escaping the town before they were cut off. Even as he watched, another of Eadric's men fell, his neck eviscerated by a stabbing sword thrust. He had to act fast. There would be no time for finesse or subtlety.

He wished he had his war-axe with him; the extra power from its weight and balance would have helped him bludgeon his way through the enemy line. But it was back in the cave in the hills near Conendovre, its blade oiled and wrapped in deerskin to keep it free from rust. He would have to make do with his sword. Just then, Leofric ran into the room, followed closely by his brother. It was the jolt Thurkill needed to unlock his indecision. With every moment that passed he felt stronger, almost as if the sickness had never happened. With those two beside him, he was ready to seize the moment.

"With me, lads. We have to break through to that door."

Forming up on either side of their lord, the two brothers interlocked their shields at an angle so that Thurkill was at the head of a little wedge. Then, roaring at the others to get out of their way, they charged forward, ducking their heads down behind their shields for protection. At the last moment, those to their front pulled apart, just as the sea had once parted for Moses.

The Normans had no time to react to this new threat. One moment they were pushing the enemy back, holding fast to their task; the next, they found themselves facing three screaming devils bearing down on them like banshees. Thurkill and the two brothers took them hard, right in the centre of their line. They stood no chance. The Saxons piled into their opponents, splitting their defensive line as if walking through a field of barley and scattering them on both sides. That was the signal for the rest of the Saxons to wade in, taking advantage of the confusion to stab, kick and punch anything that still moved.

And then, it was over. Not a single Norman remained alive. Looking around him, Thurkill saw that victory had not come cheap. Several of Eadric's men lay amongst the dead and the dying. Of his own men, only Leofgar had been injured, and thankfully not too seriously. Even now his brother was binding the wound on his sword hand as tightly as he could with strips of cloth torn from the tunic of one of the dead. Satisfied that the danger had passed, Thurkill set his mind to finding Eadric.

"Eahlmund, break down that door."

His friend did not need to be asked twice. Grabbing an axe from where it lay on the floor, he began pummelling the wood around the door frame. It took fewer than a half dozen blows before the panels splintered and finally cracked apart. Eahlmund then finished the job with the heel of his boot, smashing what remained of the door out of the way, before standing back to allow his lord to enter.

Thurkill proceeded warily, fearing that more soldiers might be waiting within, but there was none. Peering into the gloom, lit only by the reflection of the torches in the main room, Thurkill could just make out the huddled form of six bodies: three on either side of the narrow confines of the chamber. None seemed to be moving and, at first, he feared the worst. But then the shape nearest to him slowly began to uncoil itself before croaking, "You bastards took your time."

NINETEEN

The prisoners had to be helped out of their make-shift cell. It was obvious to all that they had all taken a fearful beating during their captivity and one of the six had, in fact, died of the injuries he'd sustained. Mercifully, Eadric appeared to be the least badly hurt of them all, and as soon as his bonds had been cut, he lurched down the stairs and out of the tower with a face that radiated an incandescent rage. Back out in the open, he turned to Thurkill.

"Fetch me a sword and then find me Normans to kill."

Thurkill shook his head gravely. "Look at the others, Lord. They're too weak to fight." He gestured towards the other survivors who were being led out of the tower, a man on either side to support them. "We must leave while we still can. Many have already died tonight, giving their lives that you may be free. Do not let their sacrifice be in vain, Lord. The longer we tarry, the more time the Normans have to organise their defence. FitzScrope must be somewhere in the town too, for we've not found him within the castle. If he rallies his men, they will be too strong for us."

Eadric turned his face to the sky and roared in furious frustration. For a moment, Thurkill feared he might even turn on him. But then the shadow seemed to pass just as quickly, and his expression bloomed into a broad grin. "I suppose you're right, you hairy-arsed oik. There will be time aplenty for slaughter soon enough. Lead us home then. Where's Aethelgar anyway?"

Thurkill peered into the gloom at the bottom of the mound. "There, Lord. He leads the defence against the soldiers from the town."

"Right, round the silly bugger up and let's be on our way."

Thurkill could see that they had already stayed too long. The men below were holding their own but were being forced back as more and more soldiers came running from the town. It would not be long before they were overrun. As quickly as he

124

could, Thurkill gathered his men around him. Dividing the men into three groups, he assigned a leader to each.

"Eahlmund, take six men and set torches to the tower. The flames might help divert a few from the fight below. Then join Ochta at the wall to keep the gap open at all costs. If FitzScrope has a brain, he'll send men to cut off our escape.

"Leofgar, there was another enclosure near where we found the oxen. Take six more and release the cattle you find there. Drive them towards the town. With luck they'll stampede through the soldiers coming from that direction. Then join Aethelgar and his men below.

"The rest of you, take Eadric and the others out through the wall and on to the place where we rested before the attack. Wait for us there."

Without waiting to see his orders carried out, Thurkill ran down the mound, taking care not to lose his footing or turn an ankle in his haste to join the affray. He reached the makeshift shieldwall just ahead of five other men who had followed him down the slope. Together, they would shore up the line long enough for them to retreat to safety. He joined the end nearest to where Aethelgar stood, so that he might speak to him as they fought. Before he could do that, however, he had to fight for his life. No sooner had he taken his place, forcing his large round shield in front of and overlapping with the man to his right, than he found himself under attack.

Two huge spear-wielding Normans arrived a heartbeat later and made straight for him, no doubt hoping to catch him off guard. He managed to duck behind his shield just as the first spear point was thrust directly at his head. He was not a moment too soon as he felt the blade glance off the side of his helmet. He was less lucky with the second.

Whether by luck or by plan, where the first spearman had gone high, the other went low, jamming his blade beneath the rim of his round linden board. Thurkill felt a sharp stab of pain on his thigh as the spearpoint hit his mailshirt. He prayed that the knitted iron rings had done their job as he did not have time to check. He did not think he was bleeding, but he knew that might just be the shock. Crouching, he thrust his sword blindly in the direction of the first man's groin, noting with satisfaction that the blade buried itself in the Norman's soft, yielding flesh. His opponent fell, screaming in agony as he grabbed at his ruined abdomen.

Not stopping to admire his handiwork, Thurkill turned to face the second man, only to find he had already been dispatched by Leofric who stood to his left, grinning as he held aloft his blade, dripping with fresh blood. Nodding his thanks, Thurkill glanced down at the wounded man beneath him, his screams still piercing the night. Without ceremony, he reversed his sword hilt in his hand and stabbed down hard into his neck. Abruptly, the noise ceased. Seeing the looks of those around him, Thurkill shrugged. "He was getting on my nerves."

Disheartened by the impact of the reinforcements, the Normans pulled back a short way. They seemed uncertain, as if none were there to lead them. Perhaps FitzScrope had been killed already, Thurkill mused, and his men were now in need of direction? Whatever the cause, he could not bring himself to care. The temporary lull in hostilities gave him the chance to hail Aethelgar, a few paces to his right.

"Eadric's safe. We should go back to the marshlands before they find their balls and attack once more."

Aethelgar nodded before raising his voice. "Everyone, pull back. Slow and steady. Keep the line and do not turn your back on the enemy. You'll have a spear in your arse before you know it."

They completed the withdrawal in good order, helped in part by the lack of enthusiasm on the part of the remaining Normans to engage them. Some had already turned aside to deal with the fire that was now raging through the tower, while others had peeled away to help gather the cattle that threatened to escape from the town. Without a captain to organise them, the remaining foot soldiers had lost their stomach for the fight. Several of their comrades had been killed, and with Eadric gone from his cell, there was no sense in risking further loss of life. Thurkill could not help but wonder what FitzScrope would make of their decision, though. Perhaps it would be best for them if he were already dead.

They found Ochta at the palisade, dutifully awaiting their return. From the bodies strewn around him, it was clear that they, too, had been in a fight, but the wily old weasel – his face illuminated by the roaring inferno above them – assured them that most of the dead were Norman.

"It was touch and go for a while, but when your man, Eahlmund, turned up with half a dozen lads, that swung the day in our favour. The bastards never saw them coming. Slaughtered to a man they were."

Aethelgar clapped Ochta on the back. "Excellent work, boys, excellent work. Tell me, did you see Eadric? Has he made it through safely?"

"Aye. He'll curse us for keeping him waiting, I daresay."

They found Eadric along with the other captives in the same spot where they had assembled earlier. As they arrived, men flopped to the ground where they stood, exhausted now that the exertions of the night were at an end. Thurkill knew, however, that they could not stay there. It would only be a matter of time before the surviving Normans recovered their nerve and gave chase. They had to put several miles between them and the town before the sun came up or risk annihilation.

Reading his mind, Aethelgar wasted no time rousing the men amid much grumbling and cursing. "Come on, lads. If we get caught here, your pig-loving days will be over. You saw what happened to the last one of us that FitzScrope got his hands on."

TWENTY

Richard FitzScrope stood in the centre of the smouldering embers of his beloved castle, cursing himself for his stupidity. He had underestimated the Saxon dogs thinking that, without their talismanic leader, the rest of the sorry bunch would simply slink off back into the forests and hills whence they came. Who knew that the man had some capable lieutenants amongst his followers?

If only he'd stayed within the walls of Scrobbesburh last night, then this whole mess might have been avoided. But no, he'd chosen that night, of all nights, to go off in pursuit of one of his favourite pastimes: bedding young Saxon wenches, willing or otherwise. The fact that last night's victim – he considered the word appropriate – was one of the more memorable of his recent exploits was no consolation. Worse still, the bruising he had inflicted upon her would mean it would be some time before he could sample the delights of that particular honey pot again.

He had arrived home shortly after dawn, galloping the last mile or so as he became aware of the column of smoke billowing up from his precious new keep. Fear and anger had gripped his gut. Anger that the snivelling lickspittles he had left in charge seemed to have failed him so spectacularly and fear that his prized prisoner might have escaped, just hours before William FitzOsbern was due to attend the man's hanging in the town square. FitzScrope knew he was well and truly in the shit.

He had no idea how he was going to explain this whole debacle, or how the smug bastard earl would react to the news. Even more annoying was the fact that the man he had left in charge – some wastrel newly arrived from Normandy – was dead; his charred body was found in the ruins of the tower not far from the room where Eadric was being held. The fact that the whoreson had selfishly denied him the opportunity to kill him for his abject failure just served to sour FitzScrope's mood yet further. If he could have him killed all over again, he would have.

"Lord." FitzScrope turned to face the owner of the querulous voice that had dared to break into his thoughts, his eyes burning like the fires in the deepest pits of hell.

"Well?"

"We have found their camp in the marshes to the east, about three hundred paces from the wall, but they are long gone."

"And why," his voice seethed with venom, "did no one think to pursue them at the time? Did that not occur to any of you mouse-brained buffoons?"

The unfortunate soldier who had no doubt drawn the shortest lot to have to bring this news to FitzScrope, turned pale but – to his credit – he found the courage to face down the danger that confronted him. FitzScrope made a mental note that he should consider promoting the man to replace the previous, now deceased, castellan.

"With Hugo dead and you not to be found, Lord, we were uncertain what was best. We lost several men in the attack, the tower was burning, and the cattle had been let loose. Rightly or wrongly, we chose to douse the flames to save as much of the castle as we could and to round up the livestock. We did not have the men to do more."

He's an insolent dog but, by God, the man has balls. "By what name should I call you? I like to know the names of the men I kill."

Still, the man showed no overt sign of fear. "Wakelin of Giffard, Lord. My family has long been in the service of the Scrope family, back to the earliest days of Duke Rollo."

FitzScrope grunted. There were many who could make that claim, but that alone did not devalue the man's assertion. Feeling moderately mollified, in spite of himself, he gripped the man by the forearm. "Well, Wakelin, now is the time to prove yourself where Hugo failed. I want you to organise scouting parties to find the Saxon pigs. This attack on my castle is the final insult that they shall ever hurl at me. We will spare nothing to wipe them out. Do whatever it takes to track them down. Leave no stone unturned. Search every village and hamlet. Burn down every dung-covered house and kill every last person if you but suspect them of hiding the truth from you. I care not how many die before we find this devil's spawn. Is that clear?"

Wakelin nodded, his face masking any emotion he might have felt. "Your will, Lord. I'll leave within the hour."

Turning back to survey the ruins of his keep, FitzScrope pushed thoughts of Eadric to the back of his mind. He would have his hands full sorting this mess out. The damage to the castle could be replaced, but the damage to his authority was more worrying. For the Saxons to see Scrobbesburh burned to the ground, with many of its defenders slain, was akin to lighting a beacon on every hilltop in all directions. It was an unmistakable message.

I knew it should have been built with stone. Though the truth of it was obvious, it was far simpler to say than do. There simply were not enough skilled artisans in the whole damned country to make it possible. By God, these Saxons were a backward people. Hard to believe they had become so prosperous without having mastered the art of stonemasonry. The few skilled craftsmen that they had were all employed in the major cities like Lundenburh, Wintancaester and Eoforwic. It would take years for Norman masons to train enough local men. Somewhere like Scrobbesburh might have to wait years before it could call on the services of its own guild of craftsmen, unless he could persuade a wealthy benefactor like FitzOsbern to put his hand in his coffers. After the events of this night, he had a feeling it would be some time before that route would be open to him. 'Til then, however, they would just have to rebuild in wood.

Decision made, FitzScrope stomped off in the direction of the town. The people of Scrobbesburh were going to be busy over the coming days and weeks and the sooner they got started, the better. It would be just another reason on an already long list for them to hate him. It was as well he did not care.

TWENTY-ONE

Aethelgar led them back to the caves by means of tracks narrow and ancient. Paths that would not be known to their enemy and which they would be hard-pressed to find. They wound their way through hidden gullies and valleys in between the steep-sided hills that rose high above the flat ground to the south of Scrobbesburh.

The going was slow. Not just because of the rough, uneven tracks that were pitted and broken up by exposed stones and gnarled tree roots, but also because of the wounded men who limped, stumbled, or otherwise hobbled along as best they could. Six of their men had been killed in the fighting – a figure that Thurkill regretted but, at the same time, accepted was a fair return for the damage they had inflicted. A similar number were injured. Two had been left with local farmers, their wounds so severe that they could not travel far and were unlikely to survive more than a day or two anyway. The other four could at least walk unaided, though their pace was less than that of a dawdling child.

It was close to nightfall on the next day when the landscape became familiar to Thurkill. With the strains of the battle behind him, his mind had filled with thoughts of Hild once again. His gut wrenched with worry for his wife. She had been gravely ill when he left, sweeping in and out of consciousness so much that she was unable to recognise him or even acknowledge his presence. As he walked, he prayed to God that she was recovering well and that the baby was safe. The slow pace tormented him; he wished he could run every step of the way to see her.

Perhaps sensing his growing distraction, Eahlmund fell into step beside his friend. "Fear not, Lord. She's in good hands with Eadric's people and I have no doubt the Lady Mildburh watches over her and the child as well."

Thurkill smiled, grateful for the words of comfort however useless they might be. "My thanks, friend. It's kind of you, but

I shan't be at peace until I see her and know that she is well. She is more than half of me; without her, I am much diminished."

Eahlmund grasped his shoulder, squeezing hard to convey the strength of his feeling. "Courage, Lord. Trust in God's will."

***

The first sign that something was wrong came as they reached the path that led up into the hills in which the caves were to be found. Their arrival must have been looked for since, as soon as they emerged from the dense woodland, two men ran forward, making directly for Eadric who walked at the head of the column, some way in front of Thurkill and his men. Eadric halted to embrace the two men who were overjoyed to see him safely returned, before then stepping aside a few paces from the rest of the group to talk with them.

At first Thurkill thought nothing of it, but then he became aware that Eadric had glanced at him once or twice. Fear took hold of him, its dread fingers clawing at his heart. He began to feel breathless, light-headed even; he had to lean against a tree to steady himself as he sucked great gulps of air into his lungs. Ever by his side, Eahlmund laid a comforting hand on his arm, though he too looked pale and drawn.

With every fibre of his being, Thurkill wanted to walk over to where Eadric was deep in conversation with the two men, but something held him back. He told himself that whatever they were discussing could not be true if he did not hear it for himself. If he stayed where he was – out of earshot – then it could not be happening. He knew it was stupid, a thought that only a child would invent, but it was all he had to hold on to amid the maelstrom of emotions that surged through his body.

Hild has to be alright; she must be alright. He repeated the mantra over and over again, feeling ever more helpless with each utterance.

Eventually, Eadric grasped each man by the forearm, nodding his thanks. Then he turned and walked towards Thurkill, his pace slow and heavy as though his legs were reluctant to do their master's bidding.

Hild has to be alright. She must *be alright.*

But the look on Eadric's face told him otherwise. He could

feel the colour draining from his face, his legs beginning to shake; beads of sweat broke out on his forehead. Time seemed to slow so much that he thought Eadric would never complete the short walk to where he stood. But then he was by his side, the words washing over Thurkill like a wave of ice-cold water, numbing his addled brain, so that he heard only half of what was said to him.

"...Hild... passed ... this morning.... birth... girl... too weak to... fever took hold.... nothing to be done... sorry, my friend."

He could not understand. She could not be dead. Not his Hild. Not like this. Not without saying goodbye.

Tears streamed down his face, unnoticed and without shame. Despite the severity of her illness, he had truly expected to find her singing or laughing, her blond curls bobbing in time to the movement of her head. He felt like his legs had been chopped out from under him, like a huge hand had reached into his chest, grabbed hold of his heart and wrenched it free from his body.

She couldn't be gone. This was just some nightmare from which he would surely wake soon. He'd open his eyes to see the sunlight coming through the window of their chamber, dancing across his face. And then he'd roll over under the furs so he could snuggle up against her warm back, feeling the first tinges of lust take hold of his loins. And then she would bat him away, telling him to go satiate himself with the beasts of the field for he was no better than they. A sob escaped his throat as the knowledge sunk in that never again would he hear her scold him for some minor misdemeanour.

But wait... What of the child? Had Eadric not mentioned something about a birth? Surely God had not – in all his majestic cruelty – taken the child from him too? With a voice that was hoarse and cracked with pain, he uttered the words hesitantly, fearing the answer that might come.

"Does the child live, or does it too now sit with the saints?"

Eadric gripped him by the shoulder, "I'm told that before she died, Hild gave birth to a daughter. She lives and is being cared for by Sunhilda and the other women. They tell me she seems healthy and strong, so the Lord be praised for that at least."

Thurkill could not bring himself to echo the sentiment. How

could he praise a God who caused him so much pain? To take the one thing he had left; the one thing that meant more to him than anything. More than his own life, in fact.

Feeling a new wave of grief washing over him, he sank to his knees, grabbing huge fistfuls of earth and moss in both hands as he bellowed his pain like a wounded stag run to ground by the huntsmen. Of all those around him, none by now was unaware of the cause of his anguish. Not one among them was unmoved by the stark horror of the moment, but none knew how to comfort the young Saxon. None except Eahlmund. His closest companion through all these months, he dropped down beside his friend and clasped him tight in a bear hug, moving with his friend as he heaved and jerked from the powerful sobs that wracked his body.

Eventually, Thurkill quieted, physically exhausted and his body drained of all emotion. Rising to his feet, he could see that the others had moved on, perhaps unwilling to intrude further upon his pain. Only the men of his warband remained, each of whose faces was wet with tears. He knew they would feel her loss keenly for she had been one of them. She had tolerated their boyish foolishness and joined in with their jokes and songs. It was like they had lost a sister.

One by one, they came forward to embrace him, mumbling words of comfort that they knew could not help but which had to be said all the same. For all the awkwardness of the moment, they needed to express their love for Thurkill. They could not take away his pain, but they could share the burden, at least in part.

Thurkill was as grateful for their presence in that moment as much as he'd ever been in any shieldwall. It was as if they had raised their shields around him as he lay wounded on the ground, overlapping their boards one by one until he was surrounded by an impenetrable barrier of wood and iron. He felt a fresh torrent of tears brimming behind his eyelids. Swallowing hard to force his feelings back under some semblance of control, Thurkill gathered himself.

"Let us return to the caves. I would see my wife one last time, and I have a daughter to meet."

***

Sunhilda was waiting for Thurkill at the entrance to the caves. Wordlessly, she reached out to take his hand and guided him away from the camp and through the trees instead to a clearing about fifty paces away, screened on all sides by thick brambles and bushes. In the centre of the glade, a bier had been constructed from several criss-crossing logs packed with moss and ferns and festooned with flowers on all sides.

Hild's body lay in the centre of the bier, more emaciated and frailer than he could ever remember – a legacy of the fever that had slowly sapped her strength these last several days. Her body had been wrapped in clean white linen, bound tightly around her limbs and chest as it would have been had she been but a new-born babe. Only her face was visible. And despite the ravages inflicted by the fever, he saw that his wife retained the same mesmerising beauty by which he had been struck dumb when they first met. The high cheek bones – even more pronounced now in death – the slender, almost chiselled nose, and the plump red lips, now robbed of the blood they needed and almost grey in hue. Her hair, her beautiful golden curls, were all but hidden under the white cloth cap that had been placed on her head but, here and there, errant wisps had escaped from their confinement, reminding him of his favourite of her features.

His reverie was broken when he felt Sunhilda's hand gently pushing him forward. "Go and say your goodbyes, Thurkill. I will leave you alone with her for a while."

Nodding dumbly, he lurched forward, seizing hold of one of the bier's sturdy logs to stop himself from stumbling. His legs had failed him once more, as useless as those of a new-born foal trying to stand before it has the strength to do so. As he stared down at Hild's lifeless face, the tears flowed unabated once more. Her expression held a benign serenity, giving the lie to the trauma of her last days of life. Now it looked like she had simply fallen asleep. He half expected to see her chest rising and falling in time with her breathing.

Tentatively, he reached out a hand to gently stroke her cheek. It was cold but still soft to the touch. Leaning down, he kissed her forehead before pushing away the loose strands of hair, carefully tucking them back under the edges of the cap. As he stood, looking down at his wife, he slowly became aware of the many dozens of birds rustling and twittering in the briar and bramble bushes all around him. As the noise of their song grew, he was taken back to the day of their visit to Lady Mildburh's shrine at Wenloch. Perhaps here, too, the saint had power. Perhaps she watched over him even now as he continued to stroke Hild's forehead, mumbling whatever inane or inadequate words tumbled into his mind.

A short time later, he heard footsteps rustling through the soft sward. Turning his head, he saw Sunhilda approaching him, her arms cradling the form of a baby which, like Hild, was wrapped tightly in white linen. As he stared, uncomprehending, Aethelgar's wife came to a halt just in front of him and held the child out towards him. "Your daughter, Thurkill."

The young Saxon stood transfixed, unable to move or speak. If he'd not known otherwise, he would have said that the child was Hild born once again. The eyes had both her colouring and her inquisitive sparkle. Her cheeks had the same round shape and rosy hue, like two succulent apples newly fallen from the tree. Her hair was as golden and as curly as the woman's who lay dead behind him. So similar was she to Hild that the reminiscence lanced through him more painfully than any sword might.

Haltingly, he held out his hands. Seeing his hesitation, Sunhilda told him to copy the shape of her arms so that the baby's head would be supported in the crook of his arm. Thurkill was grateful for her guidance; he had never held a baby before and was at a loss for fear that he might break something that looked so small and fragile. Eventually, happy that he had good hold of her, Sunhilda slid her hands from beneath the child and stepped back, smiling.

The tiny baby was dwarfed against the warrior's huge frame, not much bigger than one of his muscled forearms.

Once again, Thurkill was unable to move and hardly dared even to breathe. He was amazed that the child had not immediately begun to scream as soon as she left Sunhilda's comforting embrace. But now, he feared to break the spell with any sudden movement. As for his daughter, she simply stared at him while making odd gurgling sounds in her throat, a vaguely inquisitive expression on her face.

"I think she likes you."

Thurkill looked up, genuine hope in his eyes. "How can you tell?"

"Well, for one, she is not crying. That's always a good sign, I find. But more importantly, she feels safe and secure in her father's arms. A child – but especially a daughter – will always take comfort from this, no matter her age."

Thurkill nodded, accepting the wisdom of her words. He recalled how his sister, Edith, had always longed for her father's return from whatever travels he'd been on, wrapping herself around him almost before he had climbed down from his horse. Many were the nights she had cried for the lack of his presence by the hearth in his great hall. *Will this be our future too, my love?*

He somehow doubted it. So much had changed in the last few months; who could now say what the future held for the Aenglisc? As much as he might hope otherwise, could any of them truly be safe from danger under the Normans? Besides those who were intent on killing Eadric and his followers, there was the small matter of Robert FitzGilbert, too. He had escaped the battle at Gudmundcestre, and God alone knew where he was now. Though, Thurkill knew the man must still burn with the fire of vengeance for his brother's death.

And yet, Thurkill had now brought a child – a daughter no less – into this uncertain world. There was every chance he would be killed before she had left childhood, and who would care for her then? Who but he could protect her and keep her safe?

The thought of his little girl alone in the world tugged at him, worse than any toothache he had ever experienced. How could he put her in danger by continuing to fight against the Normans? Why didn't he simply walk away and find a new home in the wilds to the west? Amongst the Waelesc? Surely, they could not be as bad as the old tales suggested. Would they not find common ground in their hatred of the enemy from across the sea? Looking down at his daughter's face, he had to admit the idea was tempting.

But there were other things to consider. He was defined by his sense of duty and honour; it was no less strong than his faith in God. Without those two pillars, he was nothing, daughter or no. He could not walk away from his responsibilities. He had sworn his sword to Eadric, and beyond that, there were others who looked to him for leadership and protection. He could not desert Eahlmund, Leofric, Leofgar, Urri and Eopric. They had sacrificed so much for him, already. What sort of man would he be were he to simply abandon them? What of the memory of Copsig and Eardwulf? Could their death be allowed to be meaningless? It was a quandary he felt powerless to resolve.

"What will you name her?"

Sunhilda's question cut through his thoughts. So wrapped up in his own worries had he been that he had forgotten she was still there. In truth, the thought of a name had not even occurred to him 'til she gave voice to it, but the answer came to him without a moment's hesitation. It was only right that he honour the lady who had watched over Hild's final days and who had safely delivered their child.

"Mildryth. I name her for the Lady of Wenloch in thanks for her intercession in bringing my daughter into my arms. And I pray that she may keep watch over her for as long as she may live."

TWENTY-TWO

The days following Hild's death passed in a blur for Thurkill. All around him, Eadric's warriors prepared for war as Eadric had sworn vengeance on FitzScrope for the death of so many of his men. The insult to his pride and his reputation could not be allowed to stand unanswered. He sent messengers far and wide, even into the mountainous regions of the Waelesc to the west and north, seeking allies to join the fight. He hoped to summon a force large enough to destroy the hated Normans and evict them from his lands for good.

Thurkill played no part in the planning; he found he could not concentrate on any task for more than a few moments. No matter what he was doing, no matter how complex or simple the task, his mind was soon swamped with images of his dead wife. Every waking moment was the same; there was no escape. It was worse when he was with Mildryth. Every time he looked at her little round face, whether she be sleeping, eating or screaming at some imagined injustice, she reminded him of her mother. Her tiny features were so familiar to him, he could not help but see Hild staring back at him every time he looked at her. It became so painful that he took to avoiding her.

Everyone could see the suffering he endured, but none knew how to comfort him. Few, if any, could summon any words that might help and so they mostly left him to suffer alone. The mountain of work to be done made for a convenient excuse, saving them from the awkwardness of having to confront his pain.

Only Eahlmund dared intrude, forcing himself to sit with his friend day after day, hour after hour. At times, no words would pass between them from dawn to sunset; it was enough for Thurkill to just have the company of a friend. On other occasions, they talked long into the night; a cask of ale set between them as they sat under the stars on the balmy summer evenings. It was not unusual for the two men to be found the next morning, wrapped in their cloaks to protect them from the early morning chill, the cask empty beside them.

If it hadn't been for Eahlmund, Thurkill did not think he could have coped. Things were bad enough. He knew he stank – he had not washed or changed his clothes for days – but he did not care. His hair was unkempt and knotted through lack of attention while his skin had turned a deep brown hue partly due to the sun, but also the result of a layer of grime that had built up over the days. But none of this mattered to Eahlmund. Or, if it did, he did not let it show. All he cared about was keeping Thurkill talking, not allowing his friend to withdraw entirely into himself.

"You know you smell so foul that even the dogs don't want to know you anymore?"

It was just after noon on another blisteringly hot day. The two men lay on their backs in the sprawling shade of an ancient oak tree, the now obligatory barrel of ale between them. Thurkill glanced at his friend, seeing the anxiety in his face. Eahlmund knew the risk he was taking by asking the question.

Thurkill merely grunted, though, before helping himself to another cup. "That's as may be, but tell me, my friend. Who other than you cares?"

Undeterred, Eahlmund pressed on. "I can think of one that would and another that should."

With no response forthcoming, Eahlmund continued, too far committed now to stop. "What do you think Hild would say if she could see you now, my friend? You're a pale shadow of the man she married, the man who fought with distinction at Senlac, who took vengeance for the deaths of his aunt and sister and who defended the people of Gudmundcestre so valiantly. It saddens me to see you give up like this."

Thurkill said nothing. Shame burned his cheeks, mixing with the deep, inexorable anger that was ever close to the surface. To constrain the stinging retort that formed in his head, he ground his teeth until his jaw ached. White marks appeared on the palm of his hands where he dug his nails in deep, balling them into fists. Had he not lost everything dear to him? Was he to be allowed no time for remorse?

But Eahlmund was relentless. "I see no sign of the man I once knew. I see only a fool who drowns himself in ale and self-pity in equal measure. A fool who cares not for those around him who love him and who despair to see him like this. Where is the man who would rather die than fail in his duty? Has he forgotten those that depend on him for leadership and protection? Has he forgotten so soon the daughter who has none but her father to keep her safe? Where is the man who should care what his dead wife would think of him in this moment?"

That mention of Hild tipped Thurkill over the edge. Tears streaming down his face, he threw himself at Eahlmund, fists pummelling the other man's face and body. All the pent-up rage and emotion spilled out from him as he bellowed incoherently. But Eahlmund would not fight back. He did nothing but try to protect his face as the blows landed.

"Fight me, damn you." Thurkill's tears mixed with the snot that flowed freely from his nose, dripping on to his friend's tunic. But still, Eahlmund refused. He lay there on his back staring up at Thurkill through one eye, the other already puffed up so that only a narrow slit remained. Blood flowed from his nose, now bent at a crooked angle, and mouth, where at least one tooth had been dislodged.

Then, the anger left Thurkill just as suddenly as it had descended. Pushing himself up, he lurched away into the woods, kicking over the cask of ale as he went.

***

It was two days before Thurkill returned to find Eahlmund sitting by the stream, Mildryth nestled in the crook of his arm sucking on a strip of linen dipped in a bowl of goat's milk. Thurkill's heart melted as he watched the look of concentration on her face as she worked her tiny gums to eke out every last drop from the cloth before Eahlmund then dipped it back into the wooden bowl. She was a good feeder; just like her father, he mused. She would grow to be tall and strong, should she continue in this way.

He watched in silence as she devoured over half the contents of the bowl before beginning to tire. Laying down the bowl, Eahlmund sat her up on his lap and rubbed her back gently, laughing as she screwed up her little features into a tight grimace before letting loose with a belch that seemed to satisfy her. Then, as he laid her down to sleep, Eahlmund finally noticed Thurkill. At first his eyes, registered shock as if he feared another beating, the bruises from their last encounter still all too visible on his face. But then his concern was replaced by a smile as he took in his friend's transformation.

Gone was the grimy, dishevelled man, banished to a place of dark memories of evil times. Out of sight but never to be wholly out of mind. Stung by his friend's words, Thurkill had resolved to make amends. He'd bathed and tended to his hair so that his blond locks now shone in the sunlight as the long tresses fell loose and unknotted down to his shoulders. His clothes, whilst not wholly clean, had been scrubbed, so that at least the top layer of dirt had gone, leaving only the deeply ingrained stains that were common to all warriors, telling of long forgotten conflicts.

Even so, Thurkill knew that not all was as it seemed. Though he smiled to see Eahlmund and Mildryth, he knew there was no warmth to it, and it never reached as far as his eyes. There was a coldness to them, his gaze focussed on a point somewhere beyond Eahlmund's right shoulder.

"Well met, friend. How fares Mildryth?"

His voice sounded stiff, his manner somehow stilted, embarrassed at the memory of their last encounter. He hoped his friend would recognise the effort it took to reach out to him.

"She is well, Lord. Hale and hearty. She has an appetite for a drink... not unlike her father."

A stab of pain flickered across Thurkill's face, as he was reminded of his past behaviour. Recovering his composure, Thurkill continued, "I thank you for your care for her, Eahlmund. She is fortunate to have one such as you to stand in the place where her father should have been."

Eahlmund smiled, "Whether you are with her or not, she will always be able to turn to me for help and support, Lord. It is the least I could do in memory of her mother."

Visibly relaxing, Thurkill eased himself down by his daughter's side, idly stroking her arm as she slept. For a long while, he kept his silence, his mind apparently far away.

Eventually, he sighed and turned to face Eahlmund.

"I've been doing a lot of thinking these past days, my friend. I have come to terms with Hild's death, and my thoughts turn now to where that leaves me, you, and the others."

Eahlmund nodded but said nothing, perhaps aware that some major decision had been reached.

"Firstly, I owe you an apology. In truth, I owe it to everyone. My behaviour since Hild's death has fallen short of what should be expected of someone who carries the duties of lordship."

Eahlmund opened his mouth as if to protest, but Thurkill raised a hand to silence him. "Whatever the circumstances in which I found myself, I did not have the right to neglect my responsibilities. Many have suffered losses no less painful than mine, and yet they carry on. They deal with grief while continuing to farm the land, tend their livestock, and to care for their children. Why should I be any different? I have put my pain behind me. It will always be there but now it is private, locked away, and only to be taken out when I allow it.

"But now I must find a new purpose for my life. Whilst I shall always be grateful to Eadric for giving us shelter and protection here, I have no wish to live my life hiding in a cave. My life needs meaning, a goal. Something the scops can write tales about to sing around the hearth on cold winter nights, just as we remember the tales of Earl Brythnoth at Maldon, or even those as far back as Alfred's times."

Eahlmund grinned, infected by the passion in Thurkill's voice. Thurkill had not felt that same passion since the Normans had attacked them at Gudmundcestre when he had used it to rally the villagers to defend the town and their families. It had worked then, and he could feel it working again now.

"So, I have decided I must leave. I will tell the others soon, but I wanted to share this with you first, my oldest and closest companion to whom I owe my life. Each man shall have the choice whether to come with me or to stay here. Eadric is a good man, a strong man, and I don't doubt he can hold out for many years to come. I will bear no grudge against any man who swears allegiance to him rather than me. I shall release all of you from your oath to me so that you may freely decide your own path."

"Bollocks to that, Lord. My path is ever entwined with yours. Whither it may take me matters not." Eahlmund then paused, his brow furrowed. "Which reminds me, Lord. Where does this path of yours go?"

***

Some hours later, Thurkill sat surrounded by his warband, eyeing each man in turn, searching for a clue as to the content of their souls. He had told them his plans, asking them to reflect for a few moments before giving him an answer. Though he was prepared to leave them all behind if he had to, he desperately hoped that they would choose to follow him. But each face was as inscrutable as the next as they pondered the news.

Dusk had fallen, but the air was still warm. The summer had proven to be both long and hot, with day after day of warm sunshine, interspersed with short, sharp showers. Everywhere, the countryside was in bloom; the branches of every fruit tree were starting to droop ground-wards as the weight of their charges grew. Fields of wheat, barley and oats swayed in the gentle breeze, the plants now high enough to conceal the small children who loved to dash in amongst the swaying stalks in games of hide and go seek, until their fathers shooed them away with a clip round the ear, before they damaged the crop. It promised to be a bountiful harvest, one that would keep Eadric's people well fed through the winter.

Finally, Leofric broke the silence. "I have no love of the Normans, Lord, as you know. I would be happy to add my sword to yours. But where will your path take us, and what hope would we have to do more than we have here? I would not want to give my life for some meaningless quest."

Leofgar, who rarely disagreed with his sibling, chimed in, "What we have here may be small, but it is secure. Eadric is a strong leader who can achieve much. You saw how the men rallied to rescue him from Scrobbesburh? And even now, he gathers men to attack Henffordd. It may not reverse the tide – even Knut could not do that – but it may give the Normans pause in this shire. Is that not honourable use of our endeavours?"

Thurkill nodded, considering their advice. He could see Eopric looked as if he agreed with the brothers, though Urri's face remained a mask as the big man stared at his feet. He knew he would need to tread the ground carefully if he were to persuade them to his side, like they had picked their way through the marshy ground outside the gates of Scrobbesburh by leaping from one thick tuft of grass to the next.

"Your counsel is wise, as always, my friends. The same thoughts have occupied my head too. But what greater purpose can we serve than trying to rid this land of the Normans? There is no doubt that we have ample chance to do that here in the wilds around Scrobbesburh and Henffordd, but will what we do here resonate across the land? Who will hear of our exploits? Were we to kill FitzScrope, would the Normans not simply send another in his place?"

He paused to measure the impact of his words. Seeing nothing to encourage him, he ploughed on feeling the wet, cloying mud clinging to his boots as he forced a heavy plough share through the earth, trying to turn a furrow in the minds of his followers.

"But what if we could play a bigger role? What if we could have an impact that might be felt down the ages? Something the chroniclers might write about in years to come?"

He noted a brief flicker of interest on Leofric's face. He was ever the less cautious of the two, the more likely to jump into the unknown without a second glance. Seizing on the spark, Thurkill sought to pile kindling around it, to encourage it to become a raging inferno.

"There remain those out there that refuse to bend the knee to these foreign scum. Those that would fight to see the return of a Saxon ruler."

"Fight for the boy, Edgar, you mean?" Urri growled. "He no longer has the support of the Aenglisc. Does anyone even know where the boy has gone?"

"I speak not of Edgar, my friend. Though if he were to raise his standard, I would go. He is the rightful king of England, acclaimed by the council of nobles in Lundenburh. Perhaps his time will yet come; but for now, we have to look to others to lead where he cannot."

"Who then?"

"The Godwine family."

"Were they not all killed at Senlac Hill? You were there yourself and bore witness to the death of Harold and his brothers."

"It is true, Eopric. Harold fell, along with Gyrth and Leofwine. And with Tostig killed at Stamford the month before, that leaves only Wulfnoth who languishes in a Norman dungeon as hostage for a promise of peace from his kin."

"So, who is there to step into the breach then?"

"Fear not, Urri. The Godwine line did not die on that ridge. You are forgetting King Harold was married."

"To Ealdgyth, the sister of those craven Earls, Eadwine and Morcar? But the marriage was new, so if she'd given birth, the child would yet be suckling at its mother's teat."

"Harold was married before – to Edith Swanneshals. Together they had five children, three of them boys. The eldest, Godwine Haroldson, is a man of twenty summers, while the others – Edmund and Magnus – are not far behind."

Urri frowned. "But where are they now, Lord? And what do you know of their mind?"

"When I was away, I returned to Wenloch to pray for guidance at Lady Mildburh's shrine. That evening in the tavern where I took lodgings for the night, I met with a merchant on his way north to Chester. He told me that Harold's mother, Gytha, and her grandsons were rumoured to be gathering to the south and west of here, a land so far untouched by the Normans. If they raise the Wyvern standard of Wessex, I feel sure enough warriors will come to swear allegiance once more. It is my intention to go there. With you, if you'll follow me."

Eahlmund could stay silent no longer. He had clearly been itching to speak, fidgeting and fussing throughout the discussion. "My sword is yours to command, Lord. Whither you go, I follow." He folded his arms as if to add emphasis to his point, a look of fierce defiance on his face."

The four other men looked at each other across the fire, its flames slowly dwindling as the evening drew on. Thurkill watched as Leofric the bold fixed his eyes upon his brother, raising an eyebrow to seek confirmation. When Leofgar shrugged, his brother jumped up. "We are also with you, Lord. We will take the twists and turns of the journey together."

"In which case," Eopric added with a grin, "I'll have to come too. You're not leaving me behind."

Only Urri had not spoken, his thickly bearded face impenetrable in the orange glow of the fire. Only his eyes showed any sign of life, sparkling in the light despite being cast deep under the shadow of his heavy, protruding forehead. At last, he cleared his throat to speak. "You have my oath, Lord, of course. But what of your daughter?"

TWENTY-THREE

It was the question he had been dreading but the one which he also knew was inevitable. He had agonised over his decision for many hours and had not slept because of it. And now the moment was upon him.

Did he really have the courage to say the words? His visit to the convent at Wenloch had another purpose, over and above seeking spiritual guidance. He had spent many long hours in discussion with Abbess Coenburga, delving into his soul with her so that he might divine the right course of action. She had not sought to tell him what to do; rather, she had merely probed his mind with astute questions, the intent of which – he realised later – had been to guide him to a decision with which he could move forward. Now those convictions – so recently formed – were to be put to the test.

"Mildryth stays."

One or two of the men looked aghast while Eopric let out an involuntary gasp. Only Eahlmund remained impassive, but then he had known what was coming. Thurkill knew his friend disagreed with him on this, but that was to be expected. Eahlmund had formed a strong bond with the child, perhaps more so than even Thurkill himself had done. But he could see no alternative. To take the fight to the Normans, to join the rebellion in the south west, was not something he could inflict upon his daughter. He had a duty to keep Mildryth safe, a promise he had made standing over the grave of his dead wife not one week since. There could be no other way – no better way – to do that.

"You'd abandon her to Eadric's care?" Urri could not keep the shock and disappointment from his voice. "I would rather stay here as her guardian then have her left without a single friend." His message was clear; if her father was prepared to walk away from his child, it fell to someone else to step into his place.

Thurkill's voice was calm but there was iron resolve in his

words. "You misunderstand my intention, Urri. Mildryth will not be abandoned, not now or at any time hereafter. I have sworn a solemn oath over Hild's grave to keep our daughter safe from harm. I will not take her with me into battle. I can think of few things more irresponsible that a father could do than to willingly put their child in harm's way.

"It is for this reason that I have agreed with Abbess Coenburga for Mildryth to enter the convent at Wenloch. As she came from God – a miracle of Lady Mildburh's doing – so shall I give her back to God to serve Him for all her days in whatever way the abbess sees fit."

"However noble it may be, I find it strange, nonetheless, that a father might so willingly give up his new-born daughter, never to see her again."

Thurkill's patience was wearing thin, but he was determined to keep his anger in check. He still hoped that each of them would accompany him south, and it would serve little purpose to antagonise them further. "Who knows what the future may hold, Eopric? Mildryth will never be far from my thoughts, day or night, and maybe – God willing – I will see her again soon. I will know where to find her after all."

"So, when do we leave?" It seemed that Eahlmund had heard enough. He would have known that Thurkill's mind was not for changing on this matter; it was better for everyone to focus on the future.

"Not for a while yet, my friend," Thurkill smiled, grateful for the distraction. "First, we must help Eadric. He has done much for us since we arrived here, and I would return some of that favour by joining his attack on Henffordd, which is only days away. We wait only for the arrival of our Waelesc allies."

Leofric grunted, "Hairy-arsed sheep-shaggers."

Like many amongst the Aenglisc, Leofric held a deep-seated mistrust of the men who dwelt in the hills to the west of the ancient kingdom of Mercia. They had long been their enemies as far back as when the Saxons first arrived over six hundred years before. But now, it seemed they were to join with these same men against a common enemy. Perhaps this was the way to defeat the Normans, Thurkill mused. To put aside past differences – at least temporarily – in search of the greater goal.

For now, though, he just laughed, grateful for the opportunity to lighten the mood. "I wouldn't let Bleddyn ap Cynfyn or his brother, Rhiwallon, hear you say that."

"Who? I swear, by Almighty God, their names are as impenetrable as their mountains."

"Princes of Gwynedd, Eahlmund. Doubtless bringing scores of their hairy-arsed sheep-botherers with them."

***

Eadric rose as Thurkill and his hearth-warriors entered the cave to take their seats by the fire, a welcome source of warmth as the fresh chill of the night presaged the approaching autumn

"I'm glad to have you back with us, Thurkill. It's been a bad business, my friend, and I am pleased to see you looking more yourself again. My warband is much diminished without your sword and your voice. I've been told of the part you played at Scrobbesburh; that is the kind of leadership I will have need of in the days to come."

Thurkill grasped Eadric's outstretched arm, grateful for the warm welcome and kind words. He had worried that his recent bout of self-pity might have caused a rift between them, but he knew that, like him, Eadric had also lost his wife, albeit in more violent and altogether more horrific circumstances at the hands of FitzScrope. But at least he understood Thurkill's loss and was prepared to excuse him his time of grief.

In some ways, though, Thurkill wondered whether it might have been better if Eadric had lost patience with him. It might perhaps make what he had to say easier, make him feel less like he was letting his host down. Conscious that all eyes were on him and awaiting a response, Thurkill cleared his throat.

"My thanks, Lord Eadric. As you will know only too well, it is a pain from which I will never be free. But at least I have now learned to be its master."

Eadric nodded knowingly. But before he could speak, Thurkill ploughed on, knowing that to stop would risk losing the confidence to say his piece.

"What the last few days have also taught me is to think about my place in this world. Whilst you will forever have my gratitude and my respect for the hospitality you have shown us, I fear I must now take a different path. I stood alongside a king at Senlac, fighting to defend him against a foreign invader. But I failed in my duty, something that has nagged at me ever since. I need to make good on my failure. That I survived whilst my king did not is a stain on my name that must be assuaged."

"Nonsense, lad. What more could you have done? Your position was overrun and all those that had not already fled were lying dead or dying around you, including your own father. It is not your fault that you did not die."

"Be that as it may, Lord, my mind and my heart are united in one purpose. To stand once more, shoulder to shoulder, with a Saxon king of England."

Eadric looked confused. "There is no such thing, lad. The boy, Edgar, has submitted and is kept close to William. Who else is left that would dare stand against the Norman scum?"

So Thurkill told him what he knew of the sons of Harold. As he spoke, Thurkill saw a spark in Eadric's eyes. He could sense a powerful urge coursing through the old warrior's veins that he would give anything to take the same road as him. It seemed to him that Eadric's eyes burned with desire.

"Harold's children you say? From his first wife, Edith? And they are old enough to hold a sword and lead men in battle?" He rubbed his chin, thoughtfully. "Well, I suppose they must be, or the eldest will be, at least. Perhaps a summer or two older than you, eh?" He chuckled.

"I met Harold once, you know. Half a lifetime ago, it seems now. He came west to deal with the Waelesc who had risen in revolt. The sons of those rebels now march here to help us. Harold was a young man then, but he struck me as a good man; a capable leader whom others would gladly follow unto the gates of hell, if he but asked them to. And they would, too, for they knew that he would be there in the front rank of the shieldwall, leading the way.

"If the son, is half the man his father was, then perhaps there is hope. But will the Aenglisc rise? Who's to say that they have not had enough of slaughter by now? So many have died already, I'd wonder if there even enough staunch men left who can hold shield and spear?"

"There will be enough if men come from the Irish or even the Norse. It would take but one battle to turn the tide. It was true for William so why would it not work again?"

"It is a compelling case you make, Thurkill. I dearly hope it can succeed."

"Come with me, Lord. There will be a place for men of your standing."

Eadric turned away, making as if to warm his hands at the fire. Once more, Thurkill could sense the torrent of emotions surging through the other man's heart. Eventually, he turned back, his shoulders slumped as if wearied by life. "I would love nothing more, my friend. But my place is here with my people. They look to me for protection and prosperity. Not just keeping them safe from the Normans but also from bandits, wolves or anything else that might threaten their livelihoods. You know how life is for simple men, Thurkill. You're only ever one bad harvest away from starvation and possibly even death. I cannot abandon my people."

Thurkill nodded. He would have been surprised if Eadric had said anything else. With all his responsibilities, it was not hard to understand why he had decided to stay; but for others – those with no ties – perhaps for them it would be an easier conundrum to solve. Maybe they could summon enough men to Godwine's banner to give them a chance against William's knights. If all Saxon fighting men stood with them, he felt sure they could succeed.

"But you'll not go just yet will you, lad? I have need of you with my unfinished business with FitzScrope. I'm told he has abandoned Scrobbesburh while his men rush to rebuild what we burned. But we will find him in Henffordd, further down the river. The brothers from Gwynedd make their way here with two hundred souls at their backs. With the hundred that I can muster, that will be the largest army that has been seen in these parts since the days of Harold. You wouldn't want to miss that for the sake of Harold's bastard offspring now, would you?"

***

It was dark when Waelesc finally arrived. They could be

heard long before they were seen, singing in a language unintelligible to any but themselves. They were a wild looking bunch clad mainly in animal skins which they wore draped over leather trews and cloth tunics. Other than padded leather jerkins, they appeared to eschew armour, save for a few iron helms that looked as old as the hills whence they came. Thurkill did not doubt their courage or strength, though; they had the look of fighting men, hardened to a life of toil and brutality in the harsh mountainous regions to the west.

They halted some way off and immediately set about making their camp on an area of flat meadow at the base of the slope that led up to the caves. While the warriors busied themselves thus, a small party broke away to climb up to where Eadric and his captains awaited them. At their head walked two men, so alike that they appeared as kittens from the same mother. Both were as tall as Thurkill, but with flaming red manes that they wore plaited on either side of their heads. As they drew close, Thurkill noticed that their beards were also tied to appear like ropes. The only way in which the two men differed, in fact, was their girth. Whereas one was as lean and muscular as Thurkill, the other was almost as round as he was tall. It was as if he ate for the two of them.

"Well met, Bleddyn ap Cynfyn and Rhiwallon ap Cynfyn. You are welcome to my home."

The one called Bleddyn peered into the cave over Eadric's shoulder and chuckled. "Not much of a home from what I can see, Eadric, but I thank you for your hospitality all the same."

The formalities completed, the three men embraced, before Eadric introduced them to each of his captains in turn, ending with Thurkill.

"And this is Thurkill, son of Scalpi, favoured huscarl lately in the service of King Harold and who stood with the king until the end at Senlac."

Bleddyn eyed him up and down, taking in his great size and stature, but with an expression that was unfathomable to Thurkill's mind. Then the Lord of Gwynedd broke into a grin before pulling the Saxon to him, wrapping him in a bear hug.

"Anyone who fought with Harold is a friend of my house,

Thurkill. I am pleased, honoured even, to meet you."

Seeing Thurkill's quizzical look, Eadric stepped into to explain. "When Harold brought his army west a few years ago, he and his brother, Tostig, subdued much of the lands of the Waelesc, taking them from Gruffydd ap Llewelyn who ruled at that time. When the fighting was done, the lands were broken up between several families. The ancient kingdoms of Gwynedd and Powys passed to Bleddyn and Rhiwallon, who were sworn enemies of Gruffydd."

"And we have been friends to the Aenglisc crown ever since," Rhiwallon exclaimed. "It sorrowed us to hear of Harold's death. He was a good man and a great war leader, but he was also a fair man. He would have made a fine king had God but allowed him to live."

"But wait," Bleddyn interjected. "Eadric said you are the son of Scalpi? The same Scalpi who was one of Harold's captains?"

"The same."

"I remember him well. Never had I seen a better man in a fight, nor in his cups. He drank with the same passion as he fought. Where is the old goat? I don't see him with you."

Thurkill could not ever recall having seen his father drunk, so to hear such tales was both a surprise and a joy. He made a mental note to speak further with the brothers on the subject when the time allowed.

"I regret he is no longer with us. He gave his life at Senlac, defending his king. I feel sure though," he smirked, "he is enjoying a cup of ale with Harold even now in heaven's feasting halls."

"He died with honour, then. No man could ask for a better end than to stand by their king, sword in hand, to the death. You must be proud to bear his name."

"More than you could ever know. If I can be half the man he was, I too will die happy. Which is why I have sought Eadric's permission to leave his service to add my sword to the Godwine standard which rises once again in the south west."

"The Godwines? Who leads them?" Rhiwallon looked bemused. "The brothers are all dead or imprisoned are they not?"

"Godwine, eldest son of Harold, with two of his brothers. He is gathering his forces in Ireland and will soon cross to their ancestral lands."

Bleddyn gripped him by the forearm, staring deep into his eyes. "It is a noble cause, and one that will be worth the cost should you prevail. I wish you well, Thurkill, son of Scalpi. But first you fight with us, yes? When we are done, we will gladly sail you and your men down the Hafern and on to the northern coast of Dumnonia. From there, you can find your way to Godwine's side."

TWENTY-FOUR

Shortly after dawn, two days later, the small army made up of three hundred Saxons and Waelesc arrived, just to the north of the old border town of Henffordd. Once their camp was established, a short distance to the north of the city, Eadric set off on foot with the two Waelesc lords, Thurkill and a small escort of a dozen or so warriors, including Aethelgar, Leofric and Leofgar. Ochta was left in command of the camp with instructions to flee back north should they not return by sundown.

The scouting party left their armour and all their weapons behind, save their seaxes. It was a risk, but should they be accosted by a Norman patrol, it would go worse for them if they were caught wearing mailshirts and carrying sword and shield. As unencumbered as they were, it also meant they could travel more quickly.

They were within sight of the city walls soon after the sun had reached its zenith. Though it had begun to lose much of its strength as autumn started to take hold, it was still bright enough to force them to shield their eyes from the glare that reflected off the wide river that flowed through the southern half of the city.

They took up position on a low ridge, two arrows' flight to the north, lying down at the edge of an orchard, the branches of whose trees groaned under the weight of their opulent bounty. From where Thurkill lay, he could see why a city had grown up here. Not only did the free-flowing river provide a plentiful supply of water for mills, cloth dying and brewers, but there were also several roads converging on the city from almost every direction. It looked like the hub at the centre of a cart's wheel.

Henffordd was a daunting prospect to attack, though. A forbidding wooden palisade stretched north from the river, curving west before heading back south to end once again at the river's edge. A gateway had been built into the wall every hundred paces or so, at the point where each of the major roads dissected it. Though these might normally have been weak points in the defence, Thurkill could see that each one was protected by a pair of towers, each with room for a dozen or more archers. Even at this distance, Thurkill could see several soldiers patrolling the walls or on sentry duty in the towers, the sun glinting off their helmets and spear points like icicles hanging from the eaves of a house in the dead of winter. And this when there was no apparent threat of attack. He dreaded to think how many more could be called upon once the alarm was sounded.

It would be a tough nut to crack. Much more so than Scrobbesburh. There was no gap in the wall here, no complacency amongst its defenders. And then there was the castle. Like its twin to the north, it too was built of wood, but here it stood within its own palisade within the city walls. It was huge, at least twice as big by Thurkill's reckoning. It occupied a vast area in the south east corner of the city, its southern wall backing onto the riverbank. How on earth would they breach those defences? The longer he stared, the lower his heart sank.

"A frontal assault on the nearest gate will do the trick." Bleddyn grinned, clearly undaunted by the sight of the staunch defences.

"We'd lose a lot of men, brother, but the prize might be worth the reaper's fee."

Thurkill was aghast. Were these madmen seriously proposing this as their plan? *My God. What have I got myself into? They'll get us all killed.*

But Eadric just laughed. "You two are as deranged as your father was. Do you Waelesc not have any appreciation of subtlety? Of strategy? Not every door is to be opened by simply hammering on it until someone lets you in."

Turning to Thurkill, he continued, "What do you make of it, lad? How would you attack such a well defended position?"

Thurkill stared down at the city, trying to think what a war leader like Harold might have said. How would he have set about breaching walls as mighty as these without any siege engines?

"Trickery, Lord."

"How so?"

"We are too few to assault the city head on. The archers would massacre us before we even reached the walls. We need a more inventive way of getting inside."

Eadric rubbed his chin. "And what would you suggest?"

Thurkill's mind was a blank. He wracked his brains, willing himself to find an idea worthy of its name. Just then, a distant memory from the fight at Gudmundcestre flashed into his mind. It had worked for them from the inside to the out, so why would it not work in reverse?

"The river. It forms the southern boundary of the walled city, though I'll wager it's not defended for its entire length. See there, where the castle wall ends?" He pointed to emphasise his point. "From that point all the way west to where the wall begins again, it is given over to wharves for boats to unload their wares for market day. A few brave men – dressed as merchants, perhaps – could find their way in and make for the nearest gate and open it. The rest of us could be waiting nearby, ready to attack."

Rhiwallon sniffed. "I don't much hold much with mummery. There's no honour in it. I still say that if we throw our men against that gate, we can be through before the defenders have a chance to rally."

Eadric grunted. "That's as may be, but I'm not prepared to risk the lives of my people in such folly. The chances of victory would be slim, and many would die needlessly. I like Thurkill's odds better."

Before the disagreement could escalate further, Bleddyn stepped in, "Well, that settles it then. We send men in from the river. They should go shortly before the gates close for the night; that way, there's less time for something to go wrong."

Eadric nodded. "Agreed. No more than a half a dozen should go. Few enough to avoid raising suspicion, but enough to handle themselves should it come to it. We just need someone to lead them now."

Thurkill opened his mouth to speak, but Aethelgar jumped in first. "Lord, give me the honour. I won't let you down."

The old warrior gripped his captain's shoulder. "The honour is yours, friend. Take your hearth warriors, though be sure to leave your war gear behind. You're playing the part of merchants, so seaxes only. We'll move up in the night to the gate nearest our position here and wait in that hollow there." Eadric pointed to where the ground sloped away from the city walls, creating a blind spot about fifty or so paces from the north eastern gate. "We'll look for you in the hour before the dawn. Open the gate and we'll come running. Don't be late, though; if we are spotted in the open when the sun comes up…"

***

Thurkill shivered as he pulled his cloak more tightly around his shoulders. Autumn was well on its way. Not only was it that much colder at night, but the very air smelled different now. Stamping his feet to get some warmth back into his toes, he wondered whether the dawn might see the first frost. It certainly felt cold enough. It didn't help, that they had been in the hollow for a good while now, Eadric having insisted they move up into position soon after darkness fell.

Aethelgar had departed just as twilight was falling, timing his arrival at the wharf to coincide with the closure of the gates. It was a calculated risk; the watchmen would be flustered by their late arrival, eager to be done with their day's work and away to the taverns or whorehouses with their wages. With a night's carousing on their minds, they'd be sure to afford the newcomers less scrutiny than normal. With luck, they would tie up their borrowed boat and be safely within the city walls in a matter of moments.

The rest of the army waited. Just shy of three hundred souls, huddled together a stone's throw from the walls of Henffordd. Truth be told, Thurkill didn't like it. From where they had been watching, away up on the ridge, the hollow had seemed both longer and deeper. But Thurkill reckoned that fewer than three quarters of the men were adequately concealed. It was only the darkness that protected them from discovery. The situation was not lost on Eahlmund either.

"By the Devil's hairy ball-sack but our arses are hanging out, Lord. If we're not inside before the sun rises, we'll make for a fine collection of hedgehogs. The archers won't be able to miss."

Thurkill grunted. There was no other response possible, for the truth of the matter was plain for all to see. A natural pessimist by leaning, Thurkill fretted about it though he would not allow his worries to infect the minds of those around him. His job was to lead, not to demoralise, whatever he might personally believe.

"Don't worry, Eahlmund. We'll be long gone before sun up. You'll be eating breakfast within the city, using some dead Norman's arse as a table. You'll see."

Eahlmund sniffed. "I pray you're right, but I'd like to know what's keeping Aethelgar. Look." He gestured to the east. "The sky's beginning to lighten already."

Thurkill saw that his friend was right. The eastern horizon was now tinged with an orange glow at the point where the sky met with the distant tree line, heralding the dawn of the new day. *Where is he? The gates should have been opened by now.*

"Come on, man. Get those bastard gates open." Eadric was on his feet, up on the edge of the hollow, sword in hand. It would not be long before the light would be sufficient for the defenders on the walls to see them. If they didn't manage to get through the gate soon, they would be slaughtered to a man.

Just then, Thurkill heard a creaking and groaning sound. Spinning round, he stared at the huge gateway, just fifty yards away to his left. Finally, he could see the great wooden doors slowly crack open, a sliver of light from within at first but widening all the time.

Without hesitation, Eadric turned to roar at the men huddled together below him. "Come on, lads. Through the gate to glory. Spare none that hold a blade against us."

Thurkill jumped up and set off towards the city, not bothering to check to see if others followed. As he ran, he caught a glimpse of Aethelgar in the gap between the doors. *Better late than never, you stupid bastard.*

Yelling incoherently, Thurkill could feel the blood lust rising within him as it always did in the moments before battle. But then, something caught his eye. Something so appalling, his mind refused to register it at first. Then, a crippling fear took hold of his gut as he realised he was not mistaken.

Aethelgar was waving his arms over his head, weakly though, as if his strength had all but deserted him. Now that he looked more closely, Thurkill could see that his friend was drenched in blood. Something was horribly wrong.

Where were the others? And why was Aethelgar alone and sheeted in blood?

The answers came in a sudden and unstoppable torrent. The air was filled with the sound of hooves thundering over the ground, louder and louder with every heartbeat. Frantically, Thurkill tried to work out whence came the sound, his mind playing tricks on him as it seemed to echo all around him. And then he saw them.

Rank upon rank of Norman knights in one long column were galloping up the road from within the city. Realising what was about to happen, Thurkill screamed at Aethelgar to move, but there was no reaction. He seemed beyond reason, rooted to the spot where he stood. Time seemed to slow down for Thurkill as he watched in horror as the lead knight dropped his right shoulder a little, angling his spear point toward his friend. There was nothing he could do; he was too far away to help.

The horseman could not miss. Just before he reached Aethelgar, he stood up in his stirrups and thrust his right arm forward, using all the power of his shoulder, combined with his mount's momentum to launch a devastating blow. The point bit so deep that it protruded from the Saxon's unarmoured chest, blood spurting from the grievous wound. Aethelgar crumpled to the ground, killed almost instantaneously. In one practised move, the Norman let go of his spear haft – leaving it embedded in the dead man's body – and drew his sword, as he thundered past the prostrate body.

"Shieldwall!" Thurkill bellowed at the top of his voice, hoping he could be heard over the cacophony of charging horses and war cries. It felt like a hopeless gesture, though for the surprise was complete; the Saxons and Waelesc were completely unprepared to meet the onrushing knights. Those closest to Thurkill had the best chance. Many were able to change direction, running to him and overlapping their shields over that of the next man. Hours of practice and an iron discipline meant that a good number – fifty at least, with more joining all the time – were in position before the Normans fell upon them. But many others were less fortunate. Those that did not have the time or skill to react quickly enough were overwhelmed by the first wave of horsemen, washed away like leaves in a sudden deluge.

Far out on the wings, the Waelesc bore the brunt of it. With their minimal armour, they had little defence other than their shields, and many fell prey to the spears and swords that rained down upon them from above. Seeing so many of their comrades killed so quickly was too much for the rest of them; those that survived the initial assault turned and ran, throwing away their shields in their panic. But there was to be no respite for them as several conrois followed them, hacking at their backs and heads as they ran. As many were killed in the rout as had been during the first charge. 'Twas ever thus, Thurkill reflected as he watched the slaughter.

A trail of bodies, hewn and rent in all manner of dreadful ways, now marked the path by which the men ran, ever lengthening as they raced blindly for any form of sanctuary away from the terrible malice of their pursuers.

The fleeing Waelesc did, however, save the rest of the army. So many of the Normans were caught up in the pursuit, excited by the chance to dip their blades in the blood of their foes, that those who remained on the field were too few to break the now solid shieldwall that had formed in front of the hollow. The sight of a solid barrier, two ranks deep and bristling with deadly spear points, was enough to deter many of the horses from coming too close. Those knights who did force their beasts forward soon found themselves sprawling on the ground once their mount had been felled by a spear thrust into their chest. It was foul work, but necessary. Thurkill hated to see them suffer so, to hear their piteous screams as the blades ripped into their innocent flesh. They had not chosen to be there, and they did not deserve to die. But die they must if the Saxons were to have any hope of survival.

As the bodies of the fallen animals grew in number, they served to form a second blockade, almost as effective as the shieldwall itself. The knights had to content themselves with cantering in front of the Saxons, wheeling about time and again, looking for a gap in the wall through which to hurl their spears. It was easy work for the defenders to block the missiles as they crouched behind their shields. Thud after thud resonated along the line as more and more spears thumped into the linden boards, some sticking fast, but most clattering uselessly to the ground.

Thurkill knew that they could not stay where they were indefinitely, however. Sooner or later, the other horsemen would return to the field and lend their weight to the attack. With those numbers ranged against them, the Saxons would soon be overwhelmed. They would have to make good their escape long before that happened.

Glancing around him, he could see many others were thinking the same way. They were restless, eager to be away from there now that the plan had so comprehensively collapsed. He saw, with relief, that all his own men were gathered tightly around him, and he could hear, rather than see, Eadric a few paces to his right. He wondered what had happened to Rhiwallon and Bleddyn; whether they had been killed in the rout with their men or if they had managed to cheat death. Perhaps they had been able to join the shieldwall and were, even now, crouching behind their shields with the rest of them.

Raising his voice, Thurkill prayed that Eadric would hear him. "Lord, we need to move. We can't stay here; we will be slaughtered when the rest of the bastards return from massacring the Waelesc."

Eadric's voice boomed back at him. "What can we do, though? They have us where they want us."

"If we can't go forwards or sideways, we must go backwards".

"Back through the hollow? We'll be cut down before we've gone ten paces."

"Not if we go suddenly and quickly. The slope is steep enough to discomfit their horses. While they're picking their way down,

163

we can be across, up the other side, and into the trees beyond."

Eadric was silent for a moment; seemingly weighing up the options. "Right you are, Thurkill. We've no other choice if we are to survive. Lead the way. I'll pass the word along."

Quickly, Thurkill did the same on his side of the shieldwall, making sure each man knew what they must do. If the plan were to succeed, they would need to act in concert. Any that did not move with the rest would be cut down in moments, shorn of the protection provided by the shields of their neighbours.

When all was ready, Thurkill gave the word. Immediately, men began inching backwards, checking behind them carefully to see where the edge of the hollow began. As soon as they reached it, they halted once more. Then Thurkill bellowed, "Run!"

Within moments, five score or more men turned and hared down the slope into the bottom of the hollow. As they went, they slung their shields across their backs. It was as well that they did for the archers high on the city walls began loosing volley after volley at the fleeing Saxons. The distance was great, and most of the arrows missed their mark, thudding aimlessly into the ground or into the well-placed shields, but several more found a target. Here and there, men went down, shafts protruding from the backs of their legs, underneath their shield rims. Though painful, the wounds were not fatal, and most could be dragged along by their friends.

Thurkill was one of the first to reach the top of the rise on the far side of the hollow. Pausing to catch his breath, he risked a look back. Half a dozen bodies lay dead in the grass, victims of well-aimed or lucky shots – though it mattered not which. Beyond them, the cavalry, having recovered from the shock of the surprise retreat, had begun to make their way down the pitted slope. As he had hoped, Thurkill was pleased to see that their pace slowed to little more than a walk. What's more, the gradient was so intense that they were forced to work their way down diagonally, or risk snapping the forelegs of their horses. Already three or four beasts lay on their sides, their foolhardy riders howling in frustration by their sides.

With a grunt of satisfaction, Thurkill turned back to face the scrubland and trees beyond. They had about a hundred or so paces to cross before they would be safe from the mounted knights. With God's grace, they should cover the ground before the first Normans crested the rise.

"Come on, boys. Safety awaits us among the trees, but we must reach it before the Normans are upon us."

The men needed no urging. As soon as they had reformed on the flat ground, they set off at a trot, maintaining good order as they went. All along the line, captains harangued those that ran ahead or lagged behind. The situation might be desperate, but there was no need to allow panic to take hold.

After a few paces, they were beyond the range of all but the strongest of the archers on the walls, so the order was given for shields to be unslung and held in front in readiness. Here and there, men used their seaxes to cut away the willow shafts that had stuck into their boards. It took a few extra moments but would be worth it if it helped to make the shield less unwieldy.

Then they were off once more, and not a moment too soon. Just as they were swallowed up by the serried ranks of larches and oak trees, the knights began to thunder across the ground towards them. But the Normans were too late; their quarry had escaped. A few knights hurled their spears uselessly into the trees, more in anger than in any real hope of hitting anything.

Twenty or thirty paces deep into the wood, Thurkill and Eadric stood panting, alongside the Waelesc brothers who had managed to join the shieldwall after all. None of them spoke. There were no words to convey their fury. Instead, they simply stared at the Normans whom they could glimpse beyond the edge of the trees, seething with impotent rage.

TWENTY-FIVE

"Lord King?"

William looked up from the scroll he had been reading, concerning a grant of land in England he was planning to make to the abbey at Fecamp.

"What is it, Baldwin?"

"News from England, Lord."

William could see his steward was hesitant, as if unwilling to anger him. *This can't be good. See how he quakes in his boots as if he expects me to strike his head from his shoulders or have his tongue pulled from his mouth for the crime of causing me displeasure.*

"Out with it, man. Or do you plan to stand there all day, hopping from one foot to the other as if holding your piss? Has my new tower in Lundenburh burnt down? Or perhaps my fat brother, Odo, has eaten too much and fallen from his horse?"

"No, Lord. I mean, I don't know, Lord."

"Oh, for the sake of our Lord, Jesus Christ, just give me the god-damned parchment."

William snatched it from Baldwin's hand, almost tearing it in two in the process, causing the steward to yelp with alarm. Ignoring him, William sat back down at his pitted, oaken table, clearing a space in the centre with his forearm so that he could unroll the document more easily. The ink was faint at best, as if it had suffered from the rigours of the weather during its journey. Before he could read the text, however, William had to bring the two candlesticks closer so that their flickering light was nearer to his eyes. Although it was not yet time for vespers, the sun had already long since set, a sure indication that winter was fast approaching.

Ignoring the cold that tugged at his neck and shoulders, William once more tried to smooth the parchment flat, taking care not to smudge the ink any further. With a grunt he noted it was from William FitzOsbern, one of the two lieutenants he had left to run things in his new kingdom in his absence. Of the two,

FitzOsbern had the tougher job, pressing up – as he did – against peoples to the north and west of England. People who had yet to accept the Normans as their new overlords.

William had left strict instructions with FitzOsbern to stay his hand as far as possible – to use guile and diplomacy in place of violence and malice – but he knew that his word was being ignored at times. Reports had long since reached him of unrest among some of the remaining Saxon lords, dismayed at the heavy-handed treatment being meted out to them, and especially to their women. What was worse, there seemed to be little or no consequence for the culprits. Rarely was any man being brought to justice for his actions. *There's nothing like the rape of a man's wife or sister to stir his passions,* William mused.

He had long since known he would need to speak to FitzOsbern about the conduct of his men on his return. There was more than one way to skin a deer for the table, but both his lieutenants seemed to have chosen the least effective method. No wonder grumblings were reaching his ears.

As he scanned the text, scrawled in the imperfect Latin he'd come to expect from men who had favoured lessons of war over those of literacy, he saw that his worst fears were confirmed. For some weeks now, he had agonised over whether he had stayed too long in his homeland. It was not much more than a year since the battle at Senlac and only ten or so months since his coronation and there was much to do still, much that needed his attention. But was not the same true in Normandy also? Had he not had to fight for his birth right since he was a young boy? It seemed that trouble was always brewing only just below the surface. But now that he had added England to his domains, all he had done was double his problems.

"Baldwin, summon Bishop Remigius and Roger of Montgomery to attend me now." As Baldwin scurried off to do his bidding, William shouted after him, "And tell my Master of Ships to prepare *the Mora* to be ready to sail from Dieppe three days hence."

***

"Lord King, why risk a crossing in the dead of winter? The

waters between Normandy and England are notorious at this time of year. Many is the ship that has been lost with all hands."

William sighed, tired of explaining. "You saw the letter, Montgomery. I have no choice but to react and to do so with force and steadfast resolve, lest the people think me weak."

"There have been rumours of unrest before now. Why treat this one any different?"

"Precisely because this one is different. I have heard the same tale from several trusted sources over several weeks. It cannot be ignored any longer."

"A little local disturbance, Lord. Nothing that FitzOsbern and Odo can't deal with, surely?"

William's mind was made up. He did not care whether Montgomery was right, though he truly doubted it. He had been away too long, and he needed to impose his will before things became any worse. If nothing else, he needed to speak with FitzOsbern and Odo about their harsh interpretation of his orders. If he was heading into trouble, it was their heavy-handedness that was to blame.

For now, though, he was done with the conversation. They were returning to England and that was that. The rumours of an uprising were growing and coming from all directions. The whispers of a plot to rise up against his soldiers in the season of Lent – on Ash Wednesday no less – were too loud not to be heard in Normandy. He had to admit that it was a good choice. His nobles and many of their retinues would be attending the traditional barefoot procession through the streets. They would be ill-equipped for war and could be slaughtered in their hundreds.

On its own, it was a threat that demanded to be taken seriously. But with this latest report, the facts were now clear in his mind. Some weeks back he'd ordered riders be sent across the land to the major towns and cities, with orders to root out the rebels. Most had returned empty-handed; those that had gone to the west, however – to the old Roman fortress town of Escanceaster – had come under attack. Though none had been killed, they had been robbed of their horses, weapons and armour, and beaten bloody. A simple local disturbance it might be, but his nose told him otherwise. It spoke to him of a spark which, if not dealt with quickly and firmly, could soon become a raging inferno.

"It matters not what you think, Montgomery. I have given the order, and we sail on the tide tonight." He wetted a finger and held it up to the stiff breeze that blew into his face. "See, we'll have the wind at our backs. It will carry us across the water so quickly that, by the time you awake from your wine-induced slumber, we'll be there."

TWENTY-SIX

Thurkill groaned. Clamping his hand over his mouth, he made his way with hurried, shuffling steps to the bucking bulwark. Gripping the wooden struts hard, he leaned out as far as he dared to empty the contents of his stomach once again. He'd lost count of the number of times he'd done so in the last few hours; in fact, it was a surprise to him that there was anything left to void. Surely, his belly could hold nothing more by now.

Spitting the last flecks of effluent from his mouth, he gratefully accepted the skin of water proffered by the sympathetic but amused-looking helmsman by his side. He swilled the lukewarm, brackish liquid round his gums before spitting it over the side. He dared not swallow any, lest it return moments later. Exhausted, and not a little unsteady on his feet, he slumped back down on the bale of cloth next to Eahlmund who also looked awful. *That must be how I look too,* he thought grimly.

Of all his men, only Urri seemed unaffected, gaily whistling to himself as he wandered about the boat, admiring the view with no apparent care in the world. The rest of them lay dotted about the deck, their faces ashen white, hands pressed to their stomachs or heads as if that could somehow ease their suffering.

It was the first time Thurkill had been at sea. They had boarded the little fishing boat a few miles to the east of Henffordd, Eadric handing the captain more than twice the necessary amount of coin to secure their passage south. It was there, at the small wooden jetty, that Thurkill and his men had taken their leave of Eadric and what remained of his army.

Though the old bear had been beaten that day, he vowed he would fight on against the Normans come what may. As most of the losses had fallen upon the poorly trained and lightly armoured Waelesc, his own numbers were not greatly diminished. They owed their survival in no small part to Thurkill's quick thinking and stalwart leadership. It was for this reason, and many others besides, that Eadric had hugged

Thurkill close to his chest, real tears of sadness welling in his eyes as he bade him farewell.

At first, the journey had been pleasant enough as they meandered their way south and west along the winding river Gwy, carried along at a gentle pace by the current which flowed inexorably to the sea. The rolling hills and pleasant vistas had done little, though, to salve their souls as they reflected on the bitter defeat. The alliance had ended in disaster before it had even properly begun. So many good men had died, not least of which was Aethelgar, the first man they had met when they had come to Eadric's lands.

Thurkill still had no idea what had gone wrong in the city; perhaps Aethelgar or one of his men had been recognised by a soldier who had been at Scrobbesburh, perhaps they had been careless. It mattered little now. Those men had been caught and brutally cut down before they could reach the gates. And when they did finally open, it was only to disgorge a thundering mass of mounted knights. There were no two ways about it; they had been doomed to failure from the start.

The river had broadened as it neared the end of its course. At first, the boat coped well, swaying but gently as it came within reach of the tidal current. But then, with a suddenness that took Thurkill by surprise, they were cast forth by the land and out into the open waters of the channel that separated the land of the Waelesc from the ancient kingdom of Dumnonia in the far western reaches of Wessex.

To keep the worst of the broiling swell at bay, the helmsman beat a hard course to the south and east; the shortest line from one landfall to the other. It hadn't seemed far at first; they could see the dark green hills of the coast ahead of them. But with a strong wind blowing across their bows and the waves surging on all sides of their vessel, it seemed to take forever.

Each one of them had been soaked to the skin within moments, as wave after wave broke against the wooden prow, casting a tower of spray over the deck. At times, it had felt like the little fishing boat would be swamped and dragged down to the depths, but it proved remarkably sturdy. Whether as a result of its good design or through the skill of its captain, the helmsman was able to steer a safe passage through the surf until, eventually, they reached a point where they were no more than twenty to thirty paces from the land.

From there, they turned to take a south-westerly course to follow the coast. This close to the land, the waters were mercifully far less ferocious. But though the boat was no longer in danger, the same could not be said of Thurkill's stomach. The continual lurching as they cut a path diagonal to the direction of the waves, combined with the assault on his senses as the horizon bobbed up and down in front of his eyes, meant that he could not stop his guts from heaving.

Finally, after what felt like an age, the captain yelled an order, and the helmsman immediately yanked hard on the rudder to turn the prow towards the beach. Thurkill looked up in surprise, his woes temporarily forgotten. For the last several miles, the coast had been one long forbidding cliff face, home to nothing more than vast clouds of sea birds that seemed to swarm over its surface. Hundreds more soared in the air, held up by some unseen force as they appeared to rarely use their wings. Yet more bobbed on the surface of the water, wholly unperturbed by the constant eddying of the waves which hurled themselves forward with incredible energy until they crashed violently against the rocks.

But there it was. Just as they rounded a narrow promontory, a small cove appeared, sheltered behind a protruding finger of rock. It was tiny, probably no more than the size of a dozen boats placed end to end, around which nestled a handful of small, thatched buildings. But it was more than enough for their needs. Unerringly, the helmsman guided them towards it, while the rest of the crew worked hard to pull down the sail or bent their backs to the oars to help propel the craft to its destination. Thurkill willed them to hurry; he could not wait for the moment when he could finally put his feet back down on solid ground and put this nightmare journey behind him.

With the force of the waves to push them on, it did not take long to reach the shore. The noise of the boat's wooden keel scraping against the sand and pebbles beneath was one of the most welcome sounds Thurkill could recall hearing. No sooner had the hull shuddered to a halt than two men jumped over the sides, splashing down into the knee-deep surf. Each man carried a thick rope, one end of which was securely fastened to the bulwark. With a brute strength formed from many years of back-breaking toil, they hauled on the rope, timing each heave with the swell of the crashing waves, until the keel was firmly lodged in the soft sand, high enough to be at no danger of being swept away by the tide.

Gratefully, the warriors vaulted the side of the craft. Thurkill found his legs were like those of a new-born foal. Without their strength to support him, he tipped forward, landing on all fours, his hands gripping the wet sand with a mixture of joy and determination.

"Lord God, if it please You, spare me from ever having the misfortune to repeat such a journey for as long as I shall live."

"Amen," Urri laughed. "I have never known such feeble men. To be brought low by a mild swell such as that. Truly, I thought you were made of sterner stuff, Lord."

"We can't all have guts of iron, Urri. I have no idea how you managed to endure such torture. I honestly felt I would rather die than go on at one point."

***

Thanking him warmly, they took their leave of the captain before striking out south. As soon as they left the small hamlet behind, the going became tough. Even though they travelled light – just the six men with whatever water and provisions they could carry – they soon found themselves short of breath and weary beyond measure as they climbed up to the high ground behind the coast.

The landscape was bleak, mile after mile of undulating, soggy moorland in which their boots often sank up to the ankle. To make matters worse, a biting wind howled across the hills, carrying with it a rain that stung their faces as if hundreds of tiny needles were being pressed against their cheeks. After a couple of hours, the muscles in Thurkill's legs screamed at him to stop, but he closed his mind to their protests, put his head down to shield his face from the weather as best he could, and trudged on. Every step required a huge effort to drag each boot from the boggy soil's grip, often accompanied by a foul squelching sound, before placing it back down in another, equally sodden, patch of ground.

Just when he felt he could go no further, they happened upon a track that seemed to be heading in the right direction. It was no wider than a man could safely walk and, judging by its well-worn state, was as old as the land on which it stood. But above all else, it was dry. So well-trodden was it that the soil had been worn away practically down to the bedrock. Instantly, Thurkill felt the energy flowing back into his limbs as he stepped on to the more solid surface. Their pace quickened and mood lightened in equal measure. A little while later, the rain even conspired to cease its persistent assault on their faces. It remained grey, windy, and cold, but at least they were no longer fighting against the elements as well as the land.

The wide expanse of the beautiful green landscape reminded him of the Downs that surrounded his childhood home at Haslow, and Thurkill the memories helped him feel as though a great weight had been lifted from his shoulders. The black cloud that had dogged him since Hild's death had shifted, allowing a little light into his soul. He knew it would never completely disappear. In many ways he was glad of its presence, assuring him that he would never forget her, but he was glad that it was no longer all-consuming. It made room for the pain of his separation from Mildryth instead. Though he knew she would be well cared for at Wenloch, he regretted not having had more time with her. He prayed he would live long enough to be reunited with her soon.

But for now, at least, he had new purpose – something he had not felt for several months. Not since arriving in Gudmundcestre at the start of the year, or since standing in the front rank of the shieldwall at Senlac before that. He could see a goal now, and he could see his part in it. He and his little warband would join with the sons of King Harold and together, under the Fighting Man standard of the Godwine family, they would march to Lundenburh to cast out the usurper. They would throw his followers back into the sea whence they came. They could either swim back to Normandy or drown trying; he cared not which. The thought of it gave him the determination he needed to place one foot in front of the other, ignoring the fatigue he felt in mind and body.

It was close to dusk on the second day when the walls of the city of Escanceaster at long last came into sight. Thurkill felt his heart lift as their destination neared. Here, according to his sources, they would find those members of Harold's family that still lived – his mother, Gytha, and her three grandsons, Godwine, Edmund and Magnus. Looking down on the old fortress city, he felt a surge of optimism flowing through his veins.

"There she is, lads."

Eahlmund whistled. "By God's hairy ball-sack, would you like at the size of her? You could keep a whole army in there and still have room for their families too."

It was true. After Lundenburh and Eoforwic, it was the biggest city Thurkill had seen. Its stone walls stretched for hundreds of yards in a rectangular shape, the far side of which backed on to a river that flowed south east to the sea which could just be seen in the far distance where it reflected the golden glow of the setting sun. From what he could remember of his Latin studies as a youth, Thurkill knew that the ceaster part of the name meant that the city had been a fortress in Roman times; a fact that explained the uniform design of its layout. Though they must have been repaired and strengthened several times over the centuries, they had lost little of their essential shape and purpose.

"I very much hope that is the case, Eahlmund. From within these walls, we can grow our strength until we have an army of good Saxon men even bigger than that which King Harold led to Senlac. I've said it before, if only he had waited a while longer in Lundenburh, many more warriors would have come to his banner. Those men are still out there. We must hope they will answer the call now, so victory can be ours."

"But why here, Lord? Why in the arse end of the country so far away from anywhere that matters? We haven't seen a single sign of the Normans since we left that god-damned boat."

"And it's precisely for that reason, Urri, that we are here.

These are Godwine lands. Support for Harold's family is strongest here. We have a solid foundation here which will only grow as messengers go out to summon those others that remain loyal to join us.

"As for the Normans, they are yet to venture this far west. What you see here is England before the Normans came. A free land that answers only to Saxon lords. With luck and God's help, we can restore what exists here to the whole country."

Thurkill felt a fervour growing within him as he spoke. A sense of pride gripped hold of his heart as he thought of what might be. He had carried the burden of defeat on his shoulders, like bearing a heavy cross, since Senlac. The fact that he had not been able to stop the Norman thugs from slaughtering his king had been like a millstone around his neck. It mattered not that it was not his fault; that no one else could have done more than he in that situation. His king had died, while he yet lived. His honour would never let him cast off that shame. Perhaps now, standing alongside the sons of the dead king, he might atone for his sins and achieve the peace that his soul so desperately craved.

Urri grinned. "Well, what are we waiting for? We're good for nothing standing here and admiring the stonework."

"I bet there's a few decent taverns to be had in Escanceaster too," Eahlmund's face had a wistful look. "I've heard that most people round here don't drink ale, though. Rather, they favour a drink made from apples on account of the number of them that they grow in these parts. They had more than they could eat, so some clever bastard decided to make a drink from the rest of them."

Leofric's brow furrowed, "Why would you want to drink the juice of an apple instead of a good honest cup of ale?".

"You wait 'til you try it, my friend. I've heard it's cloudy and has bits of apple floating in it, but it will have you on your arse twice as quickly as any ale."

TWENTY-SEVEN

They reached Escanceaster's north gate just as the night watchmen were preparing to shut it for the day. Thurkill was not surprised to see a dozen men in full war gear march out to greet them; these were uncertain times, and the arrival of six armoured men carrying shield and spear demanded a show of force in return. Few in their right minds would be willing to take any chances with unknown warriors at their door, however small in number they might be.

"Hail, fellows. State your name and your business." The leader of the watch took a step forward to close the gap between them. Though he was a big man, advanced in years and doubtless well-versed in combat, he was not willing to leave the safety of his escort too far behind. Nevertheless, his greeting was brusque and to the point.

"Well met, friend. My name is Thurkill, son of Scalpi, huscarl to the late King Harold. My business is my own and to be discussed only with whomever is lord here. I would thank you to take me to him and see that my men have lodging and refreshment while they wait."

He spoke with an authority that was becoming of a leader of men. For all that had happened over the last twelve months, he no longer considered his youthfulness to be a handicap worthy of mention. This was his nineteenth winter now, and he had seen more death than most men twice his age. By the reaction of the lead watchman, he saw that he had judged his response right, for the fellow was now perplexed, uncertain how to proceed in the face of one so young but also so confident in his bearing. In the end, he erred on the side of caution. It did not pay to annoy a stranger who might turn out to have more authority than one might at first suspect.

"You are welcome to our city of Escanceaster, Lord. Gytha, Lady of Wessex and mother of King Harold, of blessed memory, commands here in place of her grandsons who have yet to arrive. I shall have one of my men escort you to her hall."

Thurkill nodded his thanks and no more, determined not to let slip the mask he had adopted. It was as well that he be treated with gravitas and respect from the beginning. He knew that news of his arrival would spread around the local taverns and markets and if it were to do so in hushed tones and with a sense of awe, that would be no bad thing. For now, however, he fell in behind a sallow-faced youth who had been detailed to lead them through the city.

Once they were inside, Thurkill was struck by the neat simplicity of the city's construction. The road on which they walked proceeded in an unerringly straight line all the way to the opposite gate in the far wall, which he could see far in the distance. On either side, smaller roads branched off at right angles every few yards, each with rows upon rows of houses, shops and other wooden buildings neatly lined up. It looked as though little had changed since the days when the Romans had first laid down the distance markers around which they had built their fortress.

He was also amazed by just how clean the streets were. In every other town he had ever been in, except for his own little village of Gudmundcestre, the roads had been choked with waste, both human and animal. In the summer months, the stench would seep into every pore and could never be fully expunged. Clouds of flies would swarm around the dung heaps, making the whole experience practically unbearable to Thurkill's mind. It was why he had always favoured the countryside, he supposed. But here, the streets were clear. Yes, there were stray dogs roaming in and out of the alleyways, but there was little evidence of their presence. *Whoever rules here does so with respect and authority,* Thurkill mused.

Just as they reached the centre of the city, their escort stopped and pointed to a large square building whose walls were made of stone to a man's height, above which wooden posts supported a roof at a much greater height. Opposite stood a stone church that was as large and as impressive as any Thurkill had seen in Lundenburh.

Having left their weapons with the gate-wardens, Thurkill and his men were ushered inside where they were immediately assailed by the warmth of the raging fire in the central hearth. Above it, was suspended a massive cauldron from which oozed the wonderful aroma of a vegetable pottage. The heat was such that, before he had even walked ten paces into the hall, Thurkill felt a line of sweat break out on his forehead. He soon wished he'd left his cloak at the door, along with his sword and spear. The thick, cloying atmosphere was made worse by the vast number of people gathered within. The hall was set out in readiness for the evening meal and every bench at every table was occupied by all manner of men and women.

They halted while their escort exchanged words with the hall steward who then announced their arrival to the assembled company in strident tones before turning back to face him. "You may approach the Lady Gytha to state your business."

The hubbub ceased as all eyes turned to look at the newcomers. Ignoring them, Thurkill focussed instead on the far end of the hall where sat the most powerful lords and ladies in Escanceaster. His eyes were drawn to a grey-haired lady in the centre, her hair pulled back tightly from her face, and covered by a green linen scarf that matched her dress. Though her face was lined through age, Thurkill could see she had lost little of the bearing and beauty she must have commanded in her prime. *This must be Harold's mother, Gytha Thorkelsdottir,* Thurkill thought, wracking his brains as to whether he'd ever had occasion to meet her before. Her face was vaguely familiar, though this was because her son's features shone out from her face – the same strong jaw and high cheek bones, the same chiselled nose that lent an air of nobility to her face. It was a nobility that came from her breeding.

Reaching the space that separated her table from the rest of the hall, Thurkill dropped to one knee and bowed his head. "Lady Gytha of Wessex, I am Thurkill, son of Scalpi, lately Lord of Gudmundcestre and loyal huscarl in the service of your son, Harold, King of England. I have come to pledge my sword and those of my men to your service."

Gytha's eyes sparkled as she listened, a smile playing across her lips. "Rise, Thurkill, son of Scalpi. You are most welcome here, for I knew your father well enough. My son often spoke fondly of him. His death at Senlac was a grave blow to us all. Please accept my condolences for your loss. But did you not stand by your father's side that day?"

Though he could not be certain whether there was any meaning behind it, the querying tone of her voice was enough to cause Thurkill to blush. It seemed he would never be rid of the perceived shame of having survived that day. Regardless, he resolved to be honest with all that she asked him.

"I was there, Lady. I saw my father cut down before me. And to my shame I was unable to save your son from death as well. But, by then, there were simply too few of us still living to be able to protect him. Though I killed a good number of the bastards, I too would have been slaughtered had I not been knocked unconscious."

Perhaps seeing the torment in his face, Gytha's expression softened, "And you should know that I do not hold you responsible, Thurkill. You stood with my son to the very end and did all that was in your power to save him. That is far more than many others can say. Many were those who fled the field before the end and many more still who did not even fight on that day. Your conscience is clear; you will stand before Our Lord on the day of judgement safe in the knowledge that you could have done no more."

Thurkill bowed once more. "I thank you, Lady. To hear these words from Harold's own mother heals my soul of the guilt it has carried since that day."

Gytha waved her hand as if swatting away a persistent fly. "Enough of such talk. Those days are in the past, consigned to the history of this land. Though I lost three sons that day, I shall mourn no more. It is time for vengeance, time to stand up and be counted. Today, we look to the future. Today, we start the journey to take back what was stolen from us. And you and your men," she spread her arms wide in a gesture of welcome to Thurkill's warband, "are now part of that quest.

"We have great need of fighters, men who know what it means to stand in a shieldwall against these Norman scum. Men who can force a blade into the heart of their foe and care nought for it. It matters not that you number but six; we have many more like you here and the promise of more to come. Rise and take your place at my table. Eat your fill of my food and drink deeply of my ale, for I accept your oath of allegiance on behalf of my grandson, Godwine Haroldsson."

Smiling broadly, Thurkill rose and walked towards the table behind which Gytha sat. Once there, he gently took her proffered hand and kissed the gold ring, embossed with the wyvern symbol of Wessex, that sat proud on her index finger. There was no going back now; his fate was tied once more to that of the Godwine family.

***

In deference to his rank and provenance, Thurkill was summoned back to the hall two days later to attend a council of leading nobles and captains. Picking a seat on the end of a bench near the back, he settled down to listen to the debate as unobtrusively as possible. He was new to this assembly and, despite the favour shown to him by the Lady Gytha, he was very aware that many others held sway over him in terms of rank, age, and experience.

"Welcome, friend." Thurkill reached out to grab the offered hand that belonged to the smiling warrior to his left. He was a young man, not much older than himself, broad of shoulder and with a shock of blond hair forming an unruly mop. "I am Eadwig, thegn of Cleavedon in the shire of Sumorsaete. My family have served the Godwines for many generations."

"I am pleased to know you, Eadwig. I am Thur-"

"Yes, I know who you are, friend. I was here two nights ago and saw you welcomed by the Lady Gytha. You are held in high esteem here."

"They do me great honour, of course, but it is the name of my father that carries the weight. I merely bask in the light cast by his reflection."

Eadwig laughed. "I like the way you say that, Thurkill, though I fear you do not do yourself justice. It may surprise you to know that songs composed after the battle of Stamford made it even as far as this backwater. I had forgotten 'til now, but as I recall, there was mention of the daring young Saxon who felled the Viking champion. The one who had held the bridge against all comers for hours. This was you, was it not? Did Harold himself not reward you with a gift of the Viking's war axe?"

Thurkill blushed; he was unused to such adulation. "I'm not sure it was hours, friend, though it is true that he had killed several fine warriors with that axe. Though it was a necessary evil, I'm not proud of my part in it. I would rather have faced him toe to toe on the bridge, but the Hardrada's army had long since crossed and time was against us."

"Ha, so it *is* true. You floated down river and stuck your spear in his arse from below the bridge?" Eadwig slapped his thighs in mirth. "I thought the scops might have made that little detail up but, no, I can see I am in the presence of true greatness."

Despite himself, Thurkill could not resist joining in with his laughter. "I suppose it was a novel solution to the problem. It certainly unblocked the bridge."

"Sounds like that was not the only thing it unblocked. But what brings you here and how many warriors follow you?"

"Including me, we number just six souls. Not the biggest warband, I'll grant you, but stout men all and not afraid of a fight. And that is why we've come hither. To join those Saxons who remain loyal to Harold's family. I stood with Harold at Senlac; I hope to banish the shame of that defeat by standing with his sons."

"I too was at Senlac, with Gyrth's men on the left. I have never felt as close to the gates of hell as I did that day." He paused, lost in his thoughts of the horrors of that day for a moment. "Do you think we can succeed where Harold failed? Even though we will have Godwine Haroldsson to lead us, we lack the king's generalship."

"If we can raise the numbers we need, who knows, Eadwig? You saw how we fought at Senlac? We are a match for them on the field, and I truly believe we could have won that day. We have to believe, or all is lost."

Just then, Lady Gytha entered the hall and took her place at the head of the table. All conversation ceased as every man rose to his feet in deference to her position.

"Welcome, all. Please take your seats." She paused until the scrapping of benches on the stone floor diminished enough for her to be heard. "I've summoned you here to discuss our position and our plans. There is news from our scouts that affects us all and I would hear your views on it, for we are all in this struggle together.

"Word has reached us that William has returned from Normandy. He landed at Winchelsea not five days since and, even now, will be within the walls of Lundenburh where he plans to spend the feast of our Lord's nativity."

The hall erupted in a cacophony of excited chatter and not a few shouts as men debated the news with their neighbours. Gytha allowed them free rein for a few moments before holding up her hands for calm.

"It is an unexpected turn of events. As you know, we believed that William would not be back until the spring; who in their right mind, after all, would risk a crossing of the salt road in winter? Though we cannot be certain, I fear our plans to fall upon the Normans on Ash Wednesday are betrayed. Word must have reached the king, causing him to change tack."

"So, what do we do now?" Thurkill was too far back to see who had spoken, though he knew it must be someone of rank to have dared interrupt.

Unperturbed, Harold's mother continued. "I fear we have but one choice; we must accelerate our plans. I will send messengers to all the major towns in the south to ask that they support us in our hour of need. If we are to succeed, we must marshal our forces more quickly than William. We must march on Lundenburh and launch an assault as soon as we can. He won't expect such a move and, if we can take him by surprise, our chance of victory will be greatly increased."

Silence reigned in the hall. Thurkill sensed a great unease among many of the assembled thegns. *What is wrong with these people?* he wondered. *Do they not wish to cast off the Norman yoke? Do they wish to be shackled to the ploughshare in service of these foreign overlords for ever?*

"We could sue for peace." It was the same speaker as before, giving voice to the feelings of several of those present. "If William knows of our intent, he is sure to come down on us hard like a smith's hammer beats a lump of iron into the shape he desires. But have we not all heard how he treats those who submit to his will with mercy and justice? I'm sure it would not be too late if we were to do likewise."

Thurkill could see that Gytha was struggling to contain her anger, perhaps determined not to lose her temper in front of so many. When she finally spoke, she did so with an icy calm, but there was no mistaking the steel that lay behind her words.

"These lands have been in my family for generations, Ulfkell. In all that time they have been subject to no man other than a Saxon lord. While there is breath in my body, I shall not permit them to be handed over to any Norman, king or otherwise. My duty to my forebears is clear; I must protect these lands so that my grandsons can inherit from their father."

Now, another voice spoke. This time on the opposite side of the hall to where Ulfkell sat. "But where are they, Lady? Why are they not here? Without them to lead us, behind whom can the men of Wessex unite?"

"Patience, Wulfnoth, patience; they are coming. It takes time to organise a fleet of ships to sail from Ireland. They will be with us within the month, I swear it. And what's more, they'll bring two thousand men with the blessing of our friend and ally, King Diarmait of Leinster."

"This is indeed welcome news, Lady, but even with those men, will it be enough to fight William's army?"

"You are a fool if you think I have no other irons in the smithy's fire, Wulfnoth. I have sent messengers to my nephew, Swein Estridsson, who rules over Danmark. Swein's mother was sister to Knut, once king of the Aenglisc before old King Edward. I am confident he will send many thousands of men to join our banner. Danish ships will once more sail up the Thames, but this time they will come to fight with their Saxon cousins against the Normans."

Thurkill could sense the mood turning. What had appeared to be a hopeless cause now seemed to be within Gytha's grasp. Her words had swayed many of the doubters to her side, though it was by no means unanimous. Glancing to his side, he saw Eadwig sporting a broad grin. Seeing Thurkill's gaze, the blond warrior punched him on the upper arm in delight.

"We can win, Thurkill. With the Danes and Irish to swell our numbers, who could stand against us? There will be a new king crowned in Lundenburh before the year is out."

Thurkill smiled back, torn between the infectiousness of Eadwig's enthusiasm and the nagging doubt in his mind that refused to be silent. "I hope you're right, my friend. I truly do."

TWENTY-EIGHT

A week later, a score of Saxons set out from Escanceaster, heading east. At their head rode Tosti, eldest son of Harold's older brother Swein Godwineson, and cousin to Godwine, Edmund and Magnus. He had arrived at the city's north gate two days previously to report that the army was delayed in Ireland. Finding enough ships to transport the warriors and all their supplies meant it would be another month, at least, before they arrived.

Gytha had borne the news well enough, determined not to let her followers see her disappointment. Though she had carried the day in the recent council, Thurkill could see the truce between her and those that favoured settlement was fragile at best. It could shatter at any moment as a pot smashes when dropped. To allow any chink of light to appear in her brittle armour, through which her opponents might seek to drive a dagger of division, would be a disaster.

Nevertheless, the tidings called for urgent action. Scouts had already confirmed that, with the nativity celebrations complete, William was preparing to march west. Any hope of falling upon the Normans in Lundenburh had gone; the best they could now hope for was to seek favourable ground of their own choosing on which to engage the Normans in battle. Even more disheartening, however, was the news that it would not just be Normans they faced, for William had summoned Aenglisc warriors to his standard as well. It was a shrewd move, designed to test the loyalty of his new subjects. Those that refused to answer his call knew that they would forfeit what lands and titles remained to them should he succeed.

So, now Thurkill and nineteen others found themselves trotting along the old Roman road that was still known to all as the Fosse Way. It would take them as far as the river Tamesis, at which point they would turn and head towards Lundenburh.

With Tosti were Ulfkell and Wulfnoth, the two men who had spoken in favour of peace during the Council. Thurkill suspected that Tosti would rather not have had them present. Although Wulfnoth had grudgingly supported Gytha's plans,

Ulfkell remained obdurate, a constant thorn in Gytha's flesh. Perhaps she thought that by entrusting him with such an important mission, he could be made to walk to heel like an obedient dog. Thurkill had his doubts, though; right from the off, Ulfkell rode apart from the others, with only Wulfnoth and his two bondsmen for company. As they rode, the four men spent hour after hour in close conversation, their heads leaning in towards each other so that they might not be overheard.

Thurkill chose to ignore them for the time being. He was content to ride with Eahlmund and alongside Eadwig and his two warriors. In the days since the council, he'd found himself spending more and more time with the thegn from Sumersaete. Though they had little in common, Thurkill found his company to be a pleasant distraction from his worries; so much so, in fact, that he made a habit of seeking the other man out each mealtime. Pleasingly, their respective warbands were also rubbing along well together. They had spent several hours training with each other, easing the rustiness from their limbs and honing their battle-craft. A competitive but healthy rivalry had grown between the two groups. Though Eadwig's men were the more skilled warriors, Thurkill was pleased that – in Urri – he had the strongest and most accomplished of them all. So far, none had been able to best him with shield, spear, or sword.

"What do you make of it, Thurkill?"

With a start, he realised that Eadwig had shot him a question. "Make of what, my friend?"

"This quest on which we now find ourselves. Folly or not?"

Thurkill paused to consider his response. "I see the logic in it, but I fear it carries great risk."

"My feelings also. What if William chooses not to believe us? What is there to stop him from cutting us down on the spot?"

"Very little, I would imagine, whether he believes us or no. As king, he can do what he likes, and few would dare challenge his authority. If he were to decide we are rebels, he could have us strung up on the spot, or worse."

"Then we must pray that those who are to speak are blessed with the power of persuasion. I, for one, am glad that this task falls not to me."

Thurkill chuckled. "There are two of us in that boat."

***

They came upon the Norman camp early in the afternoon of the third day. That it was past noon was a matter of conjecture only as the sun had not once made an appearance. Ever since the dawn, rain had fallen steadily from skies that were nought but thick, forbidding clouds as far as the eye could see. It was as if God had laid a heavy grey blanket across the world.

They had just passed the point at which the Fosse Way met the Tamesis by an abandoned town that had been built by the Romans many centuries before; a town that still went by its ancient name of Corinium. Though, little remained of the houses – the stone having mostly been robbed for other buildings in the area – Thurkill could tell it must have been a sizeable settlement.

They were greeted by sentries that had been posted along the approach roads and were escorted in under a promise of safe conduct. Once within the camp's confines, they dismounted and led their horses through row after row of tents. As he walked, Thurkill felt a cold dread descending over his heart; William's army was huge. From his own reckoning, it was at least as big, if not bigger than that which had confronted them at Senlac. It was an awe-inspiring show of strength, no doubt calculated to strike fear into the souls of those that saw it.

To make matters worse, Thurkill could see banners and hear voices that belonged to Saxon men. The fyrd had answered William's call – or at least a good portion of it had. His heart was enraged to see so many of his countrymen standing with the Normans against their own but, in his head, he could not blame them. To refuse the summons could have cost them their lands or even their lives. It was a coldly calculated test designed specifically to put them in just such a difficult position. *Who knows, though,* Thurkill wondered. W*hen push comes to shove, will they raise their sword to their fellow Saxons?*

They found William's tent in the centre of an oval-shaped area that was surrounded by grass-covered mounds. It stood just to the south east of the town and must surely have been part of that settlement, Thurkill surmised, though he knew not what purpose it would have served. Perhaps an arena of some kind. He'd heard tales in his youth of how the Romans had made sport from setting wild animals against the captives of their wars, or even set men against men for nothing more than the pleasure of those who watched.

They were left to wait in the rain in front of the king's tent. Surrounded by heavily armed soldiers, they stood, silent and unmoving, unwilling to show any emotion or weakness. Eventually, the heavy cloth drapes were pulled back by two guards within to reveal William flanked by a half dozen of his most senior captains. The king took a few steps forward and then halted, staying out of the rain under the canopy that was supported by two wooden poles on either side of the opening. His captains fanned out in a threatening semi-circle behind him.

To Thurkill's eye, William seemed tired and drawn. His face was pale and his eyes seemed sunken within his skull. Where he had been clean shaven the last time Thurkill had seen him, now he stood with several days' growth of beard casting a dark shadow over his cheeks and neck. And, even though his form was enveloped by a thick purple cloak, Thurkill could tell that the king's shoulders were hunched, as if trying to shield himself from the worst effects of the weather.

"Welcome, people of Escanceaster. What is it that you would have of your king? I trust you have come to explain the meaning of these rumours I hear of rebellion?" As he spoke, Thurkill saw that William scanned the faces of each man before him, perhaps searching for clues as to their intent. Although he could not be certain, it seemed to him that the king's eyes lingered over his face for just a fraction longer than the others. *Could it be that he remembers me?* It was true that they had met twice before; once when he had assumed the role of scout in Warengeforte and again in Beorhthanstaed when Edgar, the king elected after the death of Harold, had finally submitted to William.

Before he could think about it any further, Tosti stepped forward. "Lord King, I stand before you on behalf of Lady Gytha Thorkelsdottir, mother of the late King Harold Godwineson. The loyalty of the people of Escanceaster is unwavering and should not be doubted."

It was a canny choice of words, Thurkill thought. Tosti had not said that the city stood with William, nor had he lied openly to the king.

William opened his mouth to reply, but only succeeded in coughing; a hacking, rasping cough that continued until the man closest to him ducked back into the tent and returned with a wine goblet which he duly proffered to his lord. Recovered, William continued, his illness lending ire to his words.

"That's as may be, but it does not chime with the reports I received from my poorly-treated knights whom I sent to your city in good faith. And why, pray tell, does the Lady Gytha not do me the honour of standing here on her own behalf? Who is she that she dares send some lickspittle runt to do her bidding?"

Whether Tosti felt insulted by the slur, he showed no sign of it. "Lord, the Lady Gytha is old and frail and broken still further by the death of her sons at Senlac. She feared that to journey so far in the dead of winter would be the end of her. And, as for your men…" he shrugged theatrically. "I have no knowledge of this matter. I can only assume they met with brigands on the road, desperate men fallen on hard times, of which there are many these days, I can assure you."

It was a performance to be proud of. Thurkill hoped it was enough to convince William. Perhaps he might even consider turning his army around and marching back to Lundenburh? But before such a thin hope could take hold, Ulfkell pushed himself to the front. Thurkill might have guessed that the proud, arrogant fool would not be content to allow Tosti to take the lead role during the negotiations. Hands reached out to grasp his sleeve, but he shook himself free and did not stop until he was half a step in front of Tosti, whose brow furrowed in frustration at this new development.

"Lord King."

William turned to face Ulfkell, a look of bored bemusement on his face. "And you are? The lickspittle's lickspittle perhaps?"

The Norman lords behind the king laughed at the Saxon's discomfiture, his face colouring deeply in an obvious mix of anger and embarrassment, until William held up his hand for peace.

"Proceed."

Visibly fighting to retain his dignity, he stuttered. "Lord King, my name is Ulfkell, son of Ulfnoth. The people of Escanceaster are sorely pressed. Last year's harvest was poor, and your new taxes are beyond our means. If we were to pay what you demand, the people would starve. There will not be food enough to last the winter."

"And what concern is this of mine? Did Jesus himself not once say that all men must give Caesar what he is owed?" William yawned, apparently bored by the whole thing.

"He did, Lord. And I have no quarrel with you on the matter of taxes being due; it is simply the amount that is claimed which is under scrutiny here. Were we to give what is being asked, how would we be able to pay next year? Men would have to sell their ploughs, or their livestock in order to meet this levy, leaving them without the means of production for next year."

Thurkill began to see Ulfkell in something approaching a new light. Try as he might, he could not fault the logic of his words. How could a farmer hope to pay next year's taxes if – in order to meet this year's dues – he had to sell the oxen that pulled the plough or the plough itself? It made no sense. Raising the level of taxation was surely self-defeating in the long run.

It seemed that William also found merit in the argument as he now stood silent, pondering his response. Eventually, he cleared his throat before hawking and spitting a huge gobbet of phlegm to one side. "I swear by Almighty God this god-damned Aenglisc weather will be the death of me one day." He spat once more. "I have heard your words, Ulfkell, son of Ulfnoth, and I have made my decision. In one month, I shall come to Escanceaster to see for myself. My advisers tell me it is one of the greatest, most prosperous cities in the land, and so it is my belief that it can well afford the new levy. But I am nothing if not a reasonable man; I have sworn to govern the land fairly and treat all men justly. If you can show me that the people suffer undue hardship, then I will promise to leave your city's dues at the same level as they were under my predecessor, King Edward.

"In the meantime," he turned back to face Tosti. "I must have evidence of Escanceaster's loyalty. I will travel with my army to Gleawecastre where I shall rest until recovered. While I am there, you will send me thirty hostages made up of the sons of the greatest men in the city. They will stand as a surety of your good conduct. Should all be as you say, they shall be returned to you unharmed in twelve months. But should the city close its gates to me, or otherwise resist my just rule in this land, they will be put to death and the city razed to the ground. I should imagine that Lord FitzGilbert, here," William stepped to one side to reveal the man who had been standing largely obscured, behind him, "shall enjoy putting his sword arm to use once again, not to mention the chance to renew his acquaintance with one of your number."

As he spoke these last words, the king stared directly at Thurkill, but the Saxon was too dumbstruck to notice. He stood rooted to the spot, his mouth open in a round O of shock. He had paid no heed to the men around the king; one Norman lord was much like any other to him. But by the look on FitzGilbert's face, it was clear that he had recognised Thurkill from the start. Never had he seen a look of such malevolent venom on any man's face. His eyes seemed to burn into Thurkill's soul as if trying to kill him purely with the power of his mind alone.

TWENTY-NINE

The journey back to Escanceaster was a sombre affair. No one could remove from their mind the images they had seen that day, the sheer number of soldiers on which William could call, both Norman and Saxon. They had known the king's army would be a force to be reckoned with, but none of them had imagined they would also face men from the shires, the towns and villages from which they too were drawn. It was a heavy blow to their confidence.

For Thurkill, there was also the added complication of Robert FitzGilbert. Since the Norman whoreson had escaped from Gudmundcestre, Thurkill had often wondered what had become of him. And now he was back in his life once more. In his heart, Thurkill had known it was inevitable; whilst FitzGilbert lived, he would never truly be free from danger. The only consolation was that at least Hild was beyond his reach now.

"I hadn't expected to see that bastard again quite so soon." Eahlmund cut into this reverie, echoing Thurkill's own thoughts.

"I would have liked to have avoided it a while longer, I must admit."

"Still, did you see the scar on his face, and the way he was limping? I think he has us to thank for those small gifts."

Thurkill grinned, despite his morose mood. "It's a shame we were unable to give him more to remember us by. Perhaps we will get the chance to finish the job."

Just then, Eadwig spurred his horse forward, pulling up alongside the two men with Tosti in tow. "Hie, Thurkill. What do you make of William's last words? We've been thinking it over these last several miles and none of us has any idea to what he refers. There is none left to ask but you. Can you make sense of it?"

For a moment, Thurkill considered brazening it out but he knew there would be little point. "The FitzGilberts and I have a history that is not to be envied. It started soon after Senlac. Once I had recovered from the wounds I received that day, I finally made it home only to find that man's brother – Richard

FitzGilbert – installed in my father's hall. He and his bastard henchmen were lording it over my people and threatening my aunt and sister. I demanded he leave but he paid no heed. Things got out of hand until he callously murdered my kinswomen for no reason other than to spite me. Put simply, I avenged their deaths.

"I had thought that was an end to the matter, only to find that Richard had a brother, Robert, whom you saw today. He's sworn vengeance against me, and I'm sure he will not rest until he has killed me, or I him. He found me once before, at Gudmundcestre last year, where he proceeded to burn the town and would have killed me were it not for the men of Huntendune under Earl Aelfric. Though it saddens me not to have ended his life that day, I am heartened to see that he carries the scars of our battle. But now he has me in his grasp once again. I fear my presence here may jeopardise our common enterprise."

Tosti smiled. "I don't see why."

"Your meaning, Lord?"

"Perhaps today's subterfuge has clouded your mind, Thurkill. Our aim remains the same: to remove William from the throne and to replace him with a son of Harold. To that end, I am sure we will find ourselves face to face with the enemy soon enough. Today, we bought time to muster our forces. Harold's sons have yet to arrive from overseas with their Irish warriors, the Danes have not crossed the salt road to join us, and we wait for the men of the shires to answer our call. Only once those things have happened can we risk battle; especially now that William marches with Aenglisc men as well as Norman. But when that day comes, we will take the fight to William and we will stand against his warriors, shield to shield. What will it matter if this FitzGilbert stands with William? You can kill him just as you would kill any man that faces you. And from what I hear of your sword-skill, I'd say there is a very fair chance of you doing just that."

"But what of Ulfkell? The words he spoke made it sound as if we aim for peace and lower taxes."

Tosti glanced around him to see who was within earshot. "At first, I was worried what he might say but, then I realised his speech unwittingly served our purpose well. Like you, I think William heard a man who wants peace between Escanceaster and the Normans. William will think that the threat of rebellion has receded and that the rumours of an attack were overplayed. He may now think he is facing nothing more than greedy merchants. The fact that this is probably true of Ulfkell should not bother us unduly. We know our hearts and we have the Lady Gytha to drive us forward."

Eadwig frowned, "Though that may be, I think you would do well to watch him closely, Tosti. There are others who think the same way and were their voices to become too loud, they may yet sway a great number to their cause. They could bring down our cause from within should they be allowed to go unchecked."

Tosti didn't speak for several moments. "You speak wisely, Eadwig. In truth, I had not considered this danger but, on reflection, I see the sense in what you say. We must watch to whom he speaks and hear what he says. I shall see that it is done and keep the Lady Gytha informed. And should it come to it, we should not be afraid to end his life. We cannot allow our purpose to be undone by a man such as he."

***

As soon as they were back safe within the walls of Escanceaster, preparations began for the sending of hostages to William at Gleawecastre. They must keep up the ruse for as long as possible, Tosti declared, so as not to give the king any cause to doubt their loyalty.

Thirty young lads were chosen from amongst the best families of the city. A balance had to be struck between showing respect by selecting people of substance but without stripping the army of its best fighters. For this reason, Tosti selected younger sons of those families who were trusted most amongst the city elders, lads who were marked by their fine clothes, exquisite jewellery, and well-crafted swords but who had not yet been blooded in battle. Few wanted to go but none argued against the decision. They were wedded to the cause and knew they must play their part as surely as their elder brothers and fathers who would stand in the shieldwall. There was no pretence, however, that their duty would be any less dangerous.

195

They set off the next morning. Thirty straight-backed young men dressed in their finery, sitting tall and proud in the saddle, their long hair streaming behind them as they trotted. All along the wall, men stopped their backbreaking repair work to watch them go. A ragged cheer began far to the left, its sound barely audible to those by the gate. But like a spark in a dry, wheat field, it soon caught and spread, growing to a crescendo of love and support. Hearts filled with pride at the sight of the best of the city's future riding off into danger like the warrior heroes of old. Acknowledging the sound, the lads broke into a canter, urging their mounts forward, cloaks billowing behind them.

Thurkill watched from the parapet alongside Eadwig, Tosti, and several others of the city's council, many of whom had sons or brothers amongst the hostages. The wind whipped at his hair and face, clawing tears from his eyes with its chill fingers. He shivered, though whether it was with cold or fear, he knew not. Eadwig's youngest brother had been named in the thirty, and he watched his friend for a sign of emotion. Though there was none, he saw his face was paler than usual, the jaw clenched tight in a determined grimace. Not knowing what to say, he grasped the other man's upper arm in what he hoped would be interpreted as a gesture of encouragement. Who knew whether the two brothers would ever see each other again?

"We will not fail them. We owe it to them to raise the banner of revolt and not bring it down again unless we are victorious or there is none left to hold it aloft." Tosti's eyes glistened as he spoke, staring at the fast-diminishing shapes of the riders as they pushed on hard towards the northern horizon.

Sniffing back the tears, Tosti turned away to face the others. "Let us make good use of the time they have given us. The strengthening of the walls must continue apace. And let more riders go out to look for our allies. My cousins must have landed by now and I would have sign of them sooner rather than later, else all may be lost. We need to rouse the towns to the east of us, too. Messengers have been sent before, but we are yet to see the numbers that we had hoped for. We must shame them before God that they have not yet ridden to our side."

THIRTY

William looked out through the window of his quarters on the second floor of Sheriff Roger's hall in the middle of Gleawecastre. Below him, in the courtyard that was surrounded on three sides by the vast building, a group of thirty Saxons had just clattered across the cobbled stones and were now dismounting, their horses being taken away to the stables by the waiting ostlers.

"Hmmmpf."

"Lord King?"

William turned away from the opening, letting the heavy drape fall back into place, noticing as he did so the sharp difference in temperature now that he was shielded from the biting wind that swirled around the eaves. Though he had only looked out for a few moments, his ears, nose and cheeks had turned numb. Striding over to where the fire blazed fiercely in its hearth, he turned his back, clasping his hands behind him so that they too could be warmed.

"They're little more than boys, Roger, though they are dressed well for all that, I'll grant you. I suspect the Lady Gytha plays a canny game with me."

"You doubt her fealty, Lord?"

"Don't you? Remember the evidence we have before us. We have the rumours of the attacks that were planned for Ash Wednesday; then we have the maltreatment that befell my envoys a few weeks ago when they came to Escanceaster – though they claim to have no knowledge of that. This land has long stood for the Godwine family, and now I fear that Harold's mother, this harridan of the west, has whipped the people into a frenzy of revolt. Put yourself in their shoes, Roger – as foul smelling and as shit-stained as they may be. Would you rather a Saxon were on the throne than me? And if you saw a chance to make that so, would you not reach for it like a drowning man clutches at the floating log?"

"But why send these hostages? Why ask for clemency with

197

taxation?"

"I admit, I am not decided on this. It is possible that the rumours were false or were spread by a mere handful of malcontents. But it is equally possible that, even now, they prepare their defences and muster their supporters while I sit here enjoying the fine victuals you lay before us.

"They have sent me the hostages they promised, and in good time too, but these boys do not number among the greatest sons of the city. These are the younger siblings, the lads who have yet to grow a beard or wield a sword in anger. They will not be missed should we come to blows. But they are still sons of mothers and, by their clothes, I can see that they hail from respected families and hence arises my confusion."

William fell silent for a time, stretching up and down on his toes, feeling the muscles of his calves tighten. Eventually he shrugged and turned away from the hearth. "My plan remains the same, Roger. We rest here for a week more and then we head south and west with the army to Escanceaster. If all is well, there will have been no harm done by showing the people the strength of my arm. But if they close the gates to me, I shall know the content of their hearts and minds. And, in turn, they shall know my wrath. And the first to know it shall be these wretched hostages.

"Send FitzGilbert to me. I would have him take these boys into his care for the time being."

THIRTY-ONE

"Enough, I say! We have made our stand, and here we shall live or die."

Though she was old in years with a body made frail by sorrow, Gytha still had a voice that commanded attention and respect. The hall fell silent; the two parties on either side of the room drew apart from where they had been standing almost toe to toe as they shouted their points and insults at each other, punctuated by jabbing fingers to the chest.

To Thurkill though, she looked weary; the last year must have taken its toll. Not only was her body failing her as she advanced through her seventh decade, the stresses of her son's reign – culminating in his death and that of three more of her sons – must have taken an unimaginable toll on her. A woman with half her resolve, Thurkill mused, would have retreated from life and perhaps entered a convent to see out her days. And who could have blamed her?

Almost every day in the two weeks since the hostages had ridden off to Gleawecastre had contained nought but a litany of bad news. At a time when they expected men to be flocking to their banner, the tidings that arrived shocked them to their core. First came the messengers from the king of the Danes – Gytha's own cousin in marriage, Sweyn Estridsson. He claimed to have no warriors to spare for England as his attention was focussed on rebellious lords within his own lands. Hard on the heels of that blow came news that Gytha's grandsons had still not sailed from Ireland. Stubborn south-westerly winds kept their fleet at anchor; they would not be able to set sail until the winds changed in their favour.

Finally, as bad news tends to come in threes, word reached them that many of the messages sent out to the surrounding towns and cities, urging them to rise up, had been intercepted by the Normans. Thurkill had suspected this to be the case; though warriors had been arriving in Escanceaster every day, their numbers were far fewer than expected. They had hoped to see row upon row of campfires all around the city by now, but so far, every fighting man who had come had been able to find lodgings within the city walls.

King William could no longer be in any doubt as to their intent. Their ruse had been exposed; their lies laid bare. Already, Gytha's scouts had reported the movement of a vast army on the road leading from Gleawecastre. William was on the march and heading for the city. And it was this news that had led to this latest altercation in Gytha's hall.

On the right was Tosti and his followers, including Eadwig and Thurkill. Men who still yearned to take the fight to William. Men who wanted every last one of the foreign horde put to the sword or chased into the sea, whence they would be free to limp back home to whatever pit they had climbed from.

Against them were ranged those who stood with Ulfkell and Wulfnoth. These men abhorred the idea of war with William. They spoke of protection for their families and livelihoods. They knew of William's reputation, his wrath; they knew that any town that closed its gates to him risked destruction. Doubtless, they already imagined tongues of flame licking at the thatched rooves of their homes and workshops.

And, if he were honest, Thurkill could see their point. With so few men having come to join them, fear of what was to come was growing with each new day. How could they hope to stand against the whole Norman army, made larger still by those Saxons that marched with them? True, those men might yet refuse to kill their own, but the Norman numbers alone made that irrelevant. But still, he could not, would not, give up. He had to trust that Godwine, Edmund, and Magnus would cross the water from Ireland before it was too late. A thought which was now echoed by Gytha.

"My grandsons will come, and then we will have the strength to meet William in battle. He thinks he has us trapped here behind these walls, but he will think again when Godwine cuts through their lines like a whetted blade through roasted mutton."

But Ulfkell was not about to allow himself to be mollified by her honeyed tones. "Your pardon, Lady, but we have heard these same words for week after week now. I've heard it so often that I know not whether to believe it anymore."

"You dare insult the honour of the Godwine family, you wretch?" Gytha's voice was shrill with anger. "A promise had been made, and a promise will be kept. That has been the Godwine way for generations, and you'd do well not to forget that. Without the Godwines, you would be nothing. A peasant scrabbling for scraps to put on his table."

Though Ulfkell's cheeks shone red with shame, he could not bring himself to stand down. "Even now, William is on his way here with a force greater than that which stood with him at Senlac. What do you propose we do when he arrives here before your grandsons, as I am sure he will? What value is a Godwine promise when we are encircled by Norman soldiers?"

"Have you not seen these walls, Ulfkell? These stones have stood here since the time of the Romans; they have never been breached in all that time. We have fresh water and plentiful supplies from the harvest. If necessary, we can hold firm here until Godwine Haroldsson arrives with his brothers at the head of their army. Then you will see what it means to be a Godwine and a Saxon."

***

Next day, back in his lodgings, Thurkill sat with his warriors, making the final preparations. The Norman army could arrive any day now, and who knew what would happen when they did. Come what may, he and his men would be ready to fight. Blades would be sharpened, shield straps tightened, mail polished and clothing repaired.

"Well, here we are again, lads, eh? This is becoming a habit." Though he was grinning, Thurkill could sense an anxiety behind Eahlmund's joke.

"You have somewhere you'd rather be, friend? What could be finer than preparing to stand in battle with your hearth-companions? This is the stuff of legend, Eahlmund. Fight well and they will write songs about you."

"I can think of many places I'd rather be, Lord. The warm embrace of that dark-haired lass down at the tavern for one."

"Ah, but there you are out of luck, my friend. I can tell you on good authority, she prefers her men with a bit more meat on them." Leofgar laughed, patting his crotch suggestively.

Eahlmund threw his hands up in mock disgust. "By God's hairy ball-sack, the poor girl. What was she thinking? Rutting with an illiterate goat herder when she could have had me."

Leofric snorted. "You were ever the lucky one, brother. I was wondered where you'd been sneaking off to late at night. I don't suppose she has a sister?" he added conspiratorially.

Thurkill laughed. "I pray to God that you lot never change. May you always do your thinking with the contents of your trews."

"It beats worrying about the future. Who knows when any one of us might find ourselves in bed with a beautiful woman... or a goat in your case, Leofgar?"

The former huntsman punched Eahlmund in the stomach, not hard enough to hurt but with enough force to make him sit down with a thud, winded. "You're just jealous that neither woman nor goat will have you, yet I have my pick of both."

Urri roared with laughter. He had been following the exchange from where he sat in the corner using needle and thread to repair a gash in this tunic. "I thank the Lord that I am too old to worry about such things. Long past are the days when I used to worry about what my dick was thinking."

"Don't be so hard on yourself, old man. I'm sure there'll be a toothless old crone out there somewhere who'd be happy to have you."

It was too much for the blacksmith. Tears streamed down his cheeks as he howled, his hands pressed to his sides as if they threatened to burst. Such was the uproar that no one noticed Eadwig's arrival in the room.

The Somersaete thegn had to raise his voice to make himself heard. "It is good to find you in such good spirits. However, I regret that the news I bring may bring an end to your merriment."

Wiping his eyes, Thurkill stood to offer Eadwig the bulging mead skin that hung from a wooden hook by the door frame. "What news, my friend?"

Eadwig took a gulp before replying, swilling the sweet,

golden liquid around his mouth to rinse away the dust of the city. "Ah, that's a fine drop, Thurkill," he said appreciatively. "I'll savour it as it may be my last for some time. The Normans are here, and they are more numerous than the birds and bees in summertime."

***

Thurkill took the steps two at a time, ignoring their worn, uneven surface in his eagerness to reach the walkway that ran around the wall's perimeter. In the hazy, early morning sunlight, the rich, reddish hue of the ancient sandstone was even more striking than normal. The walls were a formidable obstacle, Thurkill reflected. Standing taller than the height of two men and with a thickness of another man's height at its base, there was surely no way the Normans could penetrate them. It was as Gytha had said; these walls had stood for hundreds of years. Surely, they would be safe here until Harold's sons came.

But whatever confidence he felt evaporated almost as soon as he looked north over the moorland that stretched all the way to the horizon. Despite himself, he was unable to prevent a sharp intake of breath at the sight that befell him. All along the north road, a massive column of mounted knights and foot soldiers was advancing upon Escanceaster. Everywhere along the seemingly unending mass of humanity, banners flapped in the wind, bearing testament to which great lords were present. Breaking up the line here and there, carts piled high with supplies were being pulled by teams of lumbering oxen, rumbling along the exposed stonework of the road. It looked like a huge snake, slithering its way over the ground, inexorably working its way towards its paralysed prey.

"Shit," Eahlmund breathed in awe.

"Look," Urri growled, pointing to a spot about halfway along the column. "Saxons. I recognise the sigil on those standards."

Thurkill grunted. It remained to be seen whether they would fight, but the fact that they were over there, instead of within the city walls spoke volumes. Already, a mere eighteen months after Harold's death, a good number of Saxon lords now reckoned their future lay on the side of the Normans.

By now, the front of the army had halted and begun to spread out to the sides. They stood about four hundred paces from the city walls and out of range of even the strongest archers. For hour after hour, the process continued as rank upon rank spread out from the road, forming an ever-widening cordon of warriors surrounding the city.

As each unit reached its designated place, the standard bearer planted the tapered end of the banner's shaft into the soft earth, pushing it down until it could stand proudly on its own. Thus, was marked the rallying point for each lord. Thurkill scanned the forest of fluttering flags, looking for designs he recalled from Senlac. There were ravens, suns, fish, all manner of shapes and colours. And there in the centre was the pale blue banner with the white cross which he had last seen the day Harold had been killed. The banner which it was said Pope Alexander had presented to Duke William in person, in recognition and support of his supposedly righteous crusade to rid England of its usurper king.

"Look." Thurkill pointed to the place. "That will be where King William stands. The bastard is still making hay from the warmth of the church's sun."

Urri growled. "I'd tear down that cloth, piss on it, and stuff it down his throat if only I could get close enough."

"Not before I take a shit and wipe my arse on it, you won't," Eahlmund re-joined, not to be outdone.

They lapsed into an uneasy silence, watching the vast army unfold before them. Dusk was falling before the immense column of soldiers ended. So huge was the army that not only was the city surrounded, but at times, the lines were several ranks deep. There could be no means of escape, no path by which messengers could be sent to other cities or shires now. They were trapped within the walls of Escanceaster; as well fortified as they were.

Their fate hung in the hands of Harold's sons; would they arrive in time to relieve them? Or were they destined for annihilation at the hands of their oppressors?

As Thurkill pondered these thoughts, the last vestiges of sunlight disappeared beneath the horizon to his left. Like a candle being snuffed out, the land was overcome by darkness.

The only light came from behind him, from the many torches affixed to walls and the braziers spaced along the perimeter to keep the watchmen warm against the winter's chill. Before long, however, little pin pricks of light pierced the night all around them as the besieging army lit their campfires.

Thurkill sniffed and turned away, heading for the stairs back down into the city. "They're settling in for the night; I'll wager we'll hear no more from them until the morning. Best get some rest, lads. Who knows what the morrow will bring?"

THIRTY-TWO

For the third time in the last hour, Thurkill carefully spread the piece of parchment flat on his thighs. The light was barely sufficient to allow him to see the words, even though he sat close to the room's one small window. Tears streamed down his cheeks, leaving ragged gunnels amidst the dust and grime that was caked onto his face from days spent without bathing. The words shimmered before his eyes, forcing him to blink repeatedly until they were cleared of their moisture. He was careful to ensure that no more tears fell onto the letter; the ink had already smudged in several places where he had been less attentive.

The letter had arrived in Escanceaster as dusk was falling the previous day, mere hours before the Normans had surrounded the city. It had taken the best part of a day to track down its intended recipient, though, so little known was he there. Ripping open the crude seal – its design unknown to him – he wondered from whom it had come? Who else knew of his presence in the city? But it took no more than the first few lines to solve the mystery.

It was the voice of Sunhilda, wife of his friend Aethelgar who had been so cruelly struck down during the attack on Henffordd, who spoke to him via the carefully formed writing. Since her husband's death, she had taken her vows and entered service within the abbey at Wenloch. Not only did this meet her need for shelter, food, and protection now that Aethelgar was no longer by her side, but it also allowed her to care for Mildryth whom Thurkill had gifted to the Abbess to raise as God's servant.

Now Sunhilda had taken it upon herself to write to him, to bring him news of his daughter. Thurkill skipped past the greetings to the words he wanted to read again.

"Be assured that Mildryth grows stronger with each day. I swear by Almighty God that she is now twice as big as when she was born. Already she can sit up on her own and roll over. I

found that out to my cost when she fell off my cot when my back was turned. You can tell that she wants to crawl now too, and I am sure it will not be long before she does. Then we will have to keep our wits about us, else she will crawl right out the front door.

All the nuns adore her, even the old abbess, though she pretends to be stern with her. Though, as young as she is, I am sure she has no understanding of the words of admonishment. Everyone wants to take turns to feed her; we give her milk from the goats and she cannot get enough of it. You've never seen a cleaner baby as everyone wants to bathe her too. She saves her best smiles for when she is splashing about in the water. I wish you could see her, Thurkill; you could not be prouder of your daughter.

Her hair has grown well. It is curly and gathers in little ringlets. Just like her mother, God rest her. You should know that I tend to her grave each week. She lies in a place that is so beautiful and peaceful. Whenever I go, the trees are always full of birds, their song like angels from heaven watching over Hild. I swear the Lady Mildburh keeps Hild in her prayers too.

I must close now, Thurkill, for there is much to be done and I can hear Mildryth calling for her milk. May the Lord God keep you safe and send you back to us one day. I can think of one young lady who would love to see you."

Memories came flooding back, filling his heart and soul with nerve-shredding emotion. When his sobbing finally ceased, his shoulders still shook with the strength of the feelings that yet wracked his body. He had been fooling himself, pretending that he had left that part of his life behind. That he had somehow boxed away the past, to be looked at only when he chose. Now he saw just how ridiculous a belief that was.

One simple letter had destroyed the barricades he had erected in his mind, like they were made of straw and had blown away in the wind. He had thought himself free to commit himself to whatever enterprise he wanted, safe in the knowledge that none would mourn his passing. But that falsehood had been laid bare, its facade cruelly stripped away and exposed for all to see. He had a daughter, and whether she was to be a nun or not, a daughter needed her father.

Yet here he was, miles away and trapped within the walls of a city surrounded by thousands of Normans – not to mention Saxons – who had come to take the town by force or otherwise. And if that were not bad enough, there was one out there who was intent on his death. Even if the siege were to be settled without loss of life, Robert FitzGilbert would find some way to confront him; a knife between the ribs in a dark alley, perhaps, should they not meet first on the field of battle.

Come what may, Thurkill knew now that he had to survive. He had to find his way back to Wenloch. *May the Lord God and the Lady Mildburh watch over me that I might see my daughter once again,* he prayed fervently.

His thoughts were interrupted by the sound of running feet thudding up the wooden stairs to his first-floor room above the tavern. The door burst open to reveal Eahlmund, breathless and red of face from exertion.

"Lord," he panted, his hands pressed into his sides to recover his breath. "There's movement in William's camp. All captains are summoned to the wall."

This is it, thought Thurkill, *the fight begins*. He had slept in his clothes in case of just such an emergency, so he needed to pause only to don his mailshirt and helmet and to pick up his shield and war axe. Then he was out through the door, clattering down the narrow staircase in pursuit of his friend.

As soon as he reached the wall, Thurkill raced up the stone steps, made slippery with an early morning frost which had turned the overnight rain to ice. At the top, he found Eadwig already waiting, blowing on his fingers and looking towards the place where Thurkill recalled William had set his banner the day before.

"What news, friend?"

Wordlessly, Eadwig pointed. Shielding his eyes from the low sun, Thurkill followed the direction of his finger. Sure enough, just in front of where the king's tent stood, lines of mounted men were forming up. All were clad in grey, knee-length mail shirts, conical helmets with the obligatory nose guard, and each carried the now-familiar kite-shaped shield and long lance. It was hard to estimate their number; Thurkill had never taken well to his numbers despite the beatings his father's priest had meted out to him. He managed to count to fifty and then reckoned there must be nigh on ten times that number. Though a small fraction of the total force available to William, it was still, nevertheless, an impressive sight.

As they watched, they saw a man come out of the king's tent. Without pausing, he stepped up onto a stool that was being held in place by a waiting boy and, in one smooth movement, swung his leg up over the horse's back before heaving himself into position. From the shock of thick dark hair atop a square-jawed face, Thurkill could see that it was William, though he looked to have put on weight since he had last seen him. *He looks to have recovered his health now,* he thought. *The business of ruling England appears to agree with him.*

Within moments of his arrival, the horsemen set off at a walk that soon became a brisk trot. As they rode, Thurkill marvelled at their discipline and skill. Not one man left his place in the line, not one pulled ahead of his fellows or fell behind. There was a symmetry and simplicity to their movement that those watching could only admire. On they came to within one hundred paces of the wall, at which point they wheeled to their left and continued their progress, maintaining the same distance from the wall the whole time.

"They mean to ride the whole length of the city wall," Eadwig said.

Thurkill nodded. "Looking for weaknesses, I shouldn't wonder."

"And taking note of our strength. Seeing if we have sufficient numbers to man the whole extent of our defences."

They continued to watch as the Normans rode out of sight to the east and south, their cheeks pinched and red as they faced the stiff westerly breeze. Then they waited, hardly breathing, for them to reappear from the far side. The distance was just under a mile and a half, so they did not have long to wait. They heard them before they saw them; the noise of two thousand hooves hammering down on the soft grassland that surrounded the city was like a thunderstorm rolling in with the wind. Moments later, they came into view, still riding in perfect formation. All along the wall, men stared, their expressions a mix of grim determination or glum resignation.

The horsemen eventually came to a halt, their mounts blowing great plumes of steam as they tossed their heads up and down. They formed up in a solid mass on either side of the road that led down to the north gate, the king in the centre of the front rank. There they stood, immobile, for what seemed an age, making no sound other than the occasional snort or whinny from one or two of the beasts, their breath visible as plumes of steam in the cold morning air. It made for an inspiring sight, but one Thurkill knew was mainly for show. Such a small force of mounted warriors would never charge the high stone walls of the city; it would be tantamount to suicide. This was a test of the defenders' resolve, no more. A test to enable William to see what sort of men held the walls against him.

Thurkill stole a glance to either side, eager to see the faces of those who stood near him. As expected, his own hearth-warriors stood impassive, bored even. They had faced these bastards before and knew what to expect. But those further on were a different story. Though there were many who scowled defiance, there were several who looked terrified, their faces drained of colour. Over to his left, he saw a man bent over the wall, the sound of his retching just about reaching his ears, followed by the splash as the contents of his stomach hit the ground far below.

He couldn't blame them; there was no shame in it. Had he himself not emptied his bowels on the morning of his first battle all those months ago? Any man who claimed not to be afraid was either a liar or a fool, neither of whom Thurkill would want next to him in the shieldwall. The real test of a man was not whether he held no fear but rather how he responded when the swords began to sing. If the man to your left could stand firm and keep you covered by his shield, then it did not matter how he felt inside. His honour and his duty to his fellow warriors were what would make him overcome the fear.

But would these men of Escanceaster stand? He reckoned that few of them would have any experience of battle. Other than the occasional sea-borne raiders looking for easy pickings, the west of the country had been spared the carnage of war for much of the last two generations. He doubted whether many of them had even seen, let alone had to fight, an army of even a tenth of this size.

Just then his thoughts were interrupted by movement to his front. A small group of knights – the king among them – had broken free of the main group and was walking slowly forward, closer to the main gate. About a dozen of them all told. They halted within hailing distance, about fifty paces away. Standing up in his stirrups to his full, considerable height, the king addressed the defenders.

"By whose order does the gate remain closed? Who dares defy the rightful king of England and stops him from entering his own city?"

His words were met with silence. Everywhere, men stood passively, facing down the enemy. Their shields were held to their front and their spear points gleamed in the sunshine like the frost sparkles on the meadow on a crisp, winter's morning.

William let the silence hang in the air happy to allow the palpable feeling of menace to grow. Finally, he continued. "Was it not but one month ago that your leaders came to me in Corinium to swear fealty. Did they not also, a few days later, send hostages to Gleawecastre as proof of that oath? What am I to make of that promise if you now refuse to open these gates? And what would you have me do with those hostages? Should they have to pay the price for the insolence and lies of your leaders? Their blood will not be on my hands if that comes to pass. My conscience will be clear."

Still, no one spoke. Thurkill could only imagine what was going through their minds. The king's words sounded like the harbingers of hell and damnation. But to their credit, not one man moved.

When he next spoke, William's voice had taken on a harder edge. It was clear that the obduracy of the defenders was beginning to wear down his patience.

"I will have an answer from you, or my next words will be delivered by my soldiers."

Suddenly, a spear flew out, launched not far from the gate itself. It sailed high, arcing into the sky before beginning its downward trajectory. Thurkill watched, mouth agape, following its course until – with an audible thud – it landed a few paces from the king and buried its point deep into the soft earth. He had no idea who had thrown it, though he suspected it might have been Tosti whom he knew to be close to whence the missile had originated. It was well thrown, though; it had been no more than a warning.

But the Normans were not to know that. A few of the horses reared in fright, throwing their riders to the ground. Others turned and bolted back to the safety of their lines. Even William had to haul back frantically on his reins, desperately trying to bring his panicked mount back under control. It was testament to his great skill as a horseman that he kept his seat.

Then, without warning, a great shout went up from the remainder of the five hundred horsemen who had been left to the rear. Perhaps believing their lord's life to be in danger, they surged forward en masse, sweeping past William and the remainder of his escort. From where he stood, Thurkill could see that the king was desperately trying to stop them but, still focussed on calming his jittery horse, he could not prevent their headlong charge. On they came, their hooves pounding the earth as they chewed up the ground towards Escanceaster.

Thurkill stared as the hurtling swathe of horse and human flesh closed in on the city walls. What were they thinking? What could they hope to achieve by such rash action? Did they think they could breach the walls just by riding them down? Perhaps they hoped to impress their king with their bravery? No wonder William had tried to prevent their foolhardiness.

As these thoughts swirled around his brain, he heard the orders being given and then repeated along the walls by every captain.

"Archers."

As one, every bowman on the north and east walls selected an arrow from the sheaf tied at their waist and nocked it in place on the bowstring.

"Aim."

Each man drew back on the string until the fingers of their right hand brushed their chins. At the same time, they raised the angle of the bow until the arrow point was aimed at their intended target.

It seemed to take forever for the final order to come. So long in fact that Thurkill feared that the men would have to relieve the pressure on their straining shoulders before it did.

"Loose."

More than two hundred shafts soared in one dense volley of iron-tipped wood. At that range they could not miss. The horses were packed so tightly together that almost every projectile found a target. In that one moment, the great skill of the riders became their undoing as their close-knit formation gave them no hope of taking evasive action. Only those on the very edges were able to wheel away, but many of those were hit before they could do so. Horse after horse crashed to the ground, their riders either dead or wounded from arrows or flung beneath the flailing hooves of the animals that stampeded over them.

Thurkill reckoned at least a quarter had been felled by that first salvo. Incredibly, however, rather than escaping from the carnage, whoever was in command turned them back in the direction whence they had come, perhaps believing that to be the quickest route to safety. He was sorely mistaken.

Straightaway, the order was repeated, but faster this time. "Nock... aim... loose." Once again, death flew out from the walls, the sound much like the wind whistling through the eaves of a lord's hall on a winter's night. And once again the screams of the dying rose to their ears, man and beast alike. It was too much to bear for some of the defenders, many of whom turned away rather than watch the death throes of so many noble beasts, animals who were innocent of men's crimes but who had no choice but to do their bidding.

After that second devastating volley, the few remaining knights lost whatever stomach they had left for the fight. Those pitiful riders who were unscathed, or just lightly wounded, trailed back to where William sat ahorse. Even at this distance, Thurkill could sense the cold fury that consumed the king. He had come there to display his strength, a taste of his power and authority. He had intended to demonstrate the skill and dexterity of his knights in order to overawe the men who stood on the walls. It had started well enough, but all that had changed in a heartbeat.

Now, well over half of the five hundred horsemen lay in front of the walls, cut down by a withering hailstorm of arrows. His best men laid low by farmers or craftsmen armed with little more than hunting bows. To add insult to injury, those part-time warriors now cheered to the skies, their raucous voices mocking the king and his army.

THIRTY-THREE

"How dare you?"

Not one of the three men ranged before William spoke. None even dared meet his eye. Rather, each man stared in shame at their feet. All three had been hauled before the king for their part in the debacle that morning. Each one of them had led a conroi of roughly one hundred men in the suicidal charge against the city walls. There would have been five men standing there but for the fact that two of them lay dead on the field, already having paid the ultimate price for their folly. And few doubted that these men would soon follow their erstwhile comrades to the afterlife.

"How dare you?" the king repeated, his anger so intense that he could not find the words to express himself any differently, resorting instead to the same barely articulate utterance. Three hundred of his best knights had been lost. Most had been killed in the arrow storm while those who had been too wounded to escape from the killing field had their throats cut by the urchins who had rushed out from the city walls to loot the bodies of anything valuable. He had watched, impotent, as mailshirts had been pulled over heads, swords, spears and helmets grabbed, and coin purses sliced free of the belts from which they had hung. Any sign of life from the owner had been met with a swift stab of a seax to the neck or face.

By Almighty God, how he hated those knives. Every bugger and his wife – not to mention their son and daughter – seemed to have one. And each one was kept deadly sharp too. Time and again, he had seen a flash as the sunlight glinted off a blade when it lashed out to end some poor bastard's feeble grip on life.

Now the architects of that disaster were stood before him, cowed and silent. It was to their credit, he supposed, that not one tried to speak; not one dared to offer any excuse or mitigation for their actions. Had they done so, he would have killed the man on the spot.

How could they have been so imbecilic to have charged the walls? Horses and men against stone that was the height of more than two men and probably just as thick? It was bound to end in a massacre. Were they trying to impress him? Did they think he would reward them for their courage? There was no doubting the bravery of the men who had followed their crazed orders, or course. But it mattered not now; those poor bastards had not deserved to die.

True, the loss was not catastrophic in terms of numbers; he had plenty more men to call upon. But it was so much more than that. They had given the Saxon dogs hope, given them the first taste of victory. If they had been wavering in the face of his great army, this episode would have emboldened them, making his task that much harder. In an equal but opposite sense, it had dented the faith and morale of William's men. They trusted him to bring them success, to not waste their lives needlessly and, above all, to bring them spoils of war.

They would have to die, of course, these three wretches. There was no question about it. He could not allow the army to see such a wanton act of stupidity and disobedience go unpunished. He had to show them that he had an iron will, that discipline underpinned everything. It was the one thing that kept the army together. And it would have to be public, so that as many saw it as possible. That was the only way for the message to hit home fully.

It was a shame; they had been promising young captains who had the makings of great leaders. One was even the grandson of his closest ally from his youth. The man who had helped keep him safe as a young man when many around him wanted him dead, wanted to stop him from coming into his father's inheritance when he came of age. But he could not have favourites, nor make exceptions. He would regret it for some time, but he would console himself that the fault was not his. If they had held station as they had been ordered, their lives would not now be forfeit.

Turning his back on the three men as if dismissing them from his mind, he wafted his hand at the waiting guards. "Take them out and hang them in view of the army."

***

Later, from his position on the heights to the north of Escanceaster, William gazed down on the city laid out beneath him. The sky had clouded over as the day had worn on and now it was as grey as the waves of the sea beyond the city walls. There was little sound but for the screeching of a few sea birds that swirled around overhead on the lookout for scraps of food, and the gentle creaking of the ropes behind him on the end of which the bodies of the three hapless captains now gently swung in the breeze.

It had been a grim business. The massed ranks of soldiers had stared silently and sullenly as the small wooden barrels were kicked out from under the feet of the condemned men. To their credit, William mused, they had died well and with honour. They were reconciled to their fate; there was no screaming, struggling or cursing. Nevertheless, the death itself was not good. Hanging rarely was. As the drop from the hastily erected gallows was too shallow to cause the neck to be broken, each man had taken several minutes to die, their legs kicking as they fought for breath, eyes bulging and faces turning slowly purple. Just before the end, an horrific stench had filled the air as two of the men lost control of their bowels as their hold on life itself faded. He pitied the poor sods whose job it would be to cut them down for burial.

But with that sordid business done, William could focus once more on the city. It was, at least, clear now that those within had no intention of surrendering to him. Not without a fight at least.

He knew he had little option other than to take the city by force. That said, he remained reluctant to spill blood unless as a last resort. Not only would he spare his own men from further senseless death if he could, but he was also mindful of his duties as king. He had not forgotten the oath he had sworn on the feast of the Lord's nativity just over a year ago. He had promised to rule fairly and justly. And while a large part of him wanted to teach the inhabitants of this God-forsaken shit hole a violent lesson, he was mindful of the message that would send. Many of the people within, he guessed, had not asked to be thrust into the middle of this conflict, and he would not be able to protect them once his men broke in. He needed to try one last time to force their surrender, even as the preparations for an assault on the walls continued apace.

"FitzGilbert?"

"Your wish, Lord King?" The weasel-faced man limped forward from where he had been standing patiently, waiting with the other lords who had assembled to watch the execution.

"Have the hostages brought to my tent at first light."

THIRTY-FOUR

Thurkill woke with the dawn, bright light streaming on to his face through the broken shutters that had been closed, futilely, across the small window. Shielding his eyes, he stared up at a sky that was no longer grey. The brisk wind that had howled like so many banshees through the night had blown the clouds away, save for the occasional wispy white puff that scudded across the heavens, blown on its way by the still powerful gale.

As he donned his mailshirt, his mind filled with images of Hild, reminding him that she had come to him in his dreams. The picture was as vivid as if she had been there in the room with him, her round face with its dimpled cheeks framed either side of her coquettishly smiling mouth. In his dream, he recalled she had been laughing at some foolery on his part, her eyes sparkling and her golden curls bouncing in time with her head as it rocked with mirth. It felt so real that it was almost as if the last few weeks had not happened.

The realisation that it was but a mirage took hold of his heart and twisted with a pain not unlike a knife. She would never be any more than a fleeting vision, a memory of happier times. All he had to remember her by was a daughter who was even now miles away while he was stranded, helpless, within the walls of a city, surrounded by Normans.

Overcome with shuddering emotion, he slumped down on the bed, bowing his head in silent prayer. *Watch over me, Hild, that I may see our daughter once again.*

Having recovered his composure, he cuffed away the tears with his sleeve, before pushing himself up off the cot. His expression set once more, he grabbed his shield, axe, and helmet and then stomped outside into the streets. Despite the earliness of the hour, the thoroughfares were already crowded. Warriors criss-crossed each other on their way to their assigned stations on the wall, pushing past tradesmen and others who sought to ply them with food and ale to keep them strong for the day.

Thurkill had no need of food, however; the familiar knot of

anxiety in the pit of his stomach had put paid to that. One or two merchants tried to hold out loaves, pastries or cuts of ham to him, but he surged past, his eyes fixed on his destination. But most left him in peace, his brooding countenance enough to warn them off.

Arriving at the wall, he found Eadwig deep in conversation with Eahlmund.

"What news?"

Eadwig smiled at Thurkill. "All quiet, my friend. Though who knows what the day will bring."

"We'll not see a repeat of yesterday's madness, for sure. Not least because those responsible are dead, either on the field beneath us or at the end of a rope."

The grassy area in front of the walls was still littered with bodies. Already, flocks of huge carrion birds had begun to feast on the flesh, pecking at eyes, noses, and ears, their beaks bloody from the grisly task. God alone knew when either side would have a chance to bury the corpses. Before long, they would start to rot, and the stench would become unbearable. Thurkill supposed they ought to be grateful that it was the midst of winter as the cold air would slow the process more than if it had been high summer.

"Look, yonder."

Eahlmund's shout made Thurkill lift his gaze towards where the Norman lines lay. At first, he could not see what his friend had spotted, but then he noticed movement around the king's tent. It took a while to work out what was happening but, once he did, his heart sank. In truth, he'd known this moment would come but that did nothing to forestall the deep sense of foreboding with which his soul was now gripped. It wasn't the horsemen – about fifty of them – that worried him, it was those who walked proudly in their midst. Heads held high, long flaxen hair flowing in the breeze.

Eahlmund gave voice to Thurkill's own thoughts. "Shit. It's the hostages."

"Fetch Tosti. He needs to be here for this."

Eahlmund nodded before hurtling down the steps and on to the great hall. Meanwhile, Thurkill turned back to watch, mesmerised by the spectacle unfolding before him. The horsemen drew to a halt not far from where they had been the previous day; close enough for the king's words to carry clearly to the watchers on the walls. The knights arranged themselves in a tight crescent around their king who sat on his horse in the middle, just to one side of the hostages. Even though they were probably facing death, the young Saxons stood tall, shoulders thrust back, and heads held high, unwilling to bring shame on their families within the city by giving in to fear.

Moments later, Tosti arrived by Thurkill's side, his face ashen as he looked down at the boys whose number – he had recently revealed – included one of his own cousins. He was followed shortly after by the Lady Gytha, her progress slowed by age and the need to use a stick with which to climb the worn stairs to the parapet.

"The bastards," Tosti hissed, just loud enough to be heard by those closest to him. "Has the Norman dog spoken yet?"

Thurkill shook his head. "I doubt he will keep us waiting long, though."

Indeed, no sooner had the words left his mouth than William tapped his heels against the flank of his mount, urging it to walk forward a couple of paces. Lifting his head a little so that his words might more easily reach those who looked down, he spoke.

"I see the gates remain closed to me. You leave me little option other than to attack your city with all the death and destruction that will entail. But before I give that order, I would allow you one last chance to bend the knee to me before I unleash the hounds of hell upon you. For once that happens, I can no longer be held responsible for your fate and that of every man, woman, and child within those walls. My captains will urge restraint, of course, but who knows whether their men will heed those words once the blood-lust is upon them?"

William paused, likely hoping that the threat alone would be enough to convince them to throw the gates open wide to admit him. He was to be sorely disappointed, though; not one person stirred, not one spoke. The lines of spearmen, interspersed with archers stood passive, immobile, just watching and waiting.

"Steady, lads. Show no weakness." Tosti's whispered command was repeated every few yards by the next captain, then the next.

With no response forthcoming, William continued, "But if my words alone are not enough to make you see reason, perhaps my actions will speak louder? You see here before you," he waved his arm behind him in the direction of the hostages, "the young men who you sent to me at Gleawecastre not two weeks hence. These lads, each one a favoured son of the greatest families of this city, were given to my safe keeping as a sign of the good faith of your leaders. A faith, whose lack I now find to be disturbing.

"What am I to do with them, now that I find the promises of their fathers to be false? Perhaps you doubt the strength of my conviction? Perhaps you think I am not a man of my word? I would prefer to have your submission without spilling any blood, but I do not fear to do so should it prove necessary. I have given you more than enough time to come to your senses; you have had every chance to change your course, to bring your ship to a safe harbour ahead of the coming storm. But still you have chosen to resist. Now you leave me no choice. I can see a stronger example is required. FitzGilbert!"

The man sat closest to the king dismounted, handing his reins to the nearest horseman. Thurkill had not noticed him before, but now that he had been named, the familiar features haunted him from beneath the rim of his iron helm. Even at this distance, the vivid red scar on his face stood out in sharp relief to the pale complexion of his beardless face. Thurkill watched as FitzGilbert limped over to where the hostages stood, huddled together in a small group for warmth and comfort against the biting wind that still ripped across the land. Without ceremony, the Norman grabbed the first boy he came to and dragged him forward to stand in front of the king. The poor lad – unprepared for the rough handling – stumbled and fell, his face planting into the soft earth.

By his side, Eadwig hissed. "See, his arms are bound behind his back, else he would have been able to put out a hand to break his fall."

A low growl greeted his words, spreading from man to man like a heathland fire in the hot, dry summer as the defenders watched, powerless and afraid for the fate of the poor wretch. They all knew what was to come, but none wanted to believe it until it had been witnessed with their own eyes.

FitzGilbert then hauled the hostage to his feet and shoved him back into position. He then glanced up to William, who gave his assent with an impatient flick of his wrist. Grinning malevolently, FitzGilbert kicked the back of his victim's legs, forcing him to his knees. Then, placing himself in front of the lad, the Norman put the palms of his gloved hands on either side of his face.

With a shock, Thurkill realised what was to follow. "The bastard," he groaned. "A quick death with a knife to the throat would have been more merciful."

Leaning forward to improve his grip and power, FitzGilbert then rested his thumbs over his victim's eyes and began to push. The scream of agony as the eyeballs were gouged from their sockets was like nothing Thurkill had ever heard before on any battlefield. It seemed to go on forever as FitzGilbert worked his thumbs into the space behind the eyes, intent on causing as much pain and damage as he possibly could. Eventually, he stepped back to inspect his handiwork. The still-screaming boy slumped back onto his haunches, blood-red pits where his eyes had once been. With his arms bound, he could not bring his hands up to his face. Not that it would have helped in any way. Eventually, mad with pain, the young lad collapsed on to his side, shaking and convulsing as if trying to flee from the torment.

By now, the rest of the hostages were crying out in shock and alarm, part in compassion for their friend and part for fear that they might be next. But William showed no signs of ordering his henchman to commit any further atrocities. Stiff backed, he sat staring at the walls, ignoring the still-jerking form beside him.

Meanwhile, those watching from the city broke free from their stupor. Howls of anger echoed around the walls, carried by the wind north to where the Norman host was arrayed. Tosti made no effort to restrain them; there was little point. Hundreds of voices joined the clamour, yelling hate and foul curses at their supposed king. All pretence of a calm and dignified resistance was gone; gone like the boy's sight, never to be regained, assuming he even survived the ordeal.

Thurkill stole a sideways glance at their war-leader. Like him, Tosti had not joined in with the others, but whereas his features remained composed, Tosti's face was ashen white. He was leaning forward against the wall, the bones of his knuckles shining white through the skin as he gripped on to the jagged stone edge of the parapet. Tears streamed from his eyes, falling unchecked to the ground far below.

My God, Thurkill gawped. *That poor bastard must be Tosti's cousin.* At that moment, he saw Tosti with a newfound respect. To stand there unflinching, while your own kin was mutilated before your eyes revealed a strength and a courage that few possessed. Thurkill knew well the pain and hurt the other man was suffering at that moment; he had experienced the same when his aunt and sister were murdered for sport. Though his own reaction had been somewhat more visceral at the time.

Without drawing attention to himself, Thurkill edged over to Tosti's side, where he laid a sympathetic hand on the other man's shoulder. It was a quiet gesture; no words were necessary. It was enough to let Tosti know that he understood his grief.

William held up his hand to speak once more, causing the uproar to subside a little. "I have delivered my message; I suggest you heed it, lest further calamity should rain down upon you. You have three days to open the gates; else I shall not be held accountable for what happens next."

More cat calls and shouts of derision greeted these final words. In amongst the tumult, Thurkill watched as Eahlmund – looking angrier than he had ever seen him before – clambered up on to the top of the wall. *What the hell is he doing?* Thurkill thought, fearfully.

Once there, his friend took a couple of steps to steady himself as the wind buffeted around him on all sides, threatening to pluck him off. Then, turning his back on the Normans he began to fumble with the ties that held his trews in place. With a look of triumph, he let them drop and then bent at the waist to let rip the most ridiculously loud fart in the king's direction. Eahlmund then hoicked up his trews and jumped back down to the inner walkway.

"You can kiss my arse, you Norman sheep-fucker," he yelled, the words chasing hard on the tail of his anal retort.

The momentary shock that had taken hold of the defenders gave way to great belly laughs. The anguish and horror that had gripped them moments before were replaced by ribaldry and ridicule.

Thurkill strode over to where his friend stood, a broad grin creasing his features. "You mad bastard, Eahlmund," he laughed. "What in God's name were you thinking? And what's more, what the devil have you been eating?" He made a show of pinching his nostrils shut against the imagined stench.

"Well, he was having it all his own way, wasn't he? Needed to do something to even the score a bit."

"You certainly managed that. Look." Thurkill pointed to where the king, a look of foul indignation etched on his face, was pulling hard on the reins to turn his horse away from the walls.

Tosti came over as well to clap Eahlmund on the back, his countenance restored. "I doubt that was quite the reaction William hoped for, but it was a good one, nonetheless. Now we shall see what else the day brings."

THIRTY-FIVE

Thurkill looked over to where Lady Gytha sat, her cloak pulled tightly around her, and furs draped around her shoulders and neck. Though it was not cold in the hall – the roaring fire in the central hearth made sure of that – her advancing years had left her susceptible to the slightest chills. And in old buildings such as these, it was not uncommon for the chill air to find its way through a gap in the wall or around the shutters that, more often than not, failed to fit snuggly in the window.

The look on her face spoke volumes. For the last hour or more, arguments had once again raged back and forth between the two factions on the council. Tosti's party continued to press for resistance despite the cruel fate meted out to the young hostage that morning. They stated that the city should have faith in its walls; they would see them safe until the long-awaited arrival of Harold's sons. Ranged against them were those who sought peace with the king for fear that the walls would crumble and that they would be slaughtered to a man. All that they had seen and heard had left them in fear for their lives. For them, the only option was to open the gates immediately and to throw themselves at William's mercy.

"Have you no shame?" Tosti roared. "Do you not care that the country of your fathers and your fathers' fathers has been overrun? That we now live at the behest of this bastard of Normandy? I, for one, will not rest until a Saxon is back on the throne of England, and it shames every one of you who demands that we settle with that whoreson for no other reason than you fear the loss of your wealth and prosperity. Shame on you all."

"It's alright for you; you have nothing to lose. You have no property, no family here. You can fight, safe in the knowledge that none will mourn your passing."

After all that had happened, this was too much for Tosti. His cheeks aflame with outrage, he stormed over to where Wulfnoth stood and punched him squarely in the face. A shocked hush descended across the hall. Violence at the council was strictly forbidden; the tradition – going back hundreds of years – was that all blades must be left by the door to ensure that arguments did not spill over to bloodshed. By common extension, it was accepted that none should ever resort to physical means to make their point. But none of that mattered to Tosti now. Into the brooding silence, he stood over his prostrate opponent and hissed a dire threat.

"How dare you? Did you not see what happened to that boy this morning? You say I have no stake in this game of chance, that I have nothing to lose? He was my cousin, so I suggest I've already paid more than anyone else. And should you wish to debate this matter further, I would gladly walk with you by the walls where we may compare the length of our swords."

For Lady Gytha, matters had now gone too far. She struggled to her feet, leaning heavily on the stick that a ceorl held out for her. "Peace, Tosti. No one here doubts your loyalty or belittles your sacrifice. I am sure that Wulfnoth meant no malice by his poorly chosen words." She stared intently at the other man, as if daring him to contradict her.

"The fact remains that our city is surrounded by the Normans," she continued, "and if we are to survive the coming days, we must stay united in purpose and heart. If we can hold on until my grandsons arrive, they will sweep the Normans from the field and cast them back into the sea. Then we will see a Godwine on the throne of England once more."

**

"Do you think they'll come, Lord?" Eahlmund stared wistfully towards the hills far to the north whence Godwin, Edmund and Magnus would hopefully appear.

"I truly cannot say, friend, but we have to hope. Without them and their army, all hope is lost here."

"And the longer this goes on," Urri growled, "the more people will lose confidence. Already, Wulfnoth's followers whisper in the taverns and in the streets, spreading their message of surrender. Their numbers will grow by the day for as long as the Godwinesons fail to show."

Silence fell between the three men as they pondered Urri's words, knowing them to be true. They stood huddled around an iron brazier in which several thick logs burned fiercely. The warmth was welcome as the temperature had plummeted as soon as the watery winter sun had set. Soon after dark, a stiff breeze had blown in thick clouds from the north from which snow had soon begun to fall; thick, heavy flakes that blew into their faces, stinging their cheeks. It was settling fast, drifting into ever growing piles against the walls of the houses below. The townspeople would wake to a landscape that was all white.

Thurkill shivered, for probably the fiftieth time. To get the blood flowing – not to mention alleviate the boredom brought on by the long hours of sentry duty – he had taken to walking to and from the brazier to his right, about twenty paces away. As he went, he stomped his feet and flapped his arms around his body which served to both warm him and ease some of the stiffness from his joints and muscles. At each turn, he stopped to exchange a few words with the other watchmen, local lads from the city who had no experience of fighting. Their armour was old, handed down from their fathers no doubt. It was ill-fitting and misshapen in places, and their weapons showed signs of age too. Thurkill could tell they were frightened, scared of what the future might hold and unsure of their part in it. He did his best to encourage them, to give them hope, but he could see that his words washed over them. There was little doubt in his mind that they would not stand when the time came. Not unless they had stout men on either side of them.

He was on his way back to his own station for the seventh or eighth time when he stopped, about halfway between the two. He turned his good ear towards the north, cupping his palm around it to try to funnel the sound. What with the wind and the snow, it would have been remarkable if any sound managed to penetrate his brain, but he could have sworn he'd heard something. Frustrated, he stared in the direction whence he thought it had come, but it was hopeless. Not only was it pitch dark, but the bright orange flames made sure that his eyes saw little but the reflection of their glare.

But there it was again. Unmistakable this time. Though what it was, he could not say. It was faint, carried to him on the wind despite the dampening effect of the snow. What he did know, however, was that no beast or bird could be responsible; the sound was too rhythmic for that. It sounded as if something was being repeatedly thumped or pounded. Nonplussed, Thurkill made his way back to where Eahlmund and Urri stood, huddled around the fire, where the crackling of the burning logs masked all other sound.

"Lads, there's something going on out there, but I can't tell what."

"How so?" Urri sounded sceptical. "Who in their right mind would be about on a night such as this?"

"I swear it, Urri, on Hild's grave. I can see nothing but there is a noise, and it's a noise that is made by man."

"What would you have us do, Lord? Should we sound the alarm?"

"I don't know, Eahlmund. Whatever it is may be far away. By God, it may even be coming from as far away as their camp; the wind is strong enough to blow sound a good distance after all." He rubbed his chin, feeling the harsh stubble scratching against his palm. "I say we do nothing for now but watch. Let us see what the dawn brings, eh? Either way, I shall report this to the Council as soon as we finish our watch."

**

First light brought nothing but the promise of more snow. Everywhere Thurkill looked was covered by a thick white carpet while the clouds above remained leaden grey, straining under the weight of the snow that they carried. But of the origins of the noise he'd heard, there was no sign. As he surveyed the land beyond the wall, the wind whipping his hair against his face, he began to doubt himself. Had he really heard anything? Had his mind been playing tricks on him? The others often mocked him for only having one ear – a legacy of the battle at Senlac – asking how he could be expected to hear anything properly? He decided to report it anyway. It would better to be safe now than sorry later.

His mind was put at rest, however, the next night. Another day had passed in peace, the Normans seemingly content to bide their time in their own camp, making only the occasional scouting sortie around the walls, though staying well out of arrow-shot range. Other than that, there was no movement, no attempt to launch another assault. Thurkill could not pretend he was not grateful; not only could they sleep uninterrupted after their night's watch duty, but also, they were a day closer to the promised arrival of the Godwines. Food, though carefully rationed, was plentiful, and the river provided all the water they could need. All was well.

But back on the wall in the darkness, Thurkill heard the noise once again. The wind had dropped, and the snow clouds blown away, so now the rhythmic thuds and scrapes floated across the night sky unhindered. It seemed louder too, somehow closer. Still, he could see nothing. The blackness of the night was thoroughly impenetrable. This time, however, he made sure that Urri and Eahlmund could hear it too, dragging them away from the warmth of their brazier, deaf to their foul-mouthed protests.

"Tell me now that my ear does not work, I dare you," he said with no small hint of triumphalism.

The same pattern continued for the next two nights, each time a little louder than before. On the second night, Tosti came up on to the wall with the other war-captains to hear for themselves.

"You are right, Thurkill. It must be the Normans. They toil to the north of us under the cover of darkness. I daresay we shall not like what is finally revealed to us, but I fear there is little we can do for now but watch and wait." Turning back towards the stairs and the cosy embrace of Lady Gytha's hall, he added, "Double the guard. We shall not be taken unawares."

***

The mystery was resolved on the morning of the fourth day. The dawn broke with a weak sun casting its glow over the land from the east, throwing long shadows over the undulating ground. A small thaw had set in over the last day or so, causing most of the snow to melt away, except where the land lay shaded from the sun. The wind had also changed, now coming from the south east, bringing slightly warmer weather with it.

Thurkill faced the sun, hoping for some of its pale light to warm his chilled face, and yawned. He was looking forward to lying on his straw-filled mattress, to burying himself under the blankets and feeling the warmth flowing back into his frozen limbs. With luck he would sleep until mid-afternoon, then avail himself of whatever hot food he could find. He decided to take one last look back towards the Norman lines before he left. As he did so, all thought of sleep evaporated.

"Alarm! Rouse the guard!" Around him, men scurried away to do his bidding, not stopping to ask why. His tone of voice was enough to instil the fear of God in them. Within moments, Tosti was at his side.

"What news, Thurkill? The Normans attack?"

Thurkill pointed towards the Norman camp where thousands of men were on the move, scurrying in all directions like a huge ants' nest that had been kicked over. Soldiers were forming up into their units beneath where their banners had been raised; the army was readying itself for an assault. From what he could see, they were all foot soldiers, a mix of heavily armoured infantry interspersed with groups of archers. Rank upon rank of them, stretching far to the left and right across their front. Of the horsemen, there was no sign. That lesson had perhaps been learned.

But in the centre of them all gathered a group of men – thirty or forty – who appeared to be carrying some sort of structure between them.

"By Satan's hairy arse crack, what is that?" Eahlmund spoke for them all.

Thurkill watched as the Normans began to approach. All around him, the men of the city rushed to take up their positions. Many looked like they had just been roused from their beds; several were still pulling on their armour or fastening their helmet straps as they arrived, panting and sweating despite the cold. By now, the enemy had covered almost half the distance from the camp to the city walls. The pace was slow, partly because of the unevenness of the sodden earth that sucked at their boots as they walked and partly because of the iron discipline imposed by the captains. Any who stepped out of line were cajoled back into place by harsh words, blows of a stick or both.

Their languid progress gave Thurkill plenty of time to study the contraption and to ponder its purpose. He guessed it to be about twenty paces long and half as wide. It had sides and a roof but was light enough to be carried by the dozen or so men on either side. Its composition eluded him, though. As they came nearer, however, he saw it was covered with animal skins that had been stretched over a wooden frame. Yet he was still no closer to divining its use. Suddenly, they stopped en masse, facing the city.

"What are they doing? Why don't they attack?" Eadwig called.

Thurkill had no answer. Surely, they were still beyond the range of the Norman archers? Even the strongest among them would see their arrows fall short at that distance. But he had reckoned without the wind. It had shifted once more, overnight, to come from the north east again, whipping its way across the open moorland, stinging the hands and faces of those on the walls.

Moments later, they heard orders being given. Without hesitation, the bowmen, in their hundreds, strung their bows and planted their arrow bundles in the ground to their front. At the next command, they reached forward to select their first missile, nocking it onto the bowstring. The third order saw them pull back on the taut string all the way until their fingers touched their chins, while aiming up into the air.

Urri snorted. "This promises to be a waste of good ash and iron. We'll be outside tonight, picking up those arrows and adding them to our stocks."

He could not have been more wrong. The final order was followed by an audible twang as hundreds of bowstrings snapped forward, slapping against the leather-sleeved forearms of the archers and launching their deadly cargo towards its target. Believing themselves to be too distant, many of the defenders shunned the safety of the walls and their shields and stood watching the coming death-storm as if it were no more than a murmuration of starlings on a summer's day. Too late they realised their mistake. Though around a quarter of the arrows fell short, most carried the distance with ease, slamming into the defenders. Man, after man fell, some screaming piteously as the arrows pierced their limbs or bellies, others falling instantly dead.

Thurkill felt a sickening thud which then reverberated all the way up his arms and across his shoulders. Horrified, he looked down to see a shaft buried into the handle of his war axe. Not overly religious by nature, he nevertheless hurriedly crossed himself and offered a silent prayer for his salvation before ducking down behind the parapet. The arrows were coming in such numbers that it sounded for all the world like a summer's downpour rattling off the roof as they clattered against the thick, stone walls. Not for the first time, he was grateful for the skill of those giants of men who had come from Rome many centuries before to build fortifications such as these. That they had stood tall and proud for so long was testament to their skill.

"Christ's bones, but you are one lucky bastard, Lord." Eahlmund, crouched by his side, was grinning wildly.

Still ashen-faced, Thurkill just nodded. Looking around, he saw men everywhere lying wounded or dead. Crazed with pain, some had lost their footing and fallen from the walls. For them, the instant death as they hit the ground would have been preferable to the unbearable agony of the metal-tipped death-bringers. In all, he reckoned fifty had been killed or seriously wounded. It was not a catastrophic number, but it was dwarfed by the impact on the morale of the survivors. The townspeople had been lulled into thinking that they were safe within the city's defences, that they simply had to wait for the promised relief. That notion had been cruelly crushed in a few moments, like a beetle succumbs to the heel of a boot.

At least those on the wall were safe from the hail of iron now, protected by the impenetrable stonework. Desperately, they yelled at those below to take cover; hundreds of arrows still sailed high over their heads to land within. Already a few unlucky folks had been struck down, causing several others to flee for the safety of their homes.

But Thurkill knew that all the while they kept their heads down below the parapet, they could not see what the Normans were doing. They were free to continue their assault unhindered. It was the perfect ploy. Taking a deep breath and trusting in God to keep him safe, Thurkill slowly lifted his head until he had a clear view of the ground below. It was just as he feared; the enemy had used the time won by the arrow-storm to good effect. Even now, the infantry had closed to within a few paces of the wall's base. Many of them, he noted, carried crudely fashioned ladders, the length of which looked plenty long enough to reach the top.

What was more, he now understood the purpose of the hide screen that he'd seen earlier. It had been placed about seventy paces away, a little off to his left, on a patch of ground that rose above a natural dip in the ground. One of its short sides faced the wall with the opposite, open end pointing towards the Norman camp. Several men had already gathered at the back, many of them stripped to the waist, despite the cold and in defiance of the Saxon soldiers high above. In their hands, they carried axes and shovels.

The realisation of their true purpose hit Thurkill as clearly as if he had dunked his head in a bucket of cold water. "Archers! Train your bows on those men at the back of the hide shelter over there".

Hearing his shout, Tosti scuttled over to Thurkill's side, bent double to keep his head down. It was as well he did as several Norman archers had already turned their fire towards the sound of the voice from above. Thurkill ducked down but not before a well-aimed arrow had struck his iron helm, glancing off the curved surface to spin uselessly down to the ground. *By Christ, I seem to have more lives than Aunt Aga's old cat.*

"What do you see, Thurkill?" Tosti dared not risk a glance over the walls as the arrows pelted the masonry around them.

"They have labourers with picks and spades. I believe they aim to dig beneath our walls."

"That would explain the noises we've heard these last several nights. They have been preparing the ground under the cover of darkness and are now close enough to complete the work. Where are those God-damned archers?"

Two captains rushed forward to receive their orders. "Lord, your command?"

"Kill as many of the men with picks as you can. And have

some of your men send fire arrows at that contraption. I'd see it in flames if you please."

The two men rushed off to organise their bowmen and before long, a steady rate of fire was arcing towards the Norman lines. In order to protect them from the enemy, each archer was assigned a spearman to hold his shield in front of the archer until he was ready to loose. But despite such precautions, a few men still fell prey to the superior marksmanship and greater enemy numbers. Still, their work was not without value; half a dozen of the workers lay dead already around the entrance to the shelter. Without the benefit of mailshirts, they were vulnerable to every missile.

Soon after, Thurkill saw the first flaming arrows. Roughly a dozen of them, smoking as they flew, carrying fragments of hot coals that would pierce and then hopefully ignite the hide. With the shelter gone, they would be able to bring down any who ventured forward to access the tunnel. Happily, he saw that about half of the arrows struck the target. But to his horror, not one achieved its aim.

"Again!" Tosti screamed in frustration.

The second volley fared no better. They could see the smoke rising from the arrows that had stuck into the leather fabric, but they obstinately refused to catch fire. Within moments, soldiers carrying pails of water arrived to douse the arrows before then pulling them out.

"They have protected it against fire." Thurkill realised that the Normans must have spent long hours soaking the skins with water so that there would be minimal, if any, chance of a flame catching light. It was a wise move and one which had proven effective.

But there was no time to dwell on the disappointment; the infantry had already begun to throw their ladders up against the walls, and the first brave men were beginning their ascent. There were so many of them, swarming up the walls like long lines of ants, that Thurkill feared for their survival. How could they hope to defeat such a vast army with little more than a handful of farmers and townspeople armed with spears and pitchforks? Where the hell were the Godwines with their warriors?

His mind was wrenched back to the present by the sound of a ladder smacking against the wall just to his side. Ignoring the threat of the arrows, he grabbed the pitchfork from the man to his left, who stood immobile, transfixed with terror. He then hooked it round the top rung which stood proud of the parapet. Glancing over the edge, he waited until the first man was three quarters of the way up – with two more following hard on his heels – and then he began to heave.

"By Christ, this is heavy. Urri, help me." The giant blacksmith needed no second bidding. With his added weight, the ladder began to push away from the wall until, with one final shove, it passed the vertical and began to tip. By now, the first soldier was almost at the top; he had guessed what was happening and had rushed to crest the wall before all was lost. But to no avail. He clung on to the sides of the ladder, a look of utter dread etched on his features. The ladder teetered for a moment and then slowly gained momentum from his weight until it crashed down below, scattering men on all sides.

Those nearby raised a ragged cheer, but Thurkill knew it would provide only a brief respite; the ladder was still serviceable and would be repositioned as soon as the injured or dead soldiers had been dragged to one side. But now it would be joined by several more. Each with two or three men climbing the rungs, swords and spears at the ready to stab at any defender who dared show his face.

"Stand firm, lads. Don't let the bastards over the wall or else all is lost." Tosti's strident tones resounded off the walls and were picked up by his captains every few yards.

Now the heads of the first wave of attackers were coming into view. A chilling scream pierced the sky to Thurkill's right, where a granite-faced Norman had managed to skewer the young lad standing directly in front of his ladder. Thurkill had spoken to him not a few moments before, calming his nerves. The poor sod had been terrified; he had not yet seen sixteen summers, and now he was dead.

Thurkill felt a surge of anger welling up within him. Slinging his shield over his back, he gripped his faithful war axe in both hands and marched over to where the lad lay in an ever-widening pool of blood. Yelling at his shocked companions to clear a path, he began to swing the long-handled blade in an ever-widening arc, timing it to perfection so that its edge connected with the Norman's neck just as he swung his leg over the wall. He watched with a satisfied grunt as the head was sliced clean away from the shoulders, tumbling down on to those below. The body stayed up right for a moment, frozen in time, before it crumpled and fell to join its severed head, blood gushing like a fountain from the gaping wound.

The effect was immediate. As if awoken from a deep slumber, the Saxons roared with delight at the spectacle. Men reached out to slap him on the back, perhaps hoping that touching him would somehow imbue them with a piece of his courage. But there was no time to celebrate; many more Normans were following the first, undaunted by the loss of just one man. Though Thurkill's example had given the defenders confidence, he knew he could not be everywhere on the wall; he could not kill every man who made it to the top of a ladder. They would have to do it for themselves.

A shout to his rear made him spin round. His heart leaped into his mouth as he saw Leofgar slumped on the ground with two soldiers stood over him and two more clambering on to the wall to join them. Eahlmund and Leofric were doing their best to hold them at bay, but the Normans were bigger and stronger, raining blows down that looked strong enough to break their arms let alone their linden-board shields.

Without stopping to think of his own safety, Thurkill charged forward, screaming incoherently. He could feel the familiar bloodlust taking hold of him and he welcomed it as he would an old friend.

Lowering his head, he ploughed straight into the first man. The Norman never saw the berserk Saxon until it was too late. The conical top of Thurkill's helm caught the smaller man square on his jaw, shattering the bone and dropping him unconscious to the ground where Leofric flicked out his spear to finish him. Using his momentum, Thurkill then launched himself at the second man, ramming the blunt end of his axe haft into the man's face, where it smashed his nose with a noise like dry twigs cracking under foot. He then reversed the blade before chopping down hard at the point where the neck and shoulder met. The soft flesh gave way, unable to form any resistance to the sharpened blade; he was dead before a sound could leave his lips.

Still, more and more soldiers were making their way on to the wall. But each one they killed seemed to be replaced by two more. It would surely only be a matter of time before they were overwhelmed. To make matters worse, the stone surface of the walkway – already worn smooth by the passage of innumerable feet over the centuries – was now slick with the blood and gore of the fallen. He knew that to lose one's balance in a hand-to-hand fight such as this would spell doom.

Thurkill buried his axe in the neck of the next man over the wall. He pulled hard on the long ash handle, but to no avail; the dead man's flesh refused to relinquish its grip on the burnished metal surface of the blade, sucking at it like a snail grips on to a plough share. Just in time, he caught a glimpse of a sword swishing towards his head. Dropping to one knee, the blade sliced the air mere inches above him, where his skull had been just moments before. Releasing his grip on the axe, he grabbed his seax from where it hung, suspended from his belt, and drove it hard into the man's groin, a warm gush of blood coating his hand.

Retrieving his axe, Thurkill took a moment to take stock. Their part of the wall was faring better than most. Urri, Leofric, and Eahlmund had seen to the remaining Normans and no more had yet dared venture where so many of their comrades had been slaughtered.

Leofgar was conscious once more but in a bad way. Thankfully, he had suffered nothing worse than a thumping blow to the head which had rendered him insensible. Had it not been for his helm, he would have surely died. Even now, he was still groggy and unable to stand. He had vomited several times, adding to foul detritus that covered that pathway, and was unable to see straight. Thurkill hoped that all he needed was rest. As soon as things had settled down a bit, he'd have someone take Leofgar down off the wall. He was more hindrance than help where he lay.

Elsewhere, however, things were not going so well. Desperate struggles were being played out between defender and attacker alike every few yards along the walkway. Every time a Norman managed to clear a space for himself on the parapet, he was immediately followed by two or three companions like wasps swarming around rotting fruit on the ground.

Tosti was doing his best to direct his warriors and to good effect. He had kept back fifty or so of the best men, holding them in readiness at the base of the wall. Now, they were being sent in groups of five or six to wherever the need was greatest. But even they were now starting to tire, their numbers already reduced by one fourth. *If this goes on much longer, the city will be lost before nightfall.*

But then, suddenly, it was over. The sound of trumpets blaring in the distance brought an end to the assault. Those Normans that could still move, scrambled down the ladders as fast as they could. Not caring to hinder their escape, the Saxons slumped to the ground where they stood, exhausted by their efforts. They were too exhausted even to harry the retreating enemy with arrows. Those that lay dead or dying on the walkway were tipped unceremoniously, over the edge to leave room for the womenfolk to treat the Saxon wounded, of which there were many.

They had survived the first attack. But for how much longer could they hold?

THIRTY-SIX

"Lord, come quickly."

Thurkill groaned. It seemed but a few moments since he had closed his eyes, having settled into his cot, draped with several furs to ward off the cold. Once they'd realised that the Normans were not planning to renew their assault, Tosti had insisted that as many men as possible rest as there was no telling how soon they'd be needed back on the walls.

"This had better be good, Eahlmund. If it's anything less than a horde of howling Normans rampaging down the main street, I'll have your ball-sack for a new purse."

When his friend didn't laugh at his crude attempt at humour, Thurkill prised open his eyes. Something was not right. It took one look at his face to confirm his worst fears. Swinging his legs out from under the covers, Thurkill pushed himself into a sitting position, stifling a yawn as he did so and shivering in the cold.

"What is it?"

Grim-faced, Eahlmund came straight to the point. "Gytha's gone."

"What do you mean, 'gone'?"

"Just that, Lord. Seems that she, along with most of her entourage, stole away in the night, disguised as merchants so they might steal a boat and take the river away through the Norman lines."

"But why? Why now? What about Tosti?"

"He remains, I'm told. But it seems Gytha grew tired of waiting for her grandsons to arrive and has looked to her own safety. The weather has been against them all winter, preventing them from sailing for these shores. The wind has them penned in at their Irish moorings."

"The news just gets better and better, doesn't it? So, with no hope of relief, she has decided to abandon the city and make good her escape?"

"Aye and leave all of us poor bastards to the mercy of the Normans. And I can't see them being too pleased that we have held them up here for the best part of two weeks, can you?"

Thurkill knew Eahlmund was right. William had a reputation for exacting cruel revenge on those that resisted his rule, and there was no reason to think that Escanceaster would fare any better than the other towns and cities that had closed their gates to the king before now. The cold forgotten, he felt an anger rising within him. He'd left all that was dear to him back in the hills around Scrobbesburh because he trusted in the Godwines. He had honestly believed that they could lead the Saxons to victory against the Norman invader. And what was worse, his hearth-warriors had followed him, pledging their swords alongside his. But now all those plans lay in tatters, let down by the Danes, thwarted by the weather and now betrayed by those who were supposed to lead them. He felt sick to his stomach.

"What should we do, Lord?"

What indeed, he mused? How was he to save them now? Stuck in a walled city, surrounded by thousands of blood-thirsty soldiers amongst whom one in particular would stop at nothing to kill him. To his mind, there was little hope of survival. But when he spoke, he adopted a determined tone that he hoped would mask his true feelings.

"We fight on, Eahlmund. What else can we do? But at the same time, we keep one eye on the back door. If or when all looks to be lost, we must be prepared to fight our way out, whatever it takes, no matter what occurs. I have a daughter, and I would see her again before I die."

***

News of Gytha's departure travelled fast among the city's inhabitants. The resulting clamour to surrender to the king grew ever louder than before. Few now wanted to continue the fight if Gytha had abandoned them, and Thurkill could see their point. With her gone, and no hope of her grandsons arriving, what was the point of carrying on? The dream of ousting William in favour of a Godwine was over.

But Thurkill feared the time for surrender was past. He could not be sure that to do so would save the people of Escanceaster from the worst ravages of the besieging enemy. There was no denying it; they had held the gates against the king, in open rebellion against his rule. They could expect no mercy from him, even were they now – belatedly – to open the gates.

Back up on the wall, Thurkill brooded over the cruel hand fate had dealt them; the playing pieces on the board were stacked heavily against them, leaving them with little hope. He burned with frustration at how events had conspired to crush his dreams of an England free of the Norman yoke. The plan had promised so much; sons of King Harold who were of an age that men could follow, supported by men from Ireland and Danmark who had sworn fealty. But one by one the pieces had toppled over, never to be righted. And now even the queen piece had left the board, leaving her protector pawns to face the marauding enemy alone.

He looked around him, at the faces of the men who had trusted his decision to come to Escanceaster. Men who had believed in his dream and promised to fight for it just as they had fought for him many times before. A part of him could not look them in the eye, ashamed of the end to which he had now brought them. They did not deserve to die for his foolish pride.

Sensing his dark mood, Urri came to stand by his side. "Well, here we are once more, Lord. On the inside of a wall, looking out at a bunch of Godless bastards who want to get in. We trusted in God and your leadership at Gudmundcestre, and I daresay the same combination will see us right once again."

Thurkill laughed, but there was no humour in his voice. "I thank you for your faith in me, Urri, but I fear this task might be beyond us. There's rather more of the Godless bastards to deal with this time."

"And here they come again." Eahlmund yelled.

The attack followed the same pattern as before. Hordes of infantry carrying countless ladders ran towards the walls under the cover of murderous volley fire from hundreds of archers, the effect of which was to keep the heads of the Saxons down below the parapet, lest they find themselves availed of new holes through which to breathe. All the while, dozens more men made for the hide-covered shelter, wherein they continued to shovel earth from the tunnel they were excavating.

Thurkill knew that the tunnel carried the greatest threat to the city and yet was the one thing about which they could do the least. The soldiers attempting to scale the walls were, once again, little more than a diversion. William must have known that the Saxons had the numbers to hold the walls. If the Normans somehow managed to gain a foothold on even one section, then that would be an unlooked-for bonus. With luck, they would be able to flood enough men through such a hole to overwhelm the city. But that outcome was unlikely. What was far more certain was the fact that, at some point soon – if not today, then almost certainly tomorrow – the diggers would reach their goal. And when they did, there would be nothing to stop the wall from collapsing. And then all would be lost. Thousands of enemy soldiers would stream through the breach, dealing death to all in their path. Already, Thurkill could see vast units forming up not far from where the tunnel entrance was. The stones tumbling down would be their signal to launch their attack.

But for now, that worry would have to wait; there were more pressing matters that demanded their attention. The ladders were going up once again, and grey-clad soldiers were once again scrabbling up the rungs as if the very devil snapped at their behinds.

Thurkill flexed his muscles, loosening some of the stiffness that had set in after the previous day's exertions. All around him, men stood ready, shield and spear held in white-knuckled grips, ready to meet whatever fate had in store for them. Gone – for the most part – was the fear he'd seen before. Most faces now showed a stalwart defiance that came with the knowledge that they had no choice but to stand and fight for as long as they were able. No one was coming to save them; they could no longer decide their own future.

"Ready, lads. It matters not that Gytha has gone. This fight is now for your honour. What happens here will determine how your name will be remembered through time. Your deeds today will decide whether the scops will sing songs of your courage in the face of the enemy."

Despite his best efforts, he knew that the words sounded hollow, but what more could he do than set an example to those around him? He was a leader, and men looked to him for courage and direction. Shrugging imperceptibly, he swivelled back to face the wall, hefting his shield into a more comfortable position. He knew its weight would become a burden the longer the day went on, but the protection afforded him by the large round board would be invaluable when the hand-to-hand fighting began. It was also for this reason that he had chosen his sword today over the axe. The balance and agility of the blade would outweigh the benefit of the heavy bludgeon.

"Ware!"

Just in time, he jerked his head to one side, feeling rather than seeing the wicked spear point that had been aimed at his face glance off the curved rim of his helm. The bastard coming up the ladder had taken him by surprise, thrusting his spear blindly over his head in the hope that a Saxon waited there for him. Taking advantage of the feint, the Norman then lunged up the final two or three rungs, aiming to cross the parapet before the defenders could recover. But Thurkill was faster. Just as the soldier reached out with his left leg, the Saxon jumped forward, smashing the hilt of his sword into his opponent's face. It was not enough to kill, or maim even, but it did succeed in hurling the man backwards and onto those who waited below.

But he was not alone; several more were, even now, cresting the stone wall from a small clutch of five or six ladders that had been deliberately grouped together. Working in pairs, the Normans strove to win a foothold. One thrust back the defenders with his long spear, while the other jumped onto the walkway, sword swinging back and forth to clear a space. The same pattern was repeated at intervals all along the wall to devastating effect. Here and there, brave men were able to repel the attackers but, all too often the attackers were able to establish themselves within the city.

Thurkill's section was one of the better defended. Working closely with each other, his war-band was succeeding in keeping the enemy at bay, for now. Even Leofgar was doing his bit, seemingly recovered from the previous day. The long hours spent training together were now reaping their rewards as they encouraged each other, howling their delight each time a

Norman was dispatched. They had formed a solid shieldwall, and settled into an easy rhythm, killing any that dared show their heads at the top of a ladder. But the same could not be said to his left, close to where the wall passed above the main gate. Several Normans – about half a dozen from what he could see – were fighting there ferociously, forcing back the few remaining Saxons so that they might reach the steps that led down to the gate. Should they succeed, it would not be long before they would let in their comrades.

"Urri, Eahlmund. With me." The walkway was narrow, only wide enough for two men to walk abreast. So Thurkill pulled Urri up alongside him and overlapped his shield with that of the blacksmith. They were roughly the same height and build and, together, formed what he hoped would be an impenetrable barrier with Eahlmund positioned behind, readying his spear to thrust between their heads.

"Stay tight, lads," Thurkill growled and then set off at a trot towards the Normans, Urri keeping pace at his side.

Luck was on their side. The Normans had their backs to them, intent on breaking through to the stairs. Two more had now joined, bringing the total to eight, and the weight of their numbers was beginning to tell. Even as they ran, Thurkill saw a young Saxon go down screaming, blood staining his kirtle from where a sword had been thrust into his guts.

Too late, the Normans finally heard them coming. The two soldiers nearest to them half turned at the sound of rushing feet, but they had no time to bring their swords or shields to bear. In unison, Urri and Thurkill brought their swords down in great hacking blows from over their heads, taking both men where their necks were exposed beneath the rim of their helms. Death was sudden and immediate, both men's heads almost completely severed.

Thurkill and Urri did not stop there. They piled into the backs of the next two men, both of whom were bundled over, being taken wholly by surprise. Behind them, Eahlmund yelled with incoherent rage as he stabbed down at the sprawling man on the right, his spear point piercing the fleshy parts of his abdomen. By now, doubt had spread to the rest of them. Even those at the front paused as they sought to understand what was happening behind them. It was a fatal error; it was all the invitation the beleaguered defenders to their front needed.

Suddenly free from attack, the battered Saxons rallied and took the fight back to the now wavering soldiers. Pressed in on both sides by screaming, snarling warriors, the surviving Normans panicked. So maddened with fear were they that they attempted to save themselves by jumping over the wall, willing to risk the drop rather than face death at the hands of these screaming fiends. All four made it over the edge, though the slowest fell to his death with Eahlmund's spear protruding from his arse.

A ragged cheer went up from the exhausted survivors, but Thurkill knew it would be no more than a brief respite. He had no doubt that more of the bastards would soon come swarming over the walls, like an inexorable tide swallowing up the beach. Their small victory was no more than a pin prick in a horse's flank, a momentary annoyance that would soon be forgotten. There were still thousands more that William could call upon, many of whom had not yet been committed to the fight.

Just then, Thurkill heard a new sound, its growing noise bringing the ragged cheering to a premature end. A rumbling like a distant thunderstorm that slowly increased in volume and intensity. As it grew, it was accompanied by a vibration that Thurkill could now feel beneath his feet. He looked over the wall, expecting to see vast hordes of horsemen hurtling towards them, but there were none.

Then it dawned on him. "The wall's about to collapse. Save yourselves!"

All around him, men began to run, streaming down the steps or running along the wall away from the epicentre. Thurkill and the others joined them, rushing back to where Leofric, Leofgar and Eopric waited. He was pleased to see that all three still lived, though Eopric's left arm was covered in blood from a gash close to the shoulder. His shield hung limply by his side, his face a mask of pain. Leofgar's head was bandaged but other than a headache ten times worse than the most awful of hangovers, he too swore he could yet fight.

Together, they ran on until they reached the next set of steps, joining the throng that had gathered at the top waiting for their turn to descend the narrow walkway. Moments later, the rumbling reached a crashing crescendo as the great stones that made up the base of the wall finally gave way, collapsing into the mine that had been dug under them these last several days. Ignoring the risk of being shot, Thurkill leaned out over the edge to stare in astonishment as a huge, yawning gap appeared, roughly twenty paces wide. Rubble was strewn on all sides as the ancient mortar that had stood for centuries cracked and broke under the weight of the stones pressing down on them from above. Several of the garrison had been killed in the collapse, their bodies broken and bent into unnatural shapes by the falling masonry.

But all that had to be forgotten. The wall had finally been breached, and their stoic resistance counted for nought. Now, there was nothing to prevent the avenging Normans from entering Escanceaster and massacring every man, woman and child they found within.

THIRTY-SEVEN

"Quickly, lads." Thurkill had to shout to make himself heard over the sound of falling masonry and the screams of the dying. "All is lost. If we want to get out of here alive, we leave now. The bastards are already running hard for the breach."

They threw themselves down the steps, though taking care not to barge other, slower men out of the way. Reaching the criss-crossing streets that divided the ramshackle rows of houses, they found that chaos reigned. Hundreds of people were running in blind panic, and the noise. There was hardly a person among them who was not screaming, crying or otherwise shouting as panic threatened to take hold. Thurkill knew that if he was to survive to see his daughter, he had to leave the city as quickly as possible. He weighed his options. There was no sense running towards the breach; even if they made it through before the enemy, they would be confronted by hundreds, if not thousands of soldiers, each looking to sate their bloodlust. Their only chance was to flee through the south gate and thence to the docks, where they might hope to take a boat away from the city.

"This way." He scurried off down one of the less busy side alleys that seemed to be heading in the right direction. The great beauty of these old Roman towns was the way in which the streets were all laid out in parallel lines, like the lines on a tafl board. There was little chance they could get lost, even amongst the cramped buildings that seemed to be piled almost one on top of another.

On they went, the six of them, each man running steadily despite the weight of their armour and weapons. Even Eopric had forgotten the pain from his arm; or at least he was hiding it well under the hastily applied strips of linen with which Urri had bound it. They had no time to collect their belongings; they could not risk being trapped within the confines of the city. It didn't matter, though; none of them had much to their name, other than the clothes, armour and weapons that they now wore or carried.

Sweat stung Thurkill's eyes as it dripped from his forehead, incongruous with the bitterly cold February weather. It flowed in little rivulets down his back, beneath the thick cloth of his woollen cloak, the heavy iron-link mailshirt and the padded kirtle that he wore under that. They had slowed to little more than a trot now, embroiled in an ever-growing tide of people flowing south to the gate, funnelled together by the narrowness of the street. But at least they had not far to go. Craning his neck to see over the masses ahead of him, Thurkill could see the stone wall towering over the houses, no more than fifty paces away.

"Come on, lads. We're nearly there." Like him, they were all panting now, chests heaving at the exertion needed to escape the enemy's clutches. But they kept going, heads down, their feet pounding the smooth cobbles that formed the ancient roadway. The fitness gained over long hours of battle-training paid dividends now, along with the will to survive the coming carnage.

But when they finally reached their goal, they found the gate closed to them. A large crowd had already gathered, clamouring to be allowed out, but the guards – some of Tosti's own men – were holding them back. They had orders to keep the gates barred against the enemy, and they would do so until told otherwise by their commander. For all they knew, packs of marauding Normans could be making their way around Escanceaster to this very point.

Growing impatient, Thurkill used his bulk to push his way to the front, his men following close behind. Reaching the captain of the guard, he realised that behind the dirt and grime, the face was familiar. "Hail, Eadwig. How do you fare?"

"Well enough, Thurkill, but for this," he waved his arm in the direction of the milling crowd. "What news? What has happened to cause such a stampede? Are the Normans within the city already?"

"They have undermined the wall, my friend, and the goat-lovers will be pouring through the breach even now. For the love of God, man, you need to stand aside and release these people before it's too late."

Eadwig' expression betrayed the conflict in his mind. "I have my orders from Tosti. Without word from him, I cannot abandon my duty."

Thurkill grabbed his forearm in a gesture of understanding. "The time for duty has passed, Eadwig. The Normans will soon be upon us, and Tosti may already have fallen for all I know. I would expect no new orders from that direction if I were you. Look at these people. They're mostly women, children, and old men. Open the gates and spare them a brutal death."

The thought of the approaching hell was obviously too much for Eadwig. Wordlessly, he nodded at his men to unbar the great wooden gates. Immediately, the inhabitants began to stream out, scattering in all directions in their haste to be away from the city.

With most of the people gone, Thurkill made ready to follow but then paused. "Come with us, Eadwig. There's no honour in staying here to be slaughtered."

"On another day, I would gladly, friend. But I would stay here to do what I can to help the people of this city. You go, Thurkill. Perhaps there will be another chance, in another time and place, to rid this country of these Norman scum."

Thurkill gripped Eadwig by the shoulder, staring deeply into his eyes. "God go with you, Eadwig. I pray we shall meet again in happier times."

The six companions trotted through the gate, some of the last to leave by that route. Thurkill took one last look at the Escanceaster, the city that had promised so much a few short weeks before. Already, he could see several tendrils of thick black smoke rising to join with the dark clouds above them – evidence that the Normans had begun the foul work of pillaging the city's houses. Tears of frustration formed in his eyes as he watched his hopes of a Saxon king disappearing along with the billowing smoke.

But for now, he had to push such thoughts to one side; his men needed him. Saving them from the marauding Normans was all he could hope to achieve now. They needed to reach the docks, where he prayed they would find a suitable ship. It would be the quickest and best way to put distance between them and the enemy.

Ignoring the acrid tang that stung his throat, Thurkill stopped to scan the waterfront. The city wall had been built within yards of the river – the Exe – which flowed south and east from the city until it reached the sea. All along its length, dozens of wooden jetties had been built, jutting into the water to allow fishermen to land their catch and merchants from Frankia, Ireland and many points besides, to unload their cargoes. Feeling hope surge in his heart, he soon found what he'd been looking for: a small fishing boat, moored fifty or so paces from where they stood.

"There, lads," he pointed. "She'll serve our purpose well."

But even as the words left his mouth, he pulled up short. So suddenly, in fact, that Eopric bundled into his back, uttering a bitter curse as he bit his lip.

"Shieldwall!" Thurkill yelled. There was no time to waste. He made a half turn to his right, raising his shield as he did so. Firmly planting his feet a shoulder's width apart, the right at an angle behind the left, he bent his knees, ready to brace for impact. With familiarity bred from hours of practice, his five warriors formed up on either side, overlapping their shields with the one to their right. It was as natural as breathing for them; they had been in too many battles for it not to be.

Thurkill had feared that escaping without hindrance would be too good to be true. And so it had proved. Ahead of them, and blocking their path to the boat, a conroi of twenty horsemen had appeared, drawn up in the lee of the wall. At first, Thurkill thought they must be there to slaughter refugees fleeing from the city, but no; they stood impassively as dozens of citizens swarmed past them, each one cowering as if they expected to be struck down at any moment. It was clear to him that they had some other purpose; a purpose that was contingent on his arrival. Even as he watched, the knights began to walk forward. A walk that soon became a trot.

A flash of hatred lanced through Thurkill, as bright as any bolt of lightning, as he recognised the man in the centre of the conroi. FitzGilbert! He'd managed to push thoughts of his nemesis to one side over the last few days, his mind more than occupied with the desperate defence of the city. But, in his heart, he'd always known that this confrontation had been unavoidable, ever since he'd laid eyes on the weasel-faced bastard in William's camp at Corinium.

Thurkill muttered a foul curse under his breath. He had to admit a grudging respect for the man. Instead of charging blindly into the city, hoping to find his quarry amid the thronged streets, FitzGilbert had reasoned that Thurkill would be more likely to be found here, at the rear of the city. Foregoing the spoils on offer to the rest of the army as they ransacked the city, the Norman had only one thing on his mind. And now his patience and foresight had been rewarded.

Howling in triumph, FitzGilbert kicked his horse into a gallop, racing ahead of his comrades who fought hard to keep pace with him. It was hopeless; the Saxons were outnumbered more than three to one. In the moments before impact, Thurkill wracked his brains, trying to find some ruse, some trick that might yet save them. He found himself wishing his father were there. He might not have had a plan either but just to fight and die by his side would have been an honour. Despite his predicament, he smiled at the thought. At least he would be reunited with Scalpi soon; he had a few stories to tell.

At the last moment, the germ of an idea – born of desperation – came into his head; perhaps it was not his fate to die that day after all. If it were to work, however, he needed to act fast.

"On my order, drop flat to the ground. And be sure you do not tarry."

He had no idea whether his men had understood what he was thinking, but there was no time to explain further. He had to trust that they would follow his orders with blind obedience as they had always done before.

By now, the Normans were almost upon them. Twenty paces, ten. He had to leave it to the last possible moment to have any chance of success. Just when it looked like they would be ridden down, he cried, "Down!"

In a heartbeat, all six men threw themselves flat, a hair's breadth in front of the onrushing horses. As well trained as they were, the war-horses instinctively leapt over the obstacle as if it were no more than a low stone wall, leaving the prone Saxons unharmed.

"Up, lads. Up and after them!" Thurkill roared. They had to press home the advantage gained by the subterfuge. They were most likely still doomed, but at least now they might make a decent fight of it.

The six warriors scrabbled to their feet, turned, and charged after the horsemen who were already hauling back on their reins, losing all their momentum and cohesion in the process. Several of the horses blundered into each other as their riders fought for space to turn in the narrow tract between wall and river. Fixing his eyes on FitzGilbert, Thurkill could see the red-faced anger in his expression. He was screaming at his men to get out of his way, using the flat of his blade to hit the knight nearest to him, whom he judged to be too slow in clearing his path and sending him tumbling to the ground with a sickening crunch.

But there was no time to revel in FitzGilbert's ire. Thurkill knew it would only be a matter of time before these expert horsemen would recover their wits and bear down on his warband once more. They had to close the gap between them before that happened, else they would be hacked to pieces.

As he ran, Thurkill wished they had more spears between them; their long reach would have allowed them to engage the knights from beyond the range of their swords. As it was, only Eahlmund and the two brothers were so equipped. No matter; they would just have to do what damage they could before they were killed.

"Into them, boys. Teach them what it means to fight Saxons. Send the bastards to hell."

They needed no further invitation. Their screams as they ran at their foes chilled Thurkill to the bone. Each man was in the grip of an all-consuming rage that blinded them to all else but the need to kill. They knew their doom was at hand and they would meet it with honour as all proud warriors must.

They hit the first two horsemen just as they completed their turn. It was the last thing the doomed knights did. Before they could lower their own weapons into position, both men found themselves transfixed on the iron points of Saxon spears. At the same time, Thurkill darted in between their horses, using the point of his seax to slash their flanks and sending them into a pain-fuelled panic that caused them to rear and kick out in rage and fear. It was but a small victory, though.

Already the rest of the conroi, enraged at the fate of their companions, had regained control. He saw Urri pulling the knight nearest to him down from his saddle before then ramming the iron-bound rim of his shield down onto the man's throat, only for the blacksmith to be felled by a hammer-like blow to the skull, the strength of which seemed to push his helm down hard on to his head. But for its protection, he would surely have been killed on the spot; but, even so, Thurkill doubted whether he could have survived such a blow.

Pure instinct made him throw up his left arm. But God – or luck – was on his side as he caught FitzGilbert's blade on the central iron boss of his shield. Sparks showered over him and his ears rang from the metallic clang that threatened to deafen him. What was worse, though, was that he could sense the muscles up as far as his shoulder going numb from the bludgeoning impact. Cursing his luck, he crouched down and tried to shake feeling back into his arm. It ached like hell, but thankfully, he could feel the strength begin to return.

Although FitzGilbert's momentum had taken him past Thurkill, the danger had not yet passed. Even now, the next two knights were bearing down on him, deadly lances aimed at his head and chest. They were almost on top of him, but it was not his way to wait for death to find him. Rising to his feet, he surged forward, batting away one spear point with his shield whilst swerving sideways to avoid the other. At the same time, he swung his sword in a blind arc at the second man's face. It was not a well-aimed strike, but it had all his strength behind it. He grinned with satisfaction to see it catch the Norman on the chin, instantly breaking his jaw and leaving the horseman's mouth hanging uselessly open.

Looking up, Thurkill saw that six more horsemen faced him. All around him, the sounds and smells of battle assailed his senses. Steel clashed with wood and iron, and he caught himself wondering how the others fared. That the conflict was still raging fiercely on all sides reassured him; at least not all of them were yet dead. But for how much longer, he could not say. They had given a good account of themselves; at least six Normans lay dead or injured to the cost of perhaps one of his, maybe more. But he knew that the weight of numbers would soon begin to tell. There was little more they could do than take as many of the goat-shaggers with them as they could.

Pulling himself up to his full height, Thurkill opened his arms wide and bellowed his defiance at the circling knights to his front, goading them to finish him. Blood dripped from his sword, mocking the knights and calling them forward to try their luck. Grinning maliciously, they were not slow to accept his challenge. Resigned to his fate, Thurkill hunkered down behind his shield for one last time, the sweat-stained, leather-bound hilt of his sword lightly gripped in his right hand. Offering a final prayer to God and the Lady Mildburh, he prepared to make the last marks on his tally book.

But as Thurkill stood waiting to meet his doom, his look of bitter determination slowly turned to astonishment as, one by one, the six knights hurtling towards him fell from their saddles, each one impaled by a throwing spear in his back. Thurkill was dumbfounded by the sudden turn in his fortunes but offered up a prayer of thanks for his deliverance, nonetheless. But then, Eadwig hove into view, followed by a dozen of his warriors – the same men who had been guarding the gate a short while before. Reaching Thurkill's side, Eadwig stopped though not before urging his men on to engage the remaining knights.

"I hope you don't mind, but I thought you could use some help." He grinned mischievously.

"Oh, I don't know. I think we had them worried," Thurkill smirked, bending at the waist to slow his breathing. Before he could utter another word, however, the air was rent by a blood curdling howl. FitzGilbert had somehow evaded Eadwig's men and was now charging straight at Thurkill, his lance aimed at the huscarl's head. The elation he felt at having survived the onslaught evaporated as quickly as it had come.

He should've known the whoreson would not go quietly to his death; he had waited too long for vengeance to see it snatched from him. Thurkill was close to exhaustion; the strains of the last few days had caught up with him. Summoning his last reserves of strength, he turned to face his oath-sworn enemy for the final time. This time, he promised himself it would be finished one way or another.

Spitting disdainfully on the ground, Thurkill strode forward to meet his nemesis.

"Come on!" he yelled, feeling the familiar anger surging through him once more. Eager to have an end to it, he began to run, closing the distance between them as quickly as he could. It was time to bring the feud to an end. His senses were filled with the sight, sound, and smell of the huge black destrier thundering towards him. He narrowed his eyes to slits, focussing on a point between FitzGilbert's face and the undulating end of his spear. He knew he would have one chance to end it, one final attack in which he would kill or be killed.

By now, FitzGilbert was almost upon him; so close was he that Thurkill could see the flecks of saliva that coated his lips as the Norman yelled unintelligible obscenities as him. Then, just when it looked as though he would be impaled on the end of the Norman's lance, Thurkill ducked and slid to his right with surprising agility for such a large man. Passing practically under the horse's head, he gathered what was left of his strength and swung his sword at FitzGilbert's back as he hurtled past.

The Norman was already off balance, twisting in his saddle to see where Thurkill had gone, when the blade caught him. So hard was the blow, that his hauberk could not save him. The steel bit through the iron rings and deep into his side, toppling him from his saddle in the process. FitzGilbert landed on his back with a force that pushed the air from his lungs with a sound like the rushing wind.

Wearily, Thurkill trudged over to where his enemy lay. Standing over him, he watched dispassionately as the blood slowly pooled around the horrific gash in his abdomen. Though FitzGilbert must have known he had but moments to live, he showed no fear. Instead, he stared at his enemy with all the baleful malice he could muster, his teeth gritted against the pain.

"Finish it, Saxon dog. Send me to meet my brother in hell."

Thurkill gazed at him, a mix of pity and contempt confusing his brain. He was spent; the urge to kill had deserted him. He had seen enough death and mutilation for a lifetime. Perhaps this could now be an end to it. His thoughts turned instead to the need to escape. Who knew how long it would be before another party of Normans found them? Wordlessly, he turned on his heel, leaving FitzGilbert to die in the dirt outside of the walls of Escanceaster. It was over. Everything was over.

Returning to Eadwig's side, Thurkill wondered how many of his hearth-warriors still lived. Waves of emotion swept through him as he thought of his brave hearth-warriors, hoping against hope that they might all yet leave this place with him. Bodies lay everywhere, limbs contorted in unnatural poses. Frantically, his eyes darted over them to see if any of his companions lay among them. No. He felt a surge of joy rising in his chest. There was Leofric bending over Eopric, tending once again to his wounded arm. And there was Eahlmund, pale-faced and holding his right hand under his armpit.

"One of the bastards got lucky with his sword," his friend grimaced. "Took the blow on the spear, but the blade ran down to my hand, taking a couple of my bloody fingers with it. Hurts like a bugger, it does."

Thurkill laughed with relief that his friend was not more grievously hurt. "We'd best get it seen to as soon as we can. Bind it for now, though, for we must leave here as soon as we can." It would need a hot iron to seal the wound, an agonising but necessary treatment. As an afterthought he added, "You may need to use your left hand to pleasure yourself for a while, too."

Eahlmund chuckled. "That'll make for a change; I reckon it will feel like someone else is doing it."

Then Thurkill saw Urri and the humour left him. The big man was still lying where he had fallen; it looked as if he hadn't moved at all. Leofgar was kneeling by his side, his own face sheathed in blood, though it was not clear whether it was his own. Thurkill placed a reassuring hand on the younger man's shoulder.

"Does he live?"

"Aye, Lord, but I fear he clings to life by no more than the tips of his fingers. I've always said he had a thick skull, and it's as well that he does. But for that and the helm he would be dead, I'm sure of it. Even so, it's too early to say whether he will pull through."

Thurkill choked back on his tears. He had grown fond of the old blacksmith, ever since those days back in Gudmundcestre when he'd become leader of the shieldwall. His friendship and his brute strength meant more than mere words could express. For now, though, he had to push his despair to one side. Escape remained their priority.

"Eadwig, help us to that boat if you will, so that we might leave here. You know you're still welcome to join us if you wish."

"My thanks, friend, but my place is here. I hear that William has sent his captains to try to stop the pillaging, so I am hopeful we may yet reach some settlement with the king to avoid any further bloodshed. There will be need of leaders to help rebuild. But I wish you God speed and safe travels to wherever you may go now."

Thurkill embraced the man, sorry to be parting from him. He knew not where the future might take him, but, right now, he knew there was but one place he must go.

EPILOGUE

Thurkill paused at the top of the snow-covered ridge, looking down happily on the familiar view below him. A great forest covered most of the land that stretched away to the north and east of him. Despite that, he could still discern the line eked out by the ancient path that wound its way through the woodland until it reached the little clearing that nestled between the surrounding hills.

Using his hand to shield his eyes from the afternoon sunshine, he could see the thatched rooves of the cluster of houses that formed the centre of the little settlement. And then, a hundred or so paces further on, there was the large stone priory which, together with its myriad outbuildings, housed the small community of nuns at Wenloch.

His heart soared to at last be so close to his journey's end. It had been two long weeks since they had put the ancient stone walls of Escanceaster behind them. Two long weeks since the dream of placing a son of Harold Godwineson on the throne of England had died amongst the rubble and the flames. Many a night on their journey north, Thurkill had tormented himself over whether he could have done any more, but the fact was that none of the promises made had been kept.

No warriors had come from Denmark to bolster their numbers. Worse still, the three brothers had not even set sail from Ireland. Without them and their warriors, the rebellion had always been doomed to failure. The optimism with which he had set out, had been eroded with every new setback until the final collapse of the city walls extinguished any final hope that had remained.

But despite all that, Thurkill did not regret his actions. He still believed in his heart that, even if there had been only the smallest chance of success, it was a price worth paying – even if it had led to his own death.

But now it was behind him, who knew what life would hold for him and his little band of loyal hearth warriors? Twisting round in his saddle, he stared back down the slope whence he had come. Like him, Leofric and Eahlmund rode sturdy little ponies, while Leofgar drove the cart in which Urri and Eopric – still recovering from their wounds – sat or lay on piles of straw amongst their shields and armour.

Eahlmund raised his hand to wave. It was still bound in strips of white linen where he'd lost the two smallest fingers, but it was mending well. The healer they'd found in the village north of Escanceaster had known her craft well. It had taken three of them to hold Eahlmund down when she burned the flesh closed, but the hot iron had done its work. The poor lad had bitten clean through the stick placed between his teeth to stop him from biting his tongue but, mercifully he'd passed out from the pain a few moments later, allowing her to finish her work in peace.

She'd been unable to do much for Urri though, other than prepare potions that would relieve his pain when he finally recovered his senses. Using her fingers to gently probe around his skull, she claimed she could feel the bone shift showing that the skull had been broken in some way. He was in the Lord's hands, she'd said, matter-of-factly. She had no skills with such things, and it would be up to His will whether the big man would live or die. Later, when they were alone, she had told Thurkill that she had never known a man to live so long with such an injury. She wondered whether the miracle suggested that God had some purpose in keeping him alive.

As if to prove her prophecy, the blacksmith had regained his senses a day or two later, but he was a shadow of the man they had known. He struggled to form words or to make himself understood and needed help with even the most basic of tasks. They had bought the cart and oxen soon after they had left the boat behind, using the last of Thurkill's coin to acquire it. But it was a price he was glad to pay to spare his friend from the rigours of the road. So now Urri lay in the back of the cart, his back propped up on some sacks of grain and covered in furs against the chilled air. Looking back at him, Thurkill could not help wondering whether the blacksmith would ever recover fully. His last hope was that the prayers of the abbess at Wenloch would somehow convince the Lady Mildburh to intercede on his behalf.

But his old friend was not the only reason he'd come back to the priory. There was the small matter of his daughter, Mildryth, too. His desire to see her, to hold her in his arms once more had grown stronger with each passing day. Almost every waking moment, his mind was awash with images of her face as he imagined how big she would be now and the things she was able to do. Although he had promised her to the priory to do God's work, she was still his own flesh, his own blood. His and Hild's. And he still felt a father's pride.

"Come on, you laggards. My stomach cramps for want of food and my throat cries out for decent cup of ale. If we don't hurry, the good abbess will have shut the gates for the night, and we shall go hungry and cold."

"Your arse won't be cold when I kick it into next week," Eahlmund called up the slope. "I'd swear you've bought the two slowest oxen in all of England. No wonder that farmer was pleased to see the back of them, and to think we paid him for them too."

Thurkill laughed. "You follow on then. I'll go on ahead and make sure they know we're coming." With that, he dug his heels into the flanks of his pony, eliciting an indignant snort before it reluctantly broke into something approaching a trot.

***

Next morning, Thurkill walked slowly towards the little shaded glade that nestled amongst the trees. In his arms, little Mildryth slept contentedly, her belly full of a thin porridge made from oats and goats' milk. The smell coming from his left shoulder reminded him of where she had not long since posited a small part of her meal as he had winded her in the way Sunhilda had shown him. Only now did he regret not accepting her offer of the linen cloth she had held out to him. But he did not really care. For the first time since Hild had died, he felt at peace with the world.

The grounds of the priory were a haven of calm and serenity, a world away from the violence and pain of the last few weeks. The abbess had made them welcome, insisting that they stay for as long as they wanted; she had plenty of work for idle hands to do in return for food and lodging. Even Urri seemed to be responding well to the abbess' care, though she too doubted he would ever return to his former self.

And then there was Mildryth, nearly six months old now and crawling everywhere. She was a happy child, quick to laugh and rarely in tears. He couldn't say whether she knew him as her father for sure, but she had held her arms out to him when Sunhilda had first brought her to him. That was enough for him, and it was all he could do to hold back the tears that brimmed in his eyes, surreptitiously brushing them away with his sleeve when her back was turned.

And now he had brought his daughter to see Hild. The low mound and little wooden cross that marked her grave were festooned with flowers, brilliant white snow drops and bluebells in little clusters. And, as he remembered from the last time he was here, the air was filled with the sound of many dozens of birds perched in the branches all around. It was a magical place, one that he could well believe was under the watchful eye of the Lady Mildburh.

Taking every care not to wake her, Thurkill adjusted his daughter's position so that she was more upright in the crook of his arm. "Here she is, my love. See how she has your golden hair and little round nose? She grows healthy and strong in the care of the nuns here – especially Aethelgar's wife, Sunhilda. It was she who cared for you during your last days, so it is fitting that she now cares for our daughter." His voice caught in his throat as the painful memories of the past flooded his mind once more, combining with his fear of what the future might hold. Outside of this abbey of Wenloch, he knew not where he belonged anymore, or what his purpose was. The tears that he had held back for so many days began to fall unchecked.

He had no kin, no wife, no home and even his daughter belonged to God rather than to him. All his hopes for an England free from the Norman invader lay in tatters as well. With every passing month, their rule would become more and more secure, leaving little hope for men such as he. Perhaps Hild would be the one to help him find a path. It couldn't hurt to try, he thought to himself.

Sniffing back the tears, he whispered. "So here we are together again, just the three of us." He sat down on the soft grass, careful not to crush any of the flowers. "I have much to tell you, wife, if you'll grant me a moment to listen to my tale."

Historical Note

Following on from Thurkill's Battle, this third volume of the Huscarl Chronicles takes us from mid-1067 until the spring of 1068.

The reality of Norman rule has begun to bite with many of the surviving Saxon landowners being deprived of their estates for having supported King Harold at Senlac. It is worth noting that, by the time the Domesday Book was compiled, roughly ninety percent of England was in the hands of Norman lords. This, if anything, represents the true impact of the Norman Conquest and it is no wonder that the seeds of rebellion soon formed in those early years.

As before, many of the characters that feature within this book are fictitious; but they are woven into the fabric of time, personalities and places that did exist. Eadric Silvaticus – or Eadric the Wild – was a Saxon landowner in Shropshire who did come to blows with Richard FitzScrope, a Norman lord based in Hereford. Though he eventually made peace with the king in 1075, his activities in the years following the conquest have parallels with the later legend of Robin Hood. The cognomen 'Silvaticus' by which the Normans referred to him wonderfully illustrates his habit of living among the trees, presumably as an outlaw.

The rebellion of the title is also a matter of historical record, as is the fact that it began in the city of Exeter and that it was led by the Lady Gytha, mother of the former King Harold. The ancient Roman town with its thick stone walls, deep in Godwine territory in south west England, would have made an ideal base from which to rally around King Harold's adult sons. In a move designed to repeat Earl Godwine's comeback in 1052, pleas for support were sent to Gytha's relations in Denmark and attempts were made to whip up support across the shires of southern England. Had they joined with a mercenary fleet from Ireland, who's to say what might have happened?

The fact is, however, that the rebellion was doomed to failure for a number of reasons. Harold's sons did not arrive from Ireland, leaving the Saxons leaderless and outnumbered; and the shires failed to respond in anything like the numbers necessary. This latter point would have been due – in no small measure – to King William cannily issuing a summons for his Saxon subjects to muster alongside his Norman troops. That so many answered his call perhaps shows that a good number of the surviving English lords could already see that the tide had forever turned, or that they were weary after the battles of 1066. Whatever the reason, they must have known that to refuse King William's command would have seen them branded as rebels in the likely event that the insurrection failed.

In the event, King William did besiege Exeter for eighteen days until its eventual surrender following the collapse of a section of the wall – most likely from having been undermined. Though it is worth noting that one version of the Anglo-Saxon Chronicle states that the citizens surrendered because 'the thegns had betrayed them' – a reference to the fact that Lady Gytha and many of her followers had escaped from the city during the siege, perhaps realising that the game was up. For the sake of dramatic licence, I chose to have the Normans break into the city to bring about the final collapse of the rebellion.

The joys of historical research sometimes allow you to stumble across small details which jump out at you from across the centuries and which demand inclusion within the pages of a novel. And so it was with the discovery that, before beginning his assault on the city, King William had one of his Saxon hostages blinded in full view of the defenders on the walls. Such a brutal act – from which the victim would have most likely died in excruciating pain – rightly inspired great anger amongst the watchers on the walls; one of whom chose to drop his trousers and bare his arse to the king, farting loudly in his general direction. I hope you'll agree, this was simply too good to leave out and felt exactly like the sort of thing that Eahlmund would have done.

Fans of Monty Python' Holy Grail film may also recognise the parallel with the insulting French Knight who also insists that King Arthur's mother was a hamster and his father smells of elderberries.

Printed in Great Britain
by Amazon